Santa's Sweetheart

More Christmas romance from Janet Dailey

Holding Out for Christmas

It's a Christmas Thing

My Kind of Christmas

Just a Little Christmas

Christmas on My Mind

Long, Tall Christmas

Christmas in Cowboy Country

Merry Christmas, Cowboy

A Cowboy Under My Christmas Tree

Mistletoe and Molly

To Santa with Love

Let's Be Jolly

Maybe This Christmas

Happy Holidays

Scrooge Wore Spurs

Eve's Christmas

Searching for Santa

Santa in Montana

JANET DAILEY

Santa's Sweetheart

KENSINGTON
PUBLISHING CORP.

www.kensingtonbooks.com

KENSINGTON BOOKS are published by

Kensington Publishing Corp.
119 West 40th Street
New York, NY 10018

All Kensington titles, imprints, and distributed lines are available at special quantity discounts for bulk purchases for sales promotion, premiums, fund-raising, educational, or institutional use.

Special book excerpts or customized printings can also be created to fit specific needs. For details, write or phone the office of the Kensington Special Sales Manager: Attn. Special Sales Department. Kensington Publishing Corp, 119 West 40th Street, New York, NY 10018. Phone: 1-800-221-2647.

The K logo is a trademark of Kensington Publishing Corp.

Library of Congress Card Catalogue Number: 2021931082

ISBN-13: 978-1-4967-2754-1
ISBN-10: 1-4967-2754-1
First Kensington Hardcover Edition: July 2021

10 9 8 7 6 5 4 3 2 1

Printed in the United States of America

Santa's Sweetheart

Chapter One

Branding Iron, Texas
Thanksgiving Day, 1996

The microwaved turkey TV dinners were the best that Sheriff Sam Delaney could manage this year. His six-year-old daughter, Maggie, hid her disappointment with a brave smile.

"It's all right, Daddy," she said, clearing the foil trays off the table. "Next year I'll be big enough to cook dinner myself, with a real turkey and everything, just like Mommy used to make."

"I'm sure you will, honey." Sam hugged her close, fighting the rush of emotion that threatened to bring tears to his eyes. Bethany, his wife and Maggie's mother, had died in a car accident a year ago, just a week before Thanksgiving. After it happened, Sam had sent Maggie to stay with her grandparents until after the holidays, while he struggled to cope with loss and grief. This year would be their first holiday season together since Bethany's passing. So far, Sam wasn't handling it well.

"Hey, at least we've got pumpkin pie," he said, picking up the frozen treat he'd grabbed at the market. "Let's see if it's thawed." He tested it with a knife. The point went in partway, then met icy resistance. "Sorry," Sam said. "I guess I should've given it more time out of the freezer."

"Let's have some anyway," Maggie said. "It'll be like eating pumpkin ice cream!"

Using the force of his big hand, Sam managed to hack out two slices of pie, slide them onto saucers, and squirt canned Reddi-wip over the top. Exchanging a thumbs-up and a smile, they each broke off a piece and took a taste.

"Yuck," Maggie said, putting down her fork. Sam did the same. Even with topping, the half-frozen pie was nothing like ice cream. It was more like mushy ice. Maybe he should have cooked it in the oven instead of just trying to thaw it.

"Sorry, honey," Sam said. "If I hadn't needed to work this morning . . ."

"I know, Daddy," Maggie said. "Your job is to keep people safe, even on Thanksgiving. That's why I'm going to make dinner next year. We've got Mom's big red and white cookbook, the one that was Grandma's. I can read and learn how. Hey, the Christmas specials are starting on TV. Want to watch them with me? We can make popcorn."

"Sure." Sam's heart had been set on football, but if his little girl, who had just eaten the worst Thanksgiving dinner ever, wanted to watch Frosty and Rudolph and Charlie Brown, who was he to spoil her day?

Maggie put the popcorn bag in the microwave and punched the buttons. As the sound of popping and the buttery smell filled the kitchen, Sam found a bowl on a high shelf and had it ready to hold the popcorn when it was done.

With the bowl between them, they settled on the couch to watch the kiddie shows. Sam sighed as the folksy voice of Burl Ives rolled out "Frosty the Snowman." Things could be worse, he told himself. At least Maggie appeared to be holding up all right. She'd always been an upbeat kid, choosing to see the sunny side of things. Or, more likely, she was just being brave. But he knew she missed her mother every day, just as he did.

As she munched her popcorn and watched her show, Sam studied her stubborn young profile. Maggie had her mother's curly auburn hair, green eyes, and the same sprinkle of freckles across her nose. But the rest of her was all Delaney. She was going to be a pretty woman one day. And tall. How tall remained to be seen.

There was a reason people referred to their sheriff as "Big Sam." At six-foot-four and a husky 250 pounds, there was no more descriptive word for him than *big*. He'd played defensive line in college and had been a likely candidate for the NFL until he'd blown his knee—blown it spectacularly in a nationally televised game. Damned knee. It still gave him a slight limp and pained him in cold weather.

With his pro football hopes gone and his athletic scholarship ended, Sam had come home to Branding Iron, married Bethany, won the election for county sheriff, and gotten on with what he'd thought of as his real life—real, until last year when a drunk driver on an ice-slicked road had changed it forever.

The program had gone to a commercial. Maggie stirred beside him. "Daddy?" she said.

"Mm-hmm?" he muttered, giving her his attention.

"I've been thinking about something. Do you know what you need?"

"What, honey?" Maybe she was going to suggest that they replace their geriatric TV or the rusting Ford pickup he drove when he wasn't on duty.

"I can tell you're lonely, Daddy," she said. "You need a wife—or maybe, for now, just a girlfriend. What do you think about finding one?"

Sam's throat jerked tight. His daughter was full of surprises. But where the hell had *that* come from?

Maggie was only in first grade. But there were two things she knew for sure. Number one: As much as she missed her mother, and as hard as she'd cried and prayed, Bethany Delaney was never coming back. And number two: The happy smile her father wore when she was around was as fake as a Halloween mask. Behind it, Big Sam was lonely and sad—and he wasn't getting better.

Nobody could ever take the place of Maggie's mother. But she couldn't let her father be unhappy forever. Now that his wife had been gone for more than a year, it was time he found a good woman to make him smile again for real. But so far, he wasn't dating—or even looking, as far as she could tell.

When she'd brought up her idea on Thanksgiving Day, while they were watching TV, he had shut her right down. "I'm not ready to think about that, Maggie," he'd told her. "Maybe I'll never be ready, but that's my choice. So please don't mention it again."

Fine, Maggie told herself. She wouldn't mention it again. But that didn't mean she was giving up. If her father wasn't ready to find a lady friend, she would find one for him. And when she found the right one, she would work on a way to get them together.

Keeping her scheme to herself, she started her search the next day. Stella Galanos, who owned the small bakery on Main Street was a pretty woman, with dark hair and eyes. Besides being nice, she was a wonderful cook. But when Maggie talked Big Sam into stopping by for a batch of glazed doughnuts, she noticed a sparkly diamond engagement ring on Stella's finger. Too bad. With a sigh, Maggie crossed Stella off her mental list.

On the way home, the same day, they paid a visit to the

Branding Iron Public Library. Both Maggie and Big Sam loved to read, and they loaded up with books—mystery and action for him, and Beverly Cleary's Ramona books for her. They were above her grade level, but Maggie had discovered that once she'd learned the basics, she could read anything she wanted to. The librarian, Clara Marsden, was a lovely woman. She would have been a perfect choice. But Maggie knew she had a husband. Their son, Ben, was in Maggie's class at school.

That night, as she watched Big Sam make chili with hamburger, canned pork, beans, and a little chili powder, Maggie tried to imagine the kind of woman who'd be right for him. She wouldn't have to be a beauty like Maggie's mother. But getting Sam interested might be easier if she was at least pretty. Of course, she would have to be nice. Being smart would help, too. And if she liked to laugh and sing and cook, she would be perfect.

But as Maggie was learning, finding a woman like that, who was single and might like to date her dad, was not as easy as she'd hoped it would be.

On the Saturday of Thanksgiving weekend, Maggie's father had to work all day. When he was working, and Maggie wasn't in school, she usually stayed with the neighbors, an older couple who were happy to have her as long as she kept herself entertained with reading, schoolwork, TV, or petting their grumpy ginger cat. She was always glad to see the big, tan Jeep Cherokee, with its oversized tires and the sheriff's logo on the door, pull up in front of the house.

Today, when Big Sam arrived home, Maggie was waiting on the neighbors' porch with her coat on and her book bag over her shoulder. She ran down the steps and across the bare grass to meet him.

"Hey," he said. "How's my best girl?"

"Did you remember, Daddy?" she asked.

"Did I remember that we're going to Buckaroo's for

burgers and shakes? You bet I did. Come on. Let's get in the truck. You can put your bag behind the seat."

Her father backed the pickup out of the driveway and headed downtown. Buckaroo's was Branding Iron's only restaurant. Its menu consisted of burgers, fries, hot dogs, pizza, sodas, shakes, and wonderful pie from Stella's bakery. The décor hadn't changed since the 1950s but the food was the best.

Maggie loved being at Buckaroo's with her dad. Everybody in the place seemed to know Big Sam, and he knew them. People often stopped by their booth to chat or just to say hello. Some had questions or even problems, and Sam was always willing to listen. That was part of his job, even when he wasn't on duty, he'd told her. Talking with people helped him know what was going on in his town and who might need his help.

Today, when they walked into the restaurant, the loudspeakers mounted above the counter were playing Christmas music. Elvis Presley was crooning the words to "Blue Christmas."

A pained expression flickered across Sam's face as they found their booth. Maggie remembered that her mother used to play that song. Back then, Maggie had liked it. Now it only made her sad. It probably made her father sad, too. Christmas was going to be a hard time this year. It would help if she could find Sam a new lady friend before the holidays. But with Christmas less than a month away, that wasn't going to be easy.

"Hi, Sam. Hi, Maggie. What can I get you?" Connie Iverson, the waitress, was young with dishwater blond hair and a smile that made her thin face almost pretty. But she was barely out of high school, too young for Sam. And everybody knew she had a boyfriend—Silas Parker—who was in the army now.

Sam ordered burgers, one loaded and one with just meat and cheese, fries, and two chocolate shakes. "How's Silas liking the military, Connie?" he asked her.

Connie's smile widened. "Fine. Silas always did like tinkering with cars. Now he's learning to be a mechanic. When he comes home next year, he wants to open a garage."

"That would be great," Sam said. "People in Branding Iron could really use a good place to take their vehicles. He'll get plenty of business. Next time Silas calls, tell him I said hello."

"Will do." Connie bustled off to give their order to the cook.

"Maybe you should run for mayor, Daddy," Maggie said.

"Why's that?" Sam asked.

"Because you're always looking out for people, and you know everything that's going on in town. Besides, if you were mayor, you wouldn't have to get up in the night to go out on calls when something bad happens."

Sam reached across the table and squeezed her hand. "If I was mayor, who'd be sheriff? That's my job, and I like it. Being mayor would be boring—sitting behind a desk and listening to people complain all day."

"Oh. Okay." The music had changed to "Here Comes Santa Claus," and now Connie was coming back with their shakes. Maybe this would be a good time to mention getting a Christmas tree. But on second thought, that could wait. Sam never wanted to talk about Christmas, and Maggie didn't want to spoil their good time. But the girlfriend thing—if she wanted that to happen by Christmas, she would have to move fast.

On Sunday morning they went to church. Fran Conroy, who played the organ, was a pretty, blond woman, and a widow. Every time she passed Big Sam in the aisle or the doorway of the church, she gave him a smile that reminded Maggie of a model in a toothpaste ad.

Maggie could tell that Fran was interested in her dad. But a few weeks ago, Fran had scolded her for running in the hall when she was late for Sunday school class. The woman had acted mean. She'd even shaken her finger, almost touching Maggie's nose. Some of the kids were scared of her. Maggie wasn't scared, but she certainly didn't want Sam to have a mean girlfriend, or especially a mean wife, should he decide to get married.

On Sunday evening, Maggie and her dad stayed home. Sam read his new mystery book while Maggie watched more Christmas specials on TV. But her thoughts weren't staying on the programs. She'd wasted three whole days and hadn't even come close to finding the right woman for her father. Tomorrow she'd be back in school, and Sam would be back on his regular work schedule. There wouldn't be much chance for either of them to get out and meet people, including single women. Maybe she was going to need more time. But it was too soon to give up. Seeing her dad happy was too important for that.

On Monday morning, Sam dropped Maggie off at school and drove to the ninety-year-old stone building that housed the mayor's office, the court, the public library, the jail, and the sheriff's office. Branding Iron was the county seat, but Mason County was small, with most of the land in farms and ranches. The population of the town was less than 2,500. Sam was the only full-time law enforcement officer. He shared the job with two on-call deputies and Helen, his sixty-year-old receptionist and office manager.

Already at her desk, she greeted Sam as he walked in.

"Anything happening?" he asked her, hanging up the leather coat that was part of his uniform.

"So far it's been pretty quiet, but you know that won't last." She shuffled a stack of reports and put them aside to be filed. "So, how was your holiday? Sorry, I know it couldn't have been an easy time for you."

"We got through it," Sam said. "Although Maggie says she's going to cook us a real dinner next year, turkey and all."

"Knowing Maggie, that wouldn't surprise me," Helen said. "That little girl can do anything she puts her mind to."

Sam shook his head. "Don't remind me. I think her new project is finding me a girlfriend. At least she was talking about it the other night."

"Well, why not, Sam? I know the two of you suffered a terrible loss. But Bethany was a loving, generous woman. You know that she wouldn't have wanted you to spend the rest of your life alone, and she wouldn't have wanted Maggie to grow up without a mother."

Sam felt the same stab at his heart that he'd experienced when Maggie brought up the subject. "Blast it, Helen, are you and my daughter ganging up on me? It's only been a year. It's too soon."

"Evidently, it isn't too soon for Maggie. Maybe you should listen to her."

"You're a fine one to talk," Sam said. "Earl's been gone for what, six or seven years? I don't see you out there cruising for men."

"That's different." Helen swiveled her chair to face him. "By the time I lost Earl, I was in my fifties. We'd raised our family, done most of the things we'd planned to. You're still young, with a daughter to raise. Besides"—she gave him a wink—"how do you know I'm not out there cruising for men? Have you put a tracker on me?"

Sam groaned. "That had better be a joke."

"You'll never know, will you?" She chuckled as Sam walked back to his private office and settled behind the desk to go over his agenda for the day. He had several ongoing cases to check, a trial appearance in the afternoon, and there were bound to be enough surprises to keep him busy the rest of the time.

Helen brought him a mug of coffee, strong and black, the way he liked it. "If you decide to take Maggie's advice, I'll be happy to spread a few subtle hints," she said. "Once the word gets out that you're looking, you'll probably have women lined up outside your door with homemade pies and pans of lasagna."

Sam sighed. "Helen, when—and if—I decide I need a woman in my life, I can find my own. I won't need any help from you, or from Maggie. Thanks for the coffee, and please close the door when you go out."

"Right." He caught her grin as she sashayed toward the door. Helen was his subordinate, but she was old enough to be his mother, which pretty much put them on an even footing. She'd lasted here through three different sheriffs, and nobody knew the job, the case histories, or the people of Branding Iron the way Helen Wilkerson did.

"Oh—" She paused in the doorway. "My son was going to Cottonwood Springs today, so I asked him to pick us up a Christmas tree and charge it to the department. He'll drop it by here on his way home."

Christmas again. Sam sighed. "Fine, Helen. As long as you're offering to decorate it."

"Don't I always?" She closed the door behind her.

Sam rose, walked to the window, and stood gazing out at the town park. The brown grass and leafless trees did nothing to improve his bleak mood. Neither did the city workers stringing colored lights across Main Street. Maybe he should have given Helen some cash and had her son pick up a second tree for him. But he knew that Maggie would want to choose the tree herself. She would want him to help her decorate it while singing along to the

Christmas music on the radio. Later there'd be shopping and wrapping and the delight of Christmas morning.

Bethany had loved Christmas.

Sam felt numb to it all.

Aside from being the tallest kid in the class, Maggie liked school. While the reading groups were meeting, her teacher, Miss Chapman, usually let Maggie go to the library and get her own book to read. Maggie liked that a lot. She was just okay at math, maybe because, compared to stories, numbers seemed boring. But science, art, and music were all fine. She was good at writing, too. But the one subject Maggie hated was physical education.

Maybe it was because her coordination hadn't caught up with last summer's growth spurt. Whatever the reason, she was no good at anything that involved catching, throwing, hitting, jumping, or dodging. And she hated being no good. She hated being the last one chosen for a team. She hated being the first one hit in dodgeball because her height made her an easy target. And she hated striking out every time she came to bat in softball. But Maggie kept trying. She kept trying because it was expected of her.

This morning, after the Pledge of Allegiance, and the announcements, Miss Chapman, whose first name was Grace, called the roll. She was young, maybe twenty-eight or thirty, with the kind of looks that could be attractive with some help. Her light brown hair was straight and pulled back with a scrunchie into a low ponytail. She dressed like a college girl in stretch pants and a baggy gray sweater, and she wore round, wire-framed glasses with almost no makeup. The glasses made her look like a nerd, which she probably was. But the brown eyes behind those glasses sparkled when she was pleased, and her smile deepened the dimples in her cheeks.

She was strict but not mean, and the students, including Maggie, liked her fine.

The first subject of the day was math. Miss Chapman liked to schedule it early, while the students were sharp. Today they were learning to subtract a single-digit number from a two-digit number. Miss Chapman demonstrated the idea and had some students work problems on the board. After that, they opened their workbooks while Miss Chapman moved up and down the rows, pausing to help anyone who appeared to be struggling.

Maggie sat in the back row. That was fine, because she got to sit next to her best friend, Brenda. Miss Chapman let friends sit together as long as they paid attention and didn't talk when they were supposed to be listening. Breaking that rule meant separation.

Maggie had almost finished her workbook pages when Brenda nudged her. "I can't figure this out," she whispered. "What am I doing wrong?"

"Here, let me help you. Look at this one, twenty-six minus four." Maggie leaned close and showed her friend how to subtract the four from the six on the right, and move down the twenty number on the left. "All right, can you do it now?" she asked.

"Uh-huh. I think so," Brenda said. "Thanks."

Maggie glanced up just then to see Miss Chapman right there next to her desk, watching. Maggie swallowed nervously. Had she done something wrong? Was she in trouble?

But Miss Chapman just smiled and nodded. "Good job, girls," she said.

Maggie watched her walk away. Some teachers were mean. But Miss Chapman made you want to do your best. Her smile, which lit her face, was like a little reward. She was nice, but not sweet; pretty but not glamorous; and young, but not too young for Maggie's father. And she was a Miss, not a Mrs. That was important.

Maggie studied her teacher as she moved to the front of the class and stood waiting for the students to close their workbooks.

Perfect! she thought.

Now all she had to do was get Sam and Miss Chapman together.

Chapter Two

An hour later it was time for recess. Maggie and Brenda put on their coats and went outside. Usually they played games with other kids, but today Maggie wanted to talk; so they just walked around the schoolyard.

Maggie had been wondering how much to tell her friend about her plan. Not everything, she decided. At least not yet. But there were things she needed to know before she went ahead. "I need to ask you something," she said to Brenda. "You said once that your brother delivers the newspaper to Miss Chapman. Do you know where she lives?"

"Uh-huh." Brenda tucked a lock of windblown hair behind her ear. The youngest of six children, she was stocky, blond, and blue-eyed like the rest of her large family. "You know that old red brick house next to the hairdresser's? The one with the big dead tree out front?"

"Where old man Warren used to live?"

"Right. Miss Chapman lives there with a couple of roommates. One of them works for the school district. I'm not sure what the other one does. They always give my brother a nice tip when he comes to collect."

So far so good, Maggie thought. "Does she have a boyfriend?"

Brenda shrugged. "How would I know that? And why are you asking?"

"Oh . . . I just wondered, that's all." She'd asked enough questions, Maggie decided. Now she needed to figure out what to do next.

They were walking back toward the building when a ruckus erupted from the far side of the schoolyard—kids shouting and running, the supervising teacher blowing her whistle.

"Hey, it's a fight!" Brenda was already sprinting toward the commotion. "Come on!"

Maggie followed, a little behind her friend. By the time she reached the scene, the teacher and the principal were pulling two second grade boys apart.

"Oh, no," Brenda whispered to Maggie. "That's Johnny Lee Willis. He's already in trouble for fighting. The last time it happened, his folks had to come to school and meet with his teacher. This time it'll be the principal for sure."

"What do you think will happen to him?" Maggie asked.

"I don't know, but he's in big trouble. Maybe he'll have to stay after school and do extra work."

As the boys grudgingly shook hands and the crowd scattered, the bell rang, signaling the end of recess. But Brenda's words had stayed with Maggie. By the time she'd hung up her coat, she'd come up with a plan to get her father and Miss Chapman to meet.

It was a daring plan. Maybe too daring. But Christmas was getting closer every day. It was time for an act of desperation.

"What's this?" Sam unfolded the note that Maggie had handed him. He read it once, then again, unable to believe his eyes. What was going on here?

"Why does your teacher want to talk to me, Maggie?" he demanded. "Are you in some kind of trouble?"

"You might say that." She looked up at him, all wounded innocence. Her expression tugged at his heart, but Sam was determined not to be moved.

"Sit down and tell me about it." The table was set, their supper of warmed-over chili heating on the stove. Sam turned the temperature down, then joined her at the kitchen table, feeling as if he were about to interrogate a suspect. "It isn't like you to be in trouble, Maggie," he said. "Tell me everything. What did you do?"

"I went on strike."

"What kind of strike?"

"I told Miss Chapman I wasn't going to phys ed anymore. And I didn't go. I stayed at my desk and read my book."

"And your teacher let you do that?"

"She told me I had to go, and I said I wouldn't. That's why she wants to talk to you."

"Maggie!" Sam shook his head. "What's wrong with you, defying your teacher like that? I thought you liked her."

"I do. But I hate phys ed. I hate being the worst one in the class. I'm not going anymore."

It was time for tough love, Sam told himself. "Fine. But until your attitude changes, young lady, you can forget about our getting a Christmas tree."

A look of utter dismay flashed across her face, but she swiftly masked it. "Whatever," she said with a shrug.

"And you're to brush your teeth and go to your room after supper. No TV." Sam could smell the chili scorching. Biting back a curse, he turned off the stove and moved the pan. He'd have to make grilled cheese sandwiches instead.

"Okay." Maggie shrugged again, an infuriating gesture. What had happened to his sweet, cheerful daughter? She was too young to be acting like a teenager.

"The note says your teacher wants to meet tomorrow after school," he said. "When I talk to her, I don't want to hear that you've misbehaved again. That includes refusing to go to phys ed."

"We don't have phys ed on Tuesdays," Maggie said. "We're having an assembly tomorrow."

"Fine." Sam fought the urge to ball up the note and fling it into the trash. "But this ends now, Maggie. No more strikes, or arguing with your teacher, or anything else. Hear?"

"Yes, Daddy." She appeared almost too meek now, too satisfied. Something was up. But what?

Sam had learned to read people. It was one of the things that made him good at his job. But his own daughter, whom he'd known from the moment of her birth, had become a mystery.

After a supper of grilled cheese sandwiches and canned tomato soup, Maggie went off to brush her teeth and go to her room. She went without a murmur of protest, but she didn't appear to be the least bit sorry for what she'd done.

Even that, Sam mused, wasn't like her at all.

He cleared the table, scraped the burned chili into the trash, and loaded the dishwasher. The note Maggie had brought home lay on the counter where he'd dropped it. He picked it up and read it again.

The document was a preprinted form with the Branding Iron Elementary School letterhead at the top, and subtitled *Request for Parent-Teacher Conference*. Only the date and time, the room number, and the teacher's name and signature had been filled in. There was a blank line at the bottom for the parent's signature. As Sam signed his name, he continued to study the scant information on the note.

Grace Chapman. He'd never met the teacher, which meant she was likely new in town. The name was old-fashioned, calling up the image of a stern, gray-haired dowager. But the scrawled signature told him the woman had gone to school after the time when students were drilled in penmanship, which would make her no older than about forty. Maggie spoke of her as *Miss* Chapman, which meant that she was unmarried. The term *old maid schoolteacher* was as outdated as it was cruel. But Sam's mental image of Grace Chapman wasn't a flattering one. She probably wore brown support stockings, kept her glasses on a chain around her neck, and lived in a house full of cats.

Maggie hadn't said much about her teacher, just that she was nice. But nice or not, Sam wasn't looking forward to their meeting. She'd probably criticize his parenting and cluck her tongue over the fact that his job often called him away from Maggie. He could almost hear her telling him that his daughter needed more parental supervision—something that he couldn't provide on his own.

Damn! In his five years as Mason County sheriff, Sam had faced down armed criminals, including a killer on the FBI's most wanted list. So why was he getting a knot in his stomach at the thought of meeting Maggie's teacher?

Grace laid out her clothes for tomorrow—sky blue shirt, tweed cardigan, and navy blue slacks—before wandering into the kitchen to join her roommates for spaghetti and garlic bread. Jess and Wynette were already at the table, dishing up the salad that Grace had made earlier, as her contribution to dinner.

"So, how was your day, Grace?" Jess Graver, a dark-eyed brunette in her late thirties, was the youth guidance counselor for the school district. She owned the house and had found her roommates with a newspaper ad. "Have the Christmas crazies started yet?"

Grace spooned spaghetti and sauce onto her plate. "So

far things have been pretty calm—except for what came out of nowhere today."

"What happened?" Blond Wynette Gustavson was currently selling beauty products while she looked for a steady job. So far, her best customers had been her roommates. "Come on, Grace, entertain us."

"I still don't know what to make of it." Grace helped herself to some salad and a slice of garlic bread. "This girl, probably the best student in the class, always well behaved, staged a strike because she didn't want to go to phys ed."

"A strike?" Jess raised her dark eyebrows. "What did she do?"

"She just sat at her desk reading. When I ordered her outside, she said she wouldn't go, and she didn't budge."

"So, what did you do?" Wynette asked.

"Well, nothing, right then. I couldn't just grab her and haul her outside. You can imagine the trouble if I were to try that. All I could do was give her a note to take home to her parents. I invited them to drop by tomorrow after school. I'm hoping we can get to the bottom of Maggie's behavior before the problem gets any worse."

"Did you say Maggie?" Jess asked. "Does she have red hair?"

"That's right. Maggie Delaney. Do you know her family, Jess?"

"Not well. But her dad's the county sheriff. His wife died in a car wreck about this time last year."

"And he's *hot!*" Wynette said. "I hear a lot of talk in my line of work. There are women out there who'd literally *die* for a date with Big Sam Delaney." She sighed. "But from what I hear, he's still mourning his wife. That little red-haired girl is all he's got."

*   *   *

That could explain a lot about Maggie, Grace mused as she cleaned up after the meal. With Christmas coming, and her mother gone, this had to be an emotional time for the sensitive girl. No wonder she was acting out.

But that didn't mean her behavior could be allowed to continue.

As for Sheriff Sam Delaney, Grace didn't care how "hot" he was. She was only interested in finding a solution to his daughter's problem. Dating the fathers of her pupils was against her personal rules—not that he'd be interested. Wynette had made that clear enough.

Besides, Grace knew better than to get involved with any man, especially in a small town. The baggage she came with included a history of running from relationships. She'd been engaged twice. The first time she'd bolted early. The second time she'd been a week from walking down the aisle when she got cold feet and cancelled everything.

That was when she'd pulled up roots, found a new teaching job, and moved to Branding Iron. So far, things were going well. She liked her job and the friendliness of the small Texas town. And one thing was for sure. She wasn't about to spoil things with yet another romantic fiasco.

After the long, somewhat stressful day, Grace was worn out. In her room, she spent an hour detailing tomorrow's lesson plans on her computer, then got ready for bed and fell asleep almost as soon as her head settled on the pillow.

The dream that rose from the shadows of her memory was as troubling as it was familiar.

She was a child, back in her old first grade class, painting a picture at the easel. She needed more blue for the sky, but when she tried to refill the paint jar, it slipped out of her hands and crashed to the floor, splattering her with blue from head to toe.

"*Don't worry about me,*" *she told her teacher as the janitor cleaned up the floor.* "*My house is just around the corner. I can run home, wash up, and put on clean clothes.*"

"*Will there be anyone at home?*" *her teacher asked.*

"*My mom and dad are both at work. But I know where the key is. I can let myself in, clean up, and come right back.*"

"*Wouldn't you like somebody to go with you?*"

"*No, I'll be fine.*" *It was a small town; she was often allowed to go places on her own.*

She left by the outside door to the classroom, cut across the schoolyard to the corner, and hurried along the sidewalk toward her house, which was partway down the block. Her clothes were a mess. Her mother would scold her when she got off work at the bank. But her father would understand that it had been an accident. He would defend her. She was his special girl. That was what he always said.

She found the key in a flowerpot on the porch, unlocked the door, and closed it behind her. As she crossed the entryway and started upstairs, she heard muffled voices overhead, coming from her parents' bedroom. For an instant, she froze. Then she recognized the sound of her father's laugh. Everything was all right, she told herself. But what was he doing at home in the daytime? Her birthday was this weekend. Maybe her parents were planning a surprise.

Then she heard another voice—a woman's, but not her mother's—giggling and moaning almost like she was being tickled. An inner voice warned Grace that something wasn't right and she should go back downstairs. But her feet kept on moving down the hallway, carrying her toward the closed door at the far end . . .

Grace woke with a gasp. Heart pounding, she lay in her

bed, staring up at the reflected moon shadow cast by the old tree outside her window. Why couldn't she purge the dream—and the awful memory—from her mind? She was a grown woman now, her mother deceased and her father gone from her life. Yet every time she dared to believe she'd moved past it, the dream came back, as real as she remembered.

As it turned out, she hadn't opened the door. She'd gone to her room, stayed until the house was empty, and never said a word about what she'd heard. But when her parents had divorced six months later, she'd never felt the need to ask why.

Sam pulled up to the curb to let Maggie off before heading on to work. "Remember, Daddy," she said as he opened the door for her. "You'll need to be here right after school to talk to Miss Chapman. I'll be waiting for you on the bench in the hall. Promise me you won't forget."

"I promise." He helped her down from the high seat and made sure she had her schoolbag. "But if I find out you've stepped over the line even once today, you'll be in big trouble."

"I know. Don't worry, Daddy." She gave him an angelic smile before she turned away and scampered up the walk toward the doors of the school. She almost seemed happy that he'd be coming for a conference with her teacher. What was going on here? Maybe he'd find out later today.

Work left him little time to think about the school appointment. His day started with a dispute between two farmers over strayed cattle and a broken fence. The situation had gotten out of hand when one man drew a gun on his neighbor and threatened him with it. Sam confiscated the gun, cited the offender, and made sure the damage would be fixed.

A domestic violence call came as he was leaving the farm. Ruth McCoy had shown up at the clinic in town, her injuries—black eye, broken wrist, and bruising—consistent with abuse. Sam interviewed her, then went to the house and arrested her husband, Ed, who was sleeping off a bender. Domestics were Sam's least favorite kind of call. Not only was it depressing to see what could happen to people who'd once promised to love and cherish each other but, with emotions running hot, there was no telling when a situation could turn dangerous and explode. In this case, Sam knew what was going to happen. Ruth would refuse to press charges. Ed would be released, and everything would be hunky-dory—until the next time.

By the time Sam had conducted a frightening search for a missing toddler—found safe, asleep in a neighbor's backyard doghouse—then written up a stack of incident reports, it was after 3:00.

Maggie's school day ended at 3:20. It was time to get moving—and to meet with the dreaded Miss Chapman. Still in uniform, he drove down Main Street, beneath the strings of colored lights that crisscrossed overhead. The speakers above the town square were blaring Christmas music. Even with the windows rolled up and his police scanner chattering, he could hear the familiar song.

"Jingle bells, jingle bells, jingle all the way . . ."

Sam suppressed a groan. He'd been dreading Christmas for months, and now it was here, bombarding him from all directions. How was he going to make it through this blasted holiday season?

The school day had just ended. Students were pouring out of the front door and spilling down the walk. Two yellow Bluebird buses were loading kids for the ride to Branding Iron's outlying farms and ranches. Sam stayed back, keeping a safe distance until the buses had left.

Then he drove around to the parking lot behind the building, chose an empty spot, and swung the big vehicle toward it.

With no warning, a boy in a red sweater darted out from between two cars, right into Sam's path. As Sam slammed on the brake and swung the wheel, missing the fool kid by inches, he heard a crunching sound. His heart sank.

Damn! He'd just done some damage.

As the boy raced out of sight, without even looking back, Sam checked his rear, backed up, and pulled straight into the parking slot. Dreading what he might see, he climbed out of the big Jeep.

Parked next to him was a ten-year-old silver Honda Civic. The rear fender on the passenger side was crumpled and hanging loose where he'd hit it with his heavy-duty bumper.

Great. He was going to owe somebody a repair job and a big apology. But at least he had the means to find out who owned the car. Taking note of the license plate, he climbed back into his vehicle and entered it into the DMV database. The information he needed came up in a few seconds.

The silver Honda was registered to . . . *oh, hell* . . . Grace Chapman.

Looking toward the building, Sam saw Maggie come out onto the back porch. She was probably worried that he might not show up. At least, from where she stood, she wouldn't be able to see the damage to her teacher's car. He gave her a wave. She waved back, dancing with impatience as he crossed the parking lot. Should he tell Grace Chapman about her car before or after the discussion of Maggie's behavior? After, he decided.

"Come on, Daddy." Grabbing his big hand with her

small one, she tugged him through the doors, toward the far end of the hall. "Miss Chapman's waiting. I told her you'd be coming."

They stopped in front of a numbered door with a printed sign that said, MISS CHAPMAN, GRADE 1. Below the sign was a taped-on cutout of a smiley face.

Great. She'll probably pull it down and rip it up when she hears about her car.

The door was open a few inches, but Sam couldn't see into the room. "Should I knock?" he asked his daughter.

"It's all right. She said we could just come in." Maggie stepped ahead of him and pushed the door open.

The woman who rose from behind the desk was younger than he'd expected, of medium height, and slim as a willow. Her delicate features and dark eyes, slightly magnified by round, wire-framed glasses, lent her a doe-like quality that Sam found strangely attractive. But never mind that. Right now his only concern was Maggie.

"Thank you for coming, Sheriff Delaney." Her low voice was strong and confident, a teacher's voice. The handshake she offered was brief and as businesslike as the tweed sweater and gabardine slacks she wore.

"Maggie," she said, glancing down at his daughter, "you can wait outside on the bench while we visit. Do you have your book?"

"Uh-huh." She held up the book, looking as self-satisfied as a kitten with cream on its face. "Take all the time you need."

"Fine. Close the door on your way out," Miss Chapman said. "Please have a seat, Sheriff."

Sam seated himself on the adult-sized wooden chair she'd placed next to the desk. She swiveled her own chair to face him.

"I'm hoping we can resolve this right here," he said.

"It's not like Maggie to misbehave in school—or anywhere else."

"You're right, it isn't like her. She's usually a model student, and she's extremely bright, as I'm sure you're aware. She's already reading at a fourth grade level."

"Maggie's mother taught her to read before she started school, and she just took off from there." Sam hadn't meant to mention Bethany, but the words had just come.

Miss Chapman leaned toward him, her voice softening. "I understand that Maggie lost her mother last year. That must've been terribly hard on her."

"It was hard on both of us. It still is, especially with Christmas coming." *Damn,* he hadn't meant to get personal.

"I understand." She leaned back in the chair, crossing her slender legs. Her feet were clad in low-heeled gray suede boots. "I was wondering if that loss might've had some bearing on yesterday's behavior."

Sam shook his head. "I had a feeling you might say that. Maggie went through some hard months after her mother died. But this year she's been happy. She's excited about Christmas, keeps asking me when we're going to get a tree."

"So, it's just the two of you at home? How do you manage?" She appeared to be studying him, her eyes soft and knowing behind the rims of her John Lennon glasses.

Sam forced a chuckle. "I'm a lousy cook, and I work a lot. But we're a team. We manage all right."

"What does she do while you're at work?"

"I've arranged for her to stay with the retired couple next door." Sam felt a prickle of annoyance. The woman was beginning to sound like somebody from Child Protective Services. "Listen, I don't know why she went on strike yesterday. I was hoping you might have some idea."

"Well . . ." A slight crown creased her forehead. "If Maggie's as happy as you say she is, and if there's nothing amiss at home, we might want to consider Maggie's stated reason for going on strike—that she hates going to phys ed."

"She really does hate it," Sam said, "especially if there's any competition involved."

"Oh, I believe her. Maggie's good at everything she does in the classroom. She's the best reader, one of the best artists, does fine at math, but . . ." Her gaze took Sam's measure. "Something tells me you didn't hate phys ed in school. Am I right?"

Sam's face felt warm. "I played college football. Might've gone pro if I hadn't blown my knee. And no, I didn't hate it. I loved it."

"Because you were good at it. But Maggie isn't good at sports. In fact, she probably sees herself as the worst one in the class, and she hates that, because she wants to be best at everything. But that doesn't excuse her from taking part."

"I didn't come here to argue," Sam said. "I agree with you. In fact, I told Maggie that, until her attitude changes, we're not getting a Christmas tree." Sam couldn't help wondering whether she approved of that tactic. Her approval shouldn't matter, he reminded himself. But somehow it did.

"And what did Maggie say to that?" she asked.

"Not much. She just dug in her heels."

"I see." Miss Chapman rose from her chair with a flowing motion. *Grace.* The name seemed a perfect fit. "Let's see what Maggie has to say about this." She strode to the door and opened it. "Come on in, Maggie."

Maggie walked in, holding her book and looking like a scolded puppy. She was the picture of contrition. But Sam knew his daughter, and he knew an act when he saw one.

The instant her gaze met Sam's, he suddenly realized what the little schemer had in mind.

He swore silently, remembering what she'd said about his needing a woman in his life.

Maggie had set him up.

Chapter Three

"Well, Maggie?" Grace took her seat again, lowering herself to eye level with the little girl. "Do you have something to say to us?"

Maggie gazed down at her red canvas sneakers. "I'm sorry, Miss Chapman. I promise not to go on strike again. But please—" She looked up again with eyes that would melt a heart of granite. "Please don't make me play sports. I feel so clumsy and stupid out there. I'll do extra work, clean up the classroom, anything."

Grace sensed Sam Delaney's eyes watching her. *Hot.* Wynette's description came back to her, and it fit. The sheriff was tall and broad-shouldered, with a square chin and gentle gray eyes. She could understand what the women of Branding Iron saw in him. But to her he was just a parent. And her only concern was his daughter's problem.

"Let me tell you a secret, Maggie," she said. "When I was your age, I was a lot like you. I loved to read, and I was a good student. But I was awful at sports, always missing the ball, or dropping it, or tripping over my own feet. I hated being laughed at and being the last one chosen for teams. But I couldn't quit because my teachers wouldn't let me. And you know what? I'm glad now. I never did get to be an athlete, but I learned a lot—things like being part of a team and being a good sport. I learned to laugh at myself when I made a mistake—and that still comes in handy sometimes. You can learn those things, too. That's why I'm going to insist that you keep on going to phys ed with your class. I'm sure your father will back me up on this." She glanced at the sheriff. He nodded.

"So it's decided. No more strikes. Are we straight, Maggie?" Grace asked.

"Straight," Maggie said. "No more strikes."

"High five?" Grace held up her hand.

"High five!" Maggie's small, open palm smacked her teacher's. Then the little girl turned to her father. "Okay, Daddy, can we go get our Christmas tree now?"

The sheriff shifted uneasily in his chair. Now what? Grace wondered. The man didn't look happy. Had she said or done something to upset him? Or was he struggling with his daughter's request for a tree? He'd already mentioned that this holiday would be difficult for him.

"We can talk about the tree after we leave, Maggie," he said. "But first, I have something else to discuss with your teacher."

Sam cleared his throat. He saw Maggie's face light up. The little matchmaker probably thought he was going to ask her teacher out on a date. But she was about to be disappointed.

Even if he'd planned to ask the woman out—which he most certainly hadn't—once Grace Chapman saw what he'd done to her car, she'd be livid. She'd probably never speak to him again, except to make sure he paid for the damage.

"Is there a problem? Can I help?" Miss Chapman's eyes were dark pools of concern. Sam felt lower than a snake's belly, but there was no way to make this any easier.

"I'm afraid the problem is with your car," he said. "I swerved into it in the parking lot when a boy ran in front of me."

Maggie gasped, her eyes wide with horror. "Daddy! You're the sheriff! What will people say?"

"Well, at least you didn't hit the boy." Miss Chapman was making an effort to stay calm, but Sam could see the strain in her face and hear it in her voice. "Is the car drivable?" she asked.

"It should be. But it won't be pretty. You're going to need a new right rear fender. Don't worry, I've got insurance to pay for it—I'll use my own policy, not the county's, since I was off duty. And I know the owner of a good body shop in Cottonwood Springs. He'll have it fixed as soon as he can get the part. Meanwhile, my insurance will cover the cost of a rental car for you, and . . ." Sam let the words trail off as he realized he was saying too much too fast. She probably thought he sounded like an idiot.

Well, blast it, he *felt* like an idiot.

With a weary sigh, she rose from her chair, slipped on the coat she'd draped over the back, and took her purse out of a desk drawer. "Let's go. I might as well see the worst of it."

Grace locked the classroom door behind her and led the way outside. Sam Delaney walked beside her. His size and masculine presence made her tingle with awareness. But never mind that. The big lug had crashed into her precious Honda, the car she'd scrimped to buy and kept in tip-top condition over the years. It was her baby and, for all she knew, it could be totaled. If it was, his insurance probably wouldn't pay enough to replace it. *Merry Christmas, Grace.*

With Maggie scampering ahead of them, they crossed

the parking lot. Grace couldn't see her car. It was hidden behind the sheriff's Jeep, which looked as big and tough as a Sherman tank. She'd bet money that it had survived the collision without so much as a scratch. While her poor, innocent little Honda . . .

She groaned as they rounded the sheriff's vehicle, and she saw the damage. The right rear fender of her car, which dangled from the chassis by a couple of bolts, was crumpled like a scrap of tinfoil.

Poor baby. Grace felt like crying.

"I'm sorry," the sheriff said.

" 'Sorry' doesn't fix it. How can I even drive it home with the fender hanging like that?"

"I've got a wrench," he said. "I can take it off for you. Or better yet, I could just call for a tow now. The tow truck can drop off your car at the body shop in Cottonwood Springs. Meanwhile, I can drive you home, and we can get you a rental car tomorrow. There's no rental agency here in Branding Iron, but I can drive you to Cottonwood Springs on my lunch hour."

"I teach school. I have to be here," she said. "One of my roommates can drive me to work, but after that, I'll need my own transportation. I want that rental sitting right here when I come out at the end of the school day." She wasn't going easy on him, but Grace didn't care. The sheriff had damaged her car, and it was up to him to make things right.

"I know this was an accident," she added when he didn't reply right away. "But it wasn't my fault, and I don't deserve to be stranded because of it. You're the sheriff. I know you have connections. Make it happen."

She studied his reaction—a silent frown. Big Sam Delaney was a hunk, with his chiseled features and superhero physique. But that was beside the point. Right now what she needed was her car fixed and something to drive in the meantime. And she had to let him know she meant business.

"Give me till tomorrow afternoon," he said. "There's a chance I can have the towing company pick up the rental and bring it from Cottonwood Springs when they come to pick up your car. I'll have to clear it with my insurance, but if that isn't an option, I'll find another way."

"Fine." Grace squelched the impulse to thank him. If he hadn't hit her car she wouldn't be needing his help.

Suddenly she felt exhausted. A few years ago a doctor had warned her that she was borderline hypoglycemic. If she felt extra tired, it could be a sign that her blood sugar was low and she needed to eat. Or maybe it was just the emotional stress of seeing her wrecked car.

The sheriff was all business now. "Clean everything you need out of your car, including the trunk. I've got some trash bags in the Jeep. I'll get you a couple of those and give you a hand. After that, you can give me the key, and I'll drive you home. All right?"

She nodded, found the key in her purse, and unlocked the car door.

"Daddy, I'm really hungry," Maggie piped up. "Can we stop at Buckaroo's when we go to Miss Chapman's house? It's right on the way."

"How about it?" The sheriff caught Grace's gaze. "It's too early for dinner, but if you could do with coffee and the best pie in three counties, we'd be glad to have you as our guest."

"Well . . ." Scooping odds and ends out of the glove box, Grace weighed the invitation. She didn't want to be obligated to the sheriff, and she didn't usually socialize with students outside of school. But Maggie and her father meant well. Turning them down would be churlish. And she did need to eat. "All right," she said. "Just pie and coffee. Thanks."

They climbed into the big vehicle. The sheriff boosted Maggie into the high backseat, then offered Grace his hand. "Watch that step, it's a long one."

"Thanks." She clasped his hand for balance as she found the foothold and hoisted her weight upward. The contact with his fingers was electric. Grace willed herself to ignore the tingle that surged through her body before pulling away to settle into the leather seat.

"Buckle up, both of you." He closed the passenger door.

"Daddy always reminds me to buckle up," Maggie said. "He's really careful that way. You can tell how much he cares about people. He's a great dad, too, and a great sheriff. Everybody likes him. You will, too, 'specially once you get to know him."

Grace fastened her seat belt. Maggie's praise of her father seemed a bit much, especially the last bit about getting to know him. What was the child up to? Heavens to Betsy, was she *matchmaking?* Had her so-called strike been a ploy to get her handsome dad to come to school and meet her teacher?

If that was true, Grace couldn't help feeling a bit flattered. But Maggie's scheme—if that's what it amounted to—was a bad idea for all sorts of reasons. Grace needed to nip it in the bud before things got awkward.

From the backseat, Maggie could see no more than the tops of their heads—her father's dark brown, her teacher's a few shades lighter. Did they like each other? It was too soon to tell. But at least her dad had invited Miss Chapman to go to Buckaroo's with them. And at least Miss Chapman had said yes. That was a good sign.

Maggie couldn't have planned better than the accident that had banged up her teacher's car. At first, she'd feared it would ruin everything. But then she'd realized it might be helpful. The two them would have to stay in touch, at least until the car was fixed. That would allow them more time to get acquainted—and more time for the magic to happen.

They wouldn't have to fall in love; just liking each other enough to ease Big Sam's loneliness would be enough for now. Was that too much to ask?

They parked at the curb outside Buckaroo's. Sam climbed out of the high vehicle and went around to the passenger side to open the door. When he offered a hand to help Miss Chapman to the sidewalk, she took it. Her fingers were long and slender, their brief clasp smooth and warm against his palm. She smelled faintly of rosemary—not perfume, maybe soap or shampoo. Whatever it was, he found himself breathing it in, savoring the sweet, clean fragrance.

Grace. She hadn't invited him to call her by her given name, but at least he could think of her that way.

Lifting Maggie by the waist, he swung her to the ground. "Can I have a chocolate shake, Daddy?" she asked. "I like shakes better than pie."

"You can have anything you want, as long as it doesn't spoil your supper." Sam watched her skip ahead of him, dancing down the sidewalk.

Overhead, seen through the bare trees that lined the street, leaden clouds were moving across the sky. The moist chill in the air warned of a coming storm. Sam made a mental note to check the weather report later. Storms always made his job harder.

"I've never been here before," Grace said as they reached the restaurant and Sam held the door.

"The food is yummy!" Maggie said, " 'specially the burgers, and the pizza, and the shakes."

Grace gave her a smile. "I'll take your word for that."

Buckaroo's wasn't crowded at this hour. But as Sam

ushered Maggie and Grace to an empty booth, he became aware of curious eyes watching them. When it came to gossip, Branding Iron was a typical small town. By tonight, the rumor that he was dating the pretty teacher would be all over town.

Not that it was true. He wasn't dating anybody, and, as far as he knew, neither was Grace. But the notion of a teacher spending time with her student's father was mildly scandalous. If word got back to her that people were talking, Grace was bound to be upset. Coming here had probably been a mistake. But there was nothing to be done about it now.

Sam gave their order to the waitress—two coffees, two slices of apple pie with ice cream, and a chocolate shake. Then they settled back to wait.

Buckaroo's reminded Grace of a place she'd known growing up. The red Formica-topped tables, the worn black-and-white tile on the floor, the smells of grilled meat and sizzling oil from behind the counter, the paper napkins and plastic bottles of ketchup and mustard all reminded her of the place her uncle had owned, where she'd worked as a waitress as soon as she was legal, and sometimes before. Even the Christmas lights strung across the ceiling and the holiday music blaring "I'll Have a Blue Christmas" from the wall-mounted speaker seemed familiar.

"That was Mom's favorite Christmas song," Maggie said. "She liked to sing along with Elvis Presley. Do you sing, Miss Chapman?"

"Only in class." Grace added creamer to the coffee the waitress had set in front of her. She'd seen the pain that had flashed across Sam's face, but when she looked up, it was gone. Grace knew about his wife. He wore no wedding ring—maybe he never had. But that didn't mean he was free.

"You said you'd never been here before," he said, breaking the awkward silence. "I take it you're new in Branding Iron. Where did you come from?"

"I grew up in Oklahoma—in a town not much bigger than this one. After college, I got a job teaching in Oklahoma City."

"Could I ask what brought you to Branding Iron?"

Was this a conversation or an interrogation? Grace wondered. But then again, maybe it was just his way of making small talk. "I needed a change of scene, and I read about the job opening. I applied, and here I am."

That was only a half truth. She'd fled Oklahoma after the last-minute cancellation of her wedding plans. Even after she'd cleaned up the mess, returned the gifts, and paid the bills, she hadn't been able to face her jilted groom or the guests who'd made an effort to be there for her. It was easier to pack up, run, and vow that she would never make the same mistake again.

"Do you have family back in Oklahoma?" The sheriff—who'd asked her to call him Sam—sipped his coffee, his gaze friendly and curious.

She shook her head. "Not anymore. My parents were divorced when I was young. My mother passed away a few years ago, and I haven't spoken with my father since he moved out of the house to marry his girlfriend."

She was revealing more than she'd meant to, but Sam Delaney was a good listener, gazing into her eyes and giving her time to talk. Maybe it was his lawman's way of opening people up.

Maggie appeared to have tuned out the conversation. She was watching the cook behind the counter and tapping her fingers in time to "Jingle Bell Rock," which was blasting out of the speakers.

"No brothers or sisters?" Sam asked.

"I do have an older brother," Grace said, remembering

how Cooper had flown in to walk her down the aisle at her botched wedding. They hadn't parted on the best of terms. "He lives in Seattle. We keep in touch, but we don't see much of each other. He—but never mind, it doesn't matter."

Grace tore her gaze away and forced herself to stop talking. If she kept looking into those gentle gray eyes of his, she'd be spilling all her past secrets—the wedding, her other broken relationships, and even the day when she'd come home spattered with easel paint and discovered that no man, not even her beloved father, could be trusted.

In the beat of awkward silence, she scrambled for a way to change the subject. But it was Maggie who broke the tension. "Yay! Here comes the waitress with our food. I'm starved. How about you?"

The pie was wonderful—the filling sweetly juicy, the crust so flaky that it crumbled at a touch. "It comes from Stella's Bakery on Main Street," Sam said. "The doughnuts and brownies there are so decadent they're almost sinful."

"But Stella's getting married, Daddy. What'll we do if she closes the place?"

Sam raised an eyebrow. "How do you know she's getting married, Maggie?"

"I saw the diamond ring on her finger the last time we were there. Didn't you notice it? You're the sheriff, Daddy. You're supposed to notice everything."

Sam gave her a smile. "I can't notice everything. That's why I have your sharp eyes to help me."

The tenderness between father and daughter tugged at Grace's heart. She remembered how her father had always made her feel like his special princess. Then everything had changed. She could only hope that Maggie would never have to feel the sting of betrayal she'd experienced as a child.

"Maybe I can learn to bake as good as Stella," Maggie said. "Then we won't need to spend money at the bakery."

"Do you know how to cook, Maggie?" Grace asked her.

"Not yet. But we have this big red and white cookbook that was my grandma's. It has everything in it—even pictures. I figure that I can read what to do and then just do it. Next year I'm going to make Thanksgiving dinner, with turkey and real pumpkin pie."

"This year we had TV dinners," Sam admitted. "And frozen pumpkin pie—still frozen."

"But that was 'cause Daddy had to work." Even with so much talking, Maggie had managed to finish her shake. "What did you do for Thanksgiving, Miss Chapman?"

"My roommates and I fixed a little dinner and invited a few friends. If I'd known, I would've asked you both to come."

"Maybe we can ask you to dinner next year," Maggie said. "Daddy, I've got an idea. When we leave here, we can go get our Christmas tree. I bet Miss Chapman would like to come with us."

Oh, no! Grace felt the pull of the adorable little manipulator reeling her in. She laid her fork next to her empty plate and shrugged into the coat she'd left to rest on her shoulders. "I really need to get home. I've got lessons to prepare, laundry to do . . ."

"Oh, please come!" Maggie begged. "It'll be so much fun! There'll be Christmas lights and music and everything! And you can pick out a tree for our class. You know that all the kids want a tree in the room."

The part about the tree got Grace thinking. The school would have a tree in the front hall, but the budget didn't cover trees for the classrooms. Any teacher who wanted a tree would have to provide her own. Grace knew her young students were excited about decorating a class tree, and she didn't mind the idea of paying for one. But with only a small car—a small *wrecked* car, she reminded herself—she had no way of getting a tree to the school. Maggie had just offered her a solution, but it would mean spending more time with this appealing father and daughter—the last thing she needed.

As if she didn't need another reminder, Sam opened his wallet to pay for their food. Grace couldn't help noticing the photo of a pretty woman with red hair like Maggie's. The photo in its plastic sleeve had been placed where he would see it anytime he opened the wallet. She remembered what Wynette had mentioned—that the sheriff was still mourning his wife.

No, this man was definitely not available.

And neither was she.

Sam had yet to weigh in on Maggie's request to go tree shopping. "We can always go tomorrow, Maggie," he hedged. "We can even pick up an extra tree for your class." He gave Grace a meaningful glance. "Miss Chapman doesn't have to be there."

"But Daddy!" Maggie argued. "Didn't you look at the sky outside? It's going to storm tomorrow, or maybe even tonight. It'll be too cold to go to the tree lot. Anyway, you've got that meeting tomorrow after work."

"Meeting?" Sam looked blank.

"You know. The one to plan the town Christmas party."

"Oh, *that* meeting." Sam suppressed a groan. "It's bound to go on half the night. Those ladies on the committee can spend hours just arguing about the decorations."

"See? You'll be too busy to get trees tomorrow," Maggie said. "We need to go now. Come on, Daddy. I've been good. I promised no more strikes."

Sam caved in with a sigh. "Okay, you win. We can drop your teacher off on the way unless . . ." Sam's pulse quickened. "Unless, of course, she'd like to come along." He turned to Grace. "We'd be happy to have you. But if you need to get home, we can still pick up your tree."

"Actually, I'd like to buy the tree myself," Grace said. "Are you sure you don't mind my coming along?"

"We don't mind a bit, do we, Maggie?" Sam felt an un-accustomed lightness as he ushered his daughter and her teacher outside and helped them into the vehicle. He was only doing a favor, he reminded himself—a favor he certainly owed Grace after damaging her car. He was being helpful, that was all. Wasn't it?

Maggie smiled as she fastened her seat belt and settled into the rear seat. So far her plan was working like a charm. Her father and Miss Chapman really seemed to like each other. And shopping for Christmas trees would be just the thing to help the romance along. Tonight wasn't what you'd call a real date, but that would be the next natural step. Maggie could hardly wait.

The Christmas tree lot was thirty minutes away, set up in a field between Branding Iron and Cottonwood Springs. With the heater blasting warmth, Sam had tuned the radio to a station that played Christmas music—another sign that he was finally getting some holiday spirit.

Humming along to "The Little Drummer Boy," she gazed out the window at the farms and ranches that separated Branding Iron from Cottonwood Springs, which had a mall with movie theaters, a hospital, and a big-box ShopMart. By now the sun was going down, casting a glow like burning coals against the sooty clouds. The Christmas tree lot would be glowing with lights strung between the high fence poles. The air would smell of fresh evergreens, and happy families would be strolling between the rows of cut trees.

Maggie remembered last year, missing her mother and

being sent off to her grandparents' for the holidays because her father was too brokenhearted to celebrate. It had been the saddest time of her life, and Sam's. That was why she'd promised herself that this Christmas would be different. She would do everything she could to make it a happy time.

Chapter Four

This had been the wrong decision, Grace scolded herself as she followed Maggie down one more row of trees. The little girl was so excited, grabbing her hand, tugging her this way and that—behavior that Grace would never have tolerated in class.

"What about this one, Miss Chapman—no, wait, here's a prettier one." She darted back and forth like a little bird, adorable in her happiness. It was all Grace could do to keep from reaching down and hugging her. But teachers had their rules, even outside the classroom. Too much familiarity tonight could become tomorrow's problem.

"Thanks for coming along tonight." Sam stood behind her, watching. "I know you might have better things to do, but you've made a little girl happy. She's taken quite a shine to you."

That's just the problem. Grace kept the words to herself. She needed to put the brakes on what was happening, but now wasn't the right time, not while Maggie was having so much fun.

"Do you need me to rein her in?" he asked. "We could be here all night."

"Let's give her time, maybe nudge her along if she doesn't

choose a classroom tree soon. Then you'll still need a tree for your house."

"Don't worry. I've already narrowed the choice down to three trees. She can choose one."

"Smart thinking." She turned and looked up at him. Big Sam. His height and broad-shouldered bulk made her feel almost petite. His eyes reflected the glow of the Christmas lights, and his smile showed a dimple in his left cheek. This was a man she could fall in love with, Grace thought. But she'd been in love before and she knew how the story would end. She didn't need any more wreckage in her life. Neither did Sam, and neither did his vulnerable little girl. When he took her home tonight, she would shut this attraction down—for good.

"I found it!" The happy shout from Maggie broke into Grace's thoughts. "Come see, Miss Chapman! It's the perfect tree!"

And so it was—full and bushy, with a nice even shape, but not too big for the classroom. With a breath of relief, Grace seized the trunk to carry the tree up to the cash register. It was heavier than it looked.

"I'll take that for you." Sam lifted the tree out of her hands, as if it weighed nothing, and carried it to the checkout table. Grace followed, her credit card in hand. She thrust it at the woman behind the table in time to make sure that Sam wouldn't offer to pay. That would be like him, and she didn't want to feel obligated.

Leaving the tree by the gate with a SOLD tag on it, Grace followed Sam back into the lot. With luck, Maggie would choose one of the trees her father had picked out. Then they could buy the winner, load the trees, and head home to Branding Iron.

By now, more families were arriving to buy their trees. Children raced up and down the rows, laughing. Fresh pine scented the cold night air. The first snowflakes of the arriving storm were drifting out of the dark sky.

Maggie had gone on ahead. When Grace and Sam found her, she was clinging to a large, lopsided tree with a scraggly top. "I want this one, Daddy," she said.

Sam looked the tree up and down, shaking his head. "Maggie, I've picked out three nice trees. You can choose the one you like best. This one is . . . ugly."

"I know." She clung to the tree, its needles jabbing her cheek. "Don't you see? Nobody else will want it. It'll be left alone in the lot, and it will be so sad."

Sam sighed. "Maggie, it's a *tree*."

"Please, Daddy." Tears glimmered in Maggie's eyes. "We can take it home and make it look pretty."

Grace watched the emotions flow across Sam's face— exasperation, patience, and yes, love. Even before he spoke, she knew what he would do.

"All right, Maggie," he said. "If this is the tree you want, it's the one we'll get." He glanced at the tag. Since the trees were priced by the foot, this gangly specimen was bound to be expensive. But Sam, to his credit, didn't flinch. Grace couldn't help liking him for that. In fact, she found herself liking this strong, gentle lawman more and more—not a good thing, in her case.

Sam paid the cashier, carried both trees out to the Jeep, and put them in the back. Maggie followed him, dancing along through the lightly blowing snow.

They piled into the vehicle, buckled up, and started for home. Snowflakes blew against the windshield. Sam turned on the wipers and cranked up the heat. Big storms were rare in Texas, and this one probably wouldn't leave much snowfall behind. But the cold was going to be fierce tomorrow—a day for slick roads, sliding vehicles, and short tempers. Sam knew what to expect, and he didn't look forward to it.

A quick look in the rearview mirror showed him that Maggie had fallen asleep in the backseat. Grace swiveled slightly, glanced back between the seats, and gave him a heartwarming smile. Sam smiled back at her. Even knowing how Maggie had set them up, he'd enjoyed the evening far more than he'd expected. Maybe his daughter was right. Maybe a new friendship was what he needed.

He wouldn't ask Grace out—not, at least, until the business with her car was settled. But the notion had taken root in his mind. He would think about it for now. Maybe after a day or two, he would come to his senses and realize that it wasn't a good idea. Or maybe not.

Grace gave him directions to her house. On the way, they stopped by the school and left the tree outside the door to her classroom. Then he drove her home. The small house was one he knew, as he knew every property in Branding Iron. The old man who'd lived here for years had died this past summer, and the place had been bought by a woman who was the youth counselor for the school district. He'd heard that she'd taken in a couple of roommates to help with expenses. Grace would be one of them.

They pulled up in front of the house, with its big, dead tree in the front yard. After checking on Maggie, who was still fast asleep, Sam got out and came around the vehicle to open the door and give Grace a hand to the ground.

"Would you mind walking me to the door?" she asked. "I need to talk with you for a minute, out of Maggie's hearing."

"Sure." He fell into step beside her. "Is something wrong?"

"That's what I'm trying to prevent." She paused at the foot of the porch steps and turned to face him. "I need to make certain that Maggie understands something. In my class, it's essential that I treat all my students the same. We had a good time tonight. But that doesn't mean I'm her new best friend, or that she can expect special treatment."

"You're right, of course," Sam said. "I'll have a talk with Maggie and make sure she understands the rules. Anything else?"

"One more thing." She took a deep breath, remembering the photo she'd seen in his wallet. "I know you meant well, taking me with you and Maggie tonight. But while we were in the restaurant, I could tell that people were staring and talking about us. As a teacher, I don't need that kind of attention."

"I was aware of it, too," Sam said. "I'm sorry you were uncomfortable."

She took another deep breath, snowflakes melting on her glasses. "Here's the thing. We both value our jobs and our reputations. I don't think we should be seen together. In fact, to be clear, I don't think we should spend any more time together at all."

Sam had half expected what was coming, but it still stung. "Grace—" he began.

"This isn't personal," she said. "You're a very nice man. In a different time and place, maybe—"

"It's all right, Grace. Something told me you might feel this way. So don't worry about it. I'll take care of your car problem, see you at Maggie's school events, and we'll call it good. Friends?" He extended his hand.

"Of course." Her smile was strained. Her hand trembled slightly in his. "Good night, Sam."

"Good night, Grace." He turned and strode back down the sidewalk, telling himself it didn't matter. Maggie would be disappointed when he gave her the news. The little schemer had put a lot of thought and effort into setting up her dad with her teacher. All for nothing—but it was probably for the best. He had his baggage, and something told him that Grace had hers as well.

Maggie had only wanted to make him happy, Sam reminded himself. Now it would be his turn to give back. His heart might not be brimming with holiday spirit, but he would do his best—ugly tree and all. Nobody deserved a happy Christmas more than his Maggie did.

When Grace walked in the door, her roommates pounced on her like a couple of cats on fresh tuna. "We saw you drive up!" Wynette tugged Grace over to the couch. "What happened? Spill! We want to hear everything!"

Grace sighed. All she really wanted was to get to her room, take off her school clothes, pull on her sweats, and try to forget the look in Sam's eyes when she'd told him she didn't want to see him again.

"There's not much to tell," she said. "It wasn't anything like a date, if that's what you're thinking. It was mostly about Maggie."

"Not much to tell? Are you saying you spent an evening with the most gorgeous man in town, and nothing happened?" Jess took Grace's coat and hung it on the rack. "He walked you to the door. That must've meant something."

Grace imagined her roommates peering through the slats of the venetian blinds, trying not to be seen. "As I said, it was mostly about Maggie. He came by for the conference after school. Maggie apologized for her behavior and promised not to do it again. She almost seemed pleased with herself."

Jess chuckled. "It wouldn't take a child psychologist to see through that. I'm betting that Maggie staged the whole act to get you and her dad together. So, did it work?"

"Hardly. The scheme might've worked better if he

hadn't hit my car in the parking lot. Believe me, when I saw that crumpled fender, the last thing on my mind was romance."

"But that's just what it sounds like!" Wynette was an avid reader of romance novels. "People in books meet that way, and it always works out fine. He could turn out to be the love of your life, Grace."

"Don't count on it." Grace pried herself off the couch. "He's going to have the car towed and fixed and have a rental waiting for me at the school by the end of the day. But that will be the end of it. We won't be seeing each other again—not socially, at least. So now that I've shared my uninteresting story, I'm going to my room to decompress."

"Not so fast," Jess said with a knowing smile. "It's almost nine o'clock. You didn't spend that much time standing around in the parking lot talking about your car."

Grace sighed. "All right. We took Maggie to Buckaroo's for treats—chocolate shake for her, apple pie and coffee for the sheriff and me, just to save you the trouble of asking. Then Maggie wanted to go and get a Christmas tree. Since I needed a tree for my classroom, I went along. If you've been to the tree lot, you know it's halfway to Cottonwood Springs, so we spent an hour just driving there and back. We dropped my tree off at the school, and he drove me home. End of story."

"But we know he walked you to the door." Wynette wasn't giving up. "After all that, I can't believe he wouldn't ask you for a date."

"Unless you didn't give him a chance," Jess added.

"As I told you, nothing happened. We shook hands and agreed to be distant friends. And speaking of friends, I'm going to need a ride to school tomorrow. Jess, could you do the honors?"

"No problem. It's right on the way to work. Will you need a ride home?"

"I'd better not need one. Sam promised me the rental car would be in the parking lot with the keys in the school office. If he's a man of his word, I should be fine."

Before Wynette and Jess could pry any more answers out of her, Grace escaped down the hallway. She liked her roommates, and she knew that the grilling they'd given her was all in fun. But between the damage to her beloved Honda and the strain of resisting her attraction to the handsome sheriff, she'd been through an emotional wringer. All she wanted to do was check tomorrow's lesson plans, undress, brush her teeth, and curl up in bed with the bestselling mystery book she was currently reading.

She'd never told her roommates about her track record of broken relationships. If she were to open up, they'd at least understand why she mustn't get involved with Sam. But the past was a closed book. Branding Iron was her chance for a fresh start. She couldn't afford to mess it up by falling in love—not even with a man like Big Sam Delaney.

By the next morning, the storm had moved on, leaving frigid blue skies and a landscape brushed with frosted white. Sam scraped the icy coating off the windows of the Jeep, buckled Maggie into the backseat, and dropped her off at school before heading to work.

The first part of last night's talk had gone all right, he thought. When he'd explained that she couldn't expect special treatment from Miss Chapman, she'd looked at him as if he were in kindergarten.

"I know that already, Daddy," she'd said. "And there's another thing, besides what you just said. If the kids in my class think I'm the teacher's pet, they won't like me. I don't want that to happen. Neither does Miss Chapman. Don't worry, I'll be fine."

The rest of their talk had been harder. When Sam had told her that he and Miss Chapman wouldn't be dating, she'd almost cried.

"But Daddy, I know she likes you. And I know you like her. I could see that last night."

"We do like each other, as friends," he said. "But when we were in Buckaroo's yesterday, we could tell that people were whispering about us. I'm the sheriff, and she's a teacher. The wrong kind of talk could be bad for both of us. So we decided it would be best not to give folks anything to gossip about."

That wasn't the whole story, but it was the best he could do for Maggie. The truth was, he'd sensed a resistance in Grace that he couldn't explain. The fear of damaging gossip had been a handy excuse, a cover-up for something deeper. At the time, he'd had little choice except to let it go. But being curious was part of his job as a lawman. Maybe she was hiding some secret from her past.

Or, what the hell, maybe she just didn't like him.

He would call the body shop and rental companies first thing when he got to work, Sam resolved. Once he'd spoken with his insurance company and arranged for the tow and the rental car delivery, he would put Miss Grace Chapman firmly out of his mind and focus on his work.

Whatever Grace was hiding, unless it was criminal, it was none of his concern. And using the database to check on her would be crossing a line—one he had no business crossing.

Preoccupied, he parked in his slot outside the city and county building and strode down the hall to the sheriff's office. Helen was already at her desk. She greeted him with a smile and brought his usual cup of hot coffee.

"Anything new?" he asked her.

"You tell me." When he gave her a blank look, she continued. "Word is that you're dating that pretty new teacher at the elementary school."

Sam swore silently. So word had already gotten around. "I'm not dating her. Maggie's one of her students. We had a meeting after school. Maggie was hungry, so I took both of them to Buckaroo's and then to buy Christmas trees. End of story."

"Mm-hmm." She gave him a knowing smile.

"Blast it, Helen, I'm not dating her. But just so you'll know, I also crashed into her car at the school. My fault. I'm arranging to get it fixed, so if you get calls about that—"

"I'll just take a message and pass it on," Helen said. "Oh, it's your turn to furnish doughnuts for the party-planning committee tonight. I've already ordered a batch from Stella's. I can pick them up after lunch if you'd like."

"Thanks. But you'd better hide them or I might be tempted to help myself early."

At least the doughnuts from Stella's Bakery would give him something to look forward to. Every year, before the holiday season, a citizens' committee held several meetings to plan Branding Iron's annual Christmas party. Not that there was much to plan. The party would be held in the high school gym, on the last Saturday before Christmas. There would be a tree and a Santa to pass out treats for the kids. People would bring their assigned dishes. They would eat at set-up tables, visit awhile, clean up the mess, and go home. It didn't make sense that a party like that would take hours of planning. But somehow it always did. Last year he'd spent an hour listening to two women debate the color scheme of the napkins and paper plates.

He knew better than to try and get out of the meeting.

As a representative of the county government, in charge of security—as if there was any need for it—being there was part of his job. At least there'd be doughnuts, and hopefully enough coffee to keep him awake.

Maybe he should have Helen order a second dozen.

After making arrangements for Grace's car, Sam waded into his day. A follow-up on the domestic had turned out just as he'd expected, with Ruth dropping charges and taking her husband home. The grocery store had taken a hit on a bad check, and the hardware and feed was missing several bags of hog chow from the storage room. Last night a deputy had arrested the town drunk in a brawl at Rowdy's Roost, the bar that was outside city limits, and therefore the county's problem.

Sam knew—and liked—the man in question. A few years ago, Hank Miller had lost his leg in a horrific hay baler accident. The pain had started him drinking, and after a year of it, his wife had had enough. She'd taken their young son, left town, and filed for divorce with full custody. Because the ranch he'd been running belonged to his wife's family, he'd lost that as well, and had nothing to live on but his monthly disability checks.

After so much pain and loss, how could anybody not *drink?* Sam asked himself as he went downstairs to the jail. He'd partied in college himself, had almost gone over the edge after blowing his knee and his football career. It had taken Bethany to pull him back. After last year's gut blow of losing her, only Maggie had kept him from turning to alcohol again.

He understood at least some of what Hank must be going through. But understanding wouldn't be enough to help the man. To change his life, Hank would have to be willing to help himself.

The only prisoner in the jail was Hank, who sat slumped

with his head in his hands. With the guard looking on from the check-in counter, Sam used his key to open the cell.

At the metallic scrape of the door, Hank raised his head. He was a year younger than Sam. They'd played football together in high school—Hank as second-string defensive tackle, Sam as the star offensive lineman who could pass the length of the field. Hank had been a good-looking young man. But he'd taken a beating from life, and he looked it. His frame was little more than skin and bones. His prosthetic leg was thrust out at an angle to relieve the painful weight on it. His bruised, unshaven face had a haunted look, the cheeks hollow, the eyes bloodshot.

"How are you feeling, Hank?" Sam asked.

"How the hell do you think I'm feeling?" Hank growled. "I've got a headache that'd knock out an elephant."

"Have you had breakfast?" The jail had no cooking facilities, but there were frozen meals in the fridge and a microwave on the counter.

Hank shook his head. "Couldn't get the crap down. But I could use a cigarette."

Sam nodded to the deputy on guard duty, who produced a pack from a drawer under the counter, along with a lighter. Smoking wasn't usually allowed in the jail, but exceptions could be made.

Sam lit the cigarette and passed the lighter back to the guard. Hank inhaled, closing his eyes as the nicotine began to flow into his system.

"So, what happened last night?" Sam asked. "The bartender said you slugged a man you didn't even know. What were you thinking?"

Hank exhaled a thin trail of smoke. "Just that I needed to hit somebody. Anybody. I got a letter from Marilyn yesterday. She's married. Her new husband wants to adopt Travis, so she wants me to sign away my parental rights.

She says the boy needs a real father—a *real* father. Hell, I'm his father. He's my flesh and blood."

"I can't tell you what to do, Hank," Sam said, hurting for the man. "But it seems to me the one question that matters is what would be best for Travis."

"Asked and answered." Hank sucked on the cigarette. "I signed the damned paper she sent and put it in the mail. And then I got drunk and punched some jerk who got in my face."

"Well, you got lucky this time," Sam said. "The man you hit declined to press charges. Otherwise you'd be facing time for assault and battery. As it is, you're free to go. As soon as the paperwork's done, I'll drive you home. We can pick up your car at Rowdy's later."

"Thanks, but I'll walk."

"It's cold out there. You don't have a warm coat, and you're already in bad shape. You could end up in the hospital. You know the drill by now. Collect your crutch and your other things, and I'll meet you by the front door."

"Have you got enough heat?" Sam asked Hank as they took a back street toward his home—a small trailer in a weedy vacant lot on the edge of town.

"My little electric heater does fine," Hank said. "Stop trying to mother hen me, Sam. You've got more important things to do. I can take care of myself."

"That's what you always say." Sam turned the corner onto a dirt road. "Then you get in trouble again. In a way, it's too bad the man you slugged didn't press charges. Six months in jail would've given you a warm place to sleep, three meals a day, and maybe some rehab."

"Rehab's for two-legged folks."

Sam knew better than to lecture the man about self-pity. Hank had heard it all. "Do you still have that schedule of AA meetings that I gave you?" he asked.

"Got it somewhere. But the last thing I need is cookies and Kool-Aid and listening to a bunch of sob stories."

Sam pulled into the lot, helped Hank out of the Jeep, and gave him a hand into the trailer. The space inside was cold. Sam gathered up the scattered food wrappers, checked the wiring on the portable electric heater, and turned it on. "Hank, you've got to keep papers and junk away from this heater, or you could burn the place down."

"Yeah, yeah, I know." Hank hobbled to the sagging couch, collapsed onto it, and closed his eyes. "You can go, Sam. I'm just gonna stretch out and sleep."

"Fine. Behave yourself." Sam took a minute to check the fridge and cupboards. He found no food except for some tuna and three cans of chicken noodle soup. He would make a run to the store for a few basics, such as bread, milk, eggs, peanut butter, and instant coffee. While Hank was out cold, he would sneak in and put everything away. Buying food for folks wasn't his job, but he cared about the well-being of everybody in his little town. Helping folks was a good use of his time. Settling fights and arresting lawbreakers was a good use of his time. So was being a father to Maggie.

But sitting through meetings like that blasted party-planning session tonight was nothing but a waste.

Chapter Five

"Have you got your book, Maggie?" Sam asked as he boosted his daughter into the Jeep.

"I've got two books, just in case," Maggie said. "Can I have an extra doughnut if I'm quiet?"

"We'll see if there's enough to go around. Buckle up."

Sam climbed into the driver's seat, switched on the headlamps, and started the powerful engine. He'd hoped to leave Maggie with the neighbors tonight, but they'd gone out of town, so she'd be coming with him to the party-planning meeting.

This arrangement was nothing new. Maggie had attended other meetings with her dad, and she knew the rules—sit in the corner, read her book, and don't interrupt. The bathroom was just down the hall, and she could go without asking permission. Otherwise she was to stay put and keep still. Most of the folks in the city and county government knew the little girl, and no one had ever complained about her being there. Maggie didn't seem to mind it either.

The drive to the city and county building was short, but it still gave Sam time to think about Grace. He'd paid extra out of pocket for the best rental car available—a late-model Cadillac. He'd given her his work and home phone numbers, hoping she'd at least let him know the car had arrived. But he hadn't heard from her.

Never mind, he'd gotten the message loud and clear. The lady wanted nothing more to do with him. And that was fine.

He pulled into the parking lot and stopped next to a tiny lime green Volkswagen bug that had been parked in the space clearly marked SHERIFF. "*Idiot,*" Sam muttered as he went around the Jeep to help his daughter out. What kind of fool would park in his slot, let alone drive a vehicle that looked as if it had been built for chipmunks? Nobody he knew, that was for sure.

The meeting would be held in the conference room next to the mayor's office. Helen had left the box of doughnuts on the table, along with the extra box that Sam had ordered as an afterthought. Reba, the mayor's secretary, always made the coffee, so that was taken care of, too.

Sam moved one chair into the corner for Maggie and made sure she was comfortable. At least it wasn't his meeting. His only job would be to sit at the table, sip coffee, offer a suggestion or two, and try not to appear too bored.

A printed agenda had been laid at each place. Scanning the items on the page, Sam pulled out his chair and sat down. When he glanced up, his mouth went dry.

Grace was sitting right across from him.

Grace's long day was getting longer by the minute. At that morning's faculty meeting, the principal, Ed Judkins, had informed her—without any prior notice—that she was to represent the school on the town committee to help plan the annual Christmas party. "I'm new in town," she'd argued uselessly. "Nobody knows me, and I don't know anything about the Christmas party they'll be planning. Wouldn't someone else be—"

"Miss Chapman, it's not rocket science." Ed Judkins, a

stocky man of about forty, with buzz-cut sandy hair, was a master of sarcasm, especially where new teachers were concerned. "It's not as if you're being asked to find a cure for cancer or negotiate world peace. Most of the planning is already done. Just show up tonight, fill the chair, and vote on suggestions. You know, like raise your hand yay or nay. You don't even have to open your pretty mouth. Understand?" He'd chuckled, probably thinking he'd made a clever joke.

"I do." *And thank you for this wonderful opportunity, you arrogant, chauvinistic jerk.*

There'd been sympathetic glances from some of the teachers, most of whom had been jabbed by the principal's barbs in the past. They stayed because they loved the students and valued their place in the community. And most of them nourished the hope that Judkins would move on to bigger things and leave the job open for someone with more than a grain of sensitivity.

The rest of the day hadn't gone much better. Maggie, at least, had been a model of decorum. But for the rest of the class, the Christmas crazies, as Jess called them, had struck. For their art lesson, Grace had shown them how to fold and cut paper snowflakes. One girl had taken her blunt-tipped scissors and trimmed off her friend's bangs. At recess, two boys had gotten into a fight, and during story time, one shy little girl had wet her panties and been teased to tears before Grace could scold the class into silence. She'd planned to move the Christmas tree into the room, but didn't want to reward her students for their wild conduct. The tree, she'd told them, would have to stay outside the door until they'd earned the right to bring it in and decorate it.

By the end of the day, Grace was getting a headache. Only as she passed the office on her way out had she remembered that Sam had promised her a rental car. Hoping for something comfortable, at least, she'd picked up the keys and paperwork at the front desk where the delivery-man had left them and walked outside.

Her eyes had scanned the parking lot for an unfamiliar car that matched the brand on her key. When she'd spot-ted it, next to the space where her Honda had been, she'd groaned. Was this Sam's idea of a joke? If so, it wasn't funny.

The VW beetle was the color of lime Jell-O, and so small she could barely squeeze into it. The upholstery was damp and reeked of air freshener, as if the car had been hastily cleaned at the last minute. Beneath the chemical smell, her nose had detected the rank, unmistakable odor of cigarette smoke.

Holding her breath, she'd rolled down the windows and gulped in the wintery air. She would freeze all the way home, but she had to breathe.

Sam had mentioned something about the meeting tonight. If he was going to be there, she would make cer-tain he knew what she thought of his car choice.

Tonight she'd arrived ahead of him and parked the wretched vehicle in his space, where he was bound to no-tice it. But now, sitting across the table and looking into his warm, gray eyes, she found herself unsure of what to say.

The meeting was about to start. People were scanning the agenda, sipping coffee, and helping themselves to the doughnuts in the open bakery box on the table. Sam reached back to hand Maggie a doughnut with icing and sprinkles, along with a napkin. Then he turned toward the table and gave Grace a smile.

"Hi," he said, keeping his voice low. "Did the car work out all right for you?"

"You didn't see it?"

"I didn't realize you'd be here. I wasn't looking."

"How could you have missed it? I parked it in your space, just so you'd notice."

"What?" His stunned expression froze. "Grace, I swear, that wasn't—"

His words were cut short by a rap of the mayor's gavel. The meeting had begun.

Maggie finished her doughnut, wiped her fingers on the napkin, and opened her book. She'd planned to start reading. But for the moment, she found herself paying more attention to the meeting than to her book.

She hadn't expected that her teacher would be here, let alone that Miss Chapman would be sitting right across from her dad. Big Sam had explained to Maggie that the two of them wouldn't be dating. But Maggie hadn't given up hope. All she needed was a little bit of luck to move things along—and this could be her lucky night.

From where she sat, she couldn't hear what they were saying. But at least they were looking at each other and talking. That had to be a good sign, didn't it?

Maggie glanced around the table, recognizing Rulon Wilkins, the mayor, who was also the bank president. A small, balding man, he had a booming voice at odds with his size. His plump, blond wife, Alice, sat next to him, ready to take notes. Maggie knew everyone else at the meeting by sight. Big Sam and Miss Chapman rounded out the group.

Like all city meetings, this one followed strict parliamentary procedure. Sam had explained to Maggie how it was used and why, but the whole business of moves and seconds and points of order sounded silly to her. Why couldn't people just talk?

The mayor called the meeting to order. As his wife stood up and began to read the minutes from last month's early-planning meeting, Maggie returned to her book and soon became lost in the story of mischievous Ramona and her big sister, Beezus.

Time passed, broken by a pause to eat the second doughnut Maggie's dad passed her. She managed to ignore most of the meeting until the indignant voice of Buffy Burton, the gym teacher, roused her from her book.

"So, we've just spent the past hour deciding to do what we've always done—same food, same decorations, same old music. Let me tell you what my students think. Most of them don't even want to go to the party. They say it's *boring*. Why can't we do something different?"

Maggie had stopped reading. This could be interesting.

"You're suggesting this *now?*" Alice Wilkins demanded. "The party's on the twenty-first, less than three weeks away. Everything's arranged. The food assignments have been made, the tree for the gym's been ordered, and we certainly can't buy new decorations. I'm all for making the party less *boring* as you say. But we don't have the time or the budget for—"

"Wait!" Maggie shot to her feet, waving her hand. The idea that had just popped into her head was so exciting that she couldn't keep still.

"Well, Maggie," the mayor said. "Since when did you become part of this meeting?"

"Permission to speak, Mr. Chairman." She remembered her parliamentary procedure. Several people at the table smiled, including her father and Miss Chapman.

"All right, Maggie, you have the floor," the mayor said. "But only for five minutes. We need to move on."

"I have an idea for the party," she said. "We could have a dance after we eat. People could dress up, in nice clothes, or even costumes, like at a ball. We could move the tables and play dance records, and it wouldn't cost anything extra at all."

As she paused, looking anxiously around for reactions,

Lois Harper's hand shot up. "I think that's a great idea! I read about something like that over in Anson. They've been doing it for years. It's called the Cowboys' Christmas Ball! They dress up in fancy western clothes and have a live band. I read that one year, they even had Michael Martin Murphey there to entertain."

"We couldn't do all that," the mayor's wife said. "Especially not with a live band."

"We wouldn't have to do all that," Buffy said. "Just add a few fun things to the party we've already planned, like western clothes for folks who wanted to dress up, and line dancing—I could teach my students and they could teach anybody who doesn't know how. I think it's a great idea."

"But what about the kids?" Doris Cullimore asked. "You can't have a dance with little ones running around unsupervised."

Miss Chapman spoke up. "We could have an activity room with games and crafts and videos. Maybe people who don't care to dance could volunteer to help—or maybe they could take turns."

A few people at the table nodded. Maggie felt a quiver of excitement. Her idea was actually catching on.

Buffy, the gym teacher, raised her hand. "I move that we accept Maggie's suggestion and turn the Christmas party into Branding Iron's own Cowboys' Christmas Ball."

"Seconded!" said Lois, the beautician.

The mayor frowned. "It's been moved and seconded . . . all in favor . . ."

The motion carried all votes except one. Alice, the mayor's wife, argued that the change was too drastic. "What's wrong with the way we've always done it?" she demanded. But the motion had already carried.

Big Sam turned and smiled at his daughter. Maggie glowed inside. She could tell he was proud of her.

"Well." The mayor hadn't voted, but he'd clearly sided

with his wife. "Since we have a new plan, that's going to mean extra meetings and new responsibilities. Miss Burton, would you be willing to choose the music for the dance and set it up to be played?"

Buffy smiled and nodded. "I'll get my students to help me choose. Don't worry, it'll be good old country, not teenage rock. I'll even make sure they know the dances and can teach them to others."

"Fine," said the mayor. "Lois, could you handle publicity—maybe put up some posters, call the radio station, and spread the word in your beauty shop?"

"It's a beauty *salon,* not a shop," said Lois. "But sure, I can do it. My daughter can make posters. She's a good little artist if I say so myself."

"Fine, we can check that off. Walt, you're already in charge of setting up the chairs and tables and putting them away. Can you also make sure the dance floor is cleared after the meal?"

"No problem," said Walt Cullimore, the feed and hardware owner.

"Now." The mayor's gaze narrowed on Miss Chapman, who suddenly looked as if she wanted to shrink under the table. "Since you're a teacher, and since you made the suggestion, you're just the one to be in charge of the kids' activity room, right?"

"Uh—right. I'm going to need help."

"You should have no trouble finding some," the mayor said dismissively, as if to say no help would be coming from him.

Clara Marsden caught Miss Chapman's eye. "I'll help," she whispered. "We'll manage fine."

The mayor cleared his throat. "With all the changes, I move that we meet again on Monday, the ninth, for a progress check. Do I hear a second?"

"Seconded," his wife echoed. With a vote, the motion carried.

"So, are we done?" Walt Cullimore asked. "Can we go now?"

"You're out of order, Walt," the mayor said. "Actually, we have one more matter to discuss. An urgent problem has come up."

The words, *urgent problem,* caught everybody's attention. A few hands reached for a third doughnut.

"As you know," the mayor said, "Archie McNab has dressed up and played Santa at the party for years. His wife even made him his own Santa costume."

A murmur of recognition went around the table. Archie was a giant of a man, as tall as Big Sam, and hefty enough to play Santa without any additional padding around the middle. He had a booming Santa laugh and seemed to love playing the part. To the people of Branding Iron, especially the kids, Archie *was* Santa.

"Unfortunately," the mayor continued, "Archie is facing hip replacement surgery this month. He'll be in no condition to play Santa at the Christmas party—or *the Christmas Ball,* as I guess we're calling it now."

A groan rose from the group around the table. "We've got to have a Santa!" It was Doris Cullimore who spoke. "My grandkids have been wanting to meet Santa for weeks. And don't ask me to take them to the mall in Cottonwood Springs. Last year the lines were halfway out the doors, and their fake Santa reeked of booze and cigarettes. Archie's the real deal, or close to it."

"It was Archie's wife who called me," the mayor said. "She and Archie are willing to lend us the Santa suit she made, along with the boots and beard. But she doesn't want anybody making alterations to it—no shortening the sleeves or the pants."

"Archie's a huge guy," Walt said. "Where are we going to find a man who'll fit into his suit?"

There was a beat of silence. Then, like steel pins drawn to a magnet, all eyes—even Maggie's and Grace Chapman's—swiveled toward Sam. It took mere seconds for him to get their silent message.

"Oh, no!" He waved the flat of his hand for emphasis. "Not me! My job's law and order. There's no way I'm showing up in a silly red suit and a beard. Besides, Santa's supposed to be jolly. I don't have a jolly bone in my body!"

"But Sam," Clara Marsden said in her gentle voice, "you're the only man in town who can wear that suit—with a couple of pillows, of course. It's you or no one at all. Think how disappointed the little ones will be if there's no Santa."

Sam groaned. "Think how they'll feel if I sneer at them instead of going 'Ho, ho, ho.' I don't have a single blasted ho-ho in me. Can't we just rent a different sized suit?"

"Not at this late date," Alice Wilkins said. "I checked the costume agencies. Santa suits have to be reserved months ahead. And don't even think about buying one. Even if we could find one for sale, the price would blow our budget for the whole holiday season."

Sam shook his head, feeling trapped. "I didn't sign on for this," he said. "Playing Santa isn't part of my job description."

"We can't force you," the mayor said. "But there's an election coming up next fall. Nobody's going to vote for a sheriff who refused to play Santa for their kids."

Sam swore silently. The mayor had just taken the issue to a whole new level. This wasn't just persuasion. This was extortion. And the mayor's threat had put him in a tough spot. If he caved in now and agreed to play Santa, it would appear that he was doing it for political reasons. If he stuck to his principles and refused to be threatened, he would come off as a curmudgeon who didn't care about the kids—and he'd probably lose next year's election to boot.

With his pride at stake, neither choice was good.

Sam could feel the pressure. People were watching him, waiting for his answer. He could ask for more time, but that would only prolong the tension. He needed to decide now.

He felt a light touch on his shoulder. Maggie had left her chair to stand beside him.

"Please, Daddy," she said in a voice that only he could hear. "You'll make a great Santa. I know you will. And the kids will be so happy. I know Christmas makes you sad, but do it for them."

It was the answer he needed. Sam's arm went around her. "All right, I'll do it," he said. "But only for this year and only for the kids."

An audible sigh of relief went around the table. "The suit's at the cleaner's," Alice said. "We'll have it for you in plenty of time."

"Fine," Sam said. "And I can furnish my own pillows. So, with that settled, I move that we adjourn."

"Seconded," Maggie added.

"Moved, seconded . . . all in favor," the mayor said. The decision to adjourn was unanimous.

Grace fell into step with Sam and Maggie as they walked out to the door. She'd planned on confronting him about the car he'd rented. But somehow that problem didn't seem so important now.

"I don't know whether to congratulate you or give you my sympathy," she said. "But for the record, I think you'll make a great Santa. You just don't know it yet."

He gave her a wry chuckle. "That's one way to look at it. But you got handed a pretty big job yourself."

"And I don't even know where to begin. I should've let somebody else make that suggestion."

Sam held the door for her and Maggie. They stepped out into the brittle air. Earlier, the night had been clear. But now a low bank of fog was flowing in. Grace could taste its dampness on her tongue.

"Over time, I've learned that the only way to survive those meetings is to stay quiet," Sam said. "If you speak up, the mayor will think you're asking for a job."

"That strategy didn't help you tonight, did it?"

"Not this time."

They'd reached the spot where Grace had parked the ugly little Volkswagen. Sitting in the circle of light from an overhead lamp, the small car looked even more pathetic than she remembered.

"So help me, Grace, this isn't the car I ordered for you. I asked for a Cadillac. Somebody pulled a switch. I'll call the agency tomorrow and take a piece out of their hide."

"Thanks. I'll give you the benefit of the doubt." Grace had been fuming when she'd parked the car in Sam's spot. But over the course of the meeting, her anger had faded. Maybe watching Sam agree to play Santa—the last job he would want—had something to do with it. "If the car were in better shape, I wouldn't mind," she said. "But the tires are almost bald. And the inside has got this *smell*. I have to drive with the windows down. Otherwise I can barely stand to breathe."

"Don't worry, I'll take care of it," Sam said. "I'll make this right if I have to drive to Cottonwood Springs and raise hell in person."

"Poor little car," Maggie said. "It looks sad."

"Cars don't have feelings, Maggie," Sam said. "Neither do Christmas trees."

"You should read more books, Dad." Turning, Maggie

gave Grace a heart-melting smile. "Shouldn't he, Miss Chapman?"

"That, or maybe see more Disney movies." Grace gave Sam a teasing grin and felt her heart skip when he smiled back at her. She found herself wishing the evening would last longer, giving them a chance to get better acquainted. But she'd been down that road before, and she knew where it would end. Besides, tomorrow was a school day, and Maggie was already out past what Grace assumed to be her bedtime.

"I was really proud of you tonight, Maggie," she said. "Your idea about having a dance was a great one. You spoke right up, and people listened."

"I was proud of you, too, Maggie," Sam said. "Your idea will make a difference for the whole town—maybe for years to come."

"Wow, I never thought of that," Maggie said.

"Before you and your dad go, Maggie, maybe you can help me with a different idea," Grace said. "I need to come up with some games and activities for the kids at the dance. I've never done anything like this before, and I don't know who to ask for help. Does anyone come to mind?"

Maggie was silent for a moment. Then she laughed out loud. "That's easy," she said. "You've already got a whole classroom full of helpers. We can all help you with ideas. We can even make some of the crafts. And some of us might be able to help with the littlest kids at the party."

Grace shook her head in amazement. "That's perfect! You're a wonder, Maggie Delaney. We can make that our big Christmas project for the class." Her gaze met Sam's gentle gray eyes. Again, he was smiling—and once more, her heart did flip-flops. Not good. She needed to get out of here—now.

"I'd better be going," she said. "And I know you two need to get home, too. Good night, and thanks again for your help, Maggie." She turned away and headed for the car at a brisk stride.

"Be careful. That fog's moving in fast," Sam called after her. "You'll have a better car tomorrow. That's a promise!"

Maggie opened the door of the tiny car and squeezed herself into the driver's seat. Before closing the door, she rolled both windows down, shivering as the chill poured in. The starter gurgled, then died. On the second try she had better luck. The engine caught and started with a roar.

As she turned on the headlights and headed out of the parking lot, she glanced in her rearview mirror to see Sam and Maggie standing next to the sheriff's big Jeep. Maggie was waving. Then they vanished behind her in the fog.

Grace sighed and turned on the radio. "Grandma Got Run Over by a Reindeer" boomed out of the speakers, so loud it made her nerves jump.

She switched the radio off and sighed again. Ready or not, the Christmas crazies had arrived.

Chapter Six

Sam was boosting Maggie into the Jeep when she gave a little cry. "Daddy, I forgot my books! Can we go back inside and get them?"

"You stay here. I'll go." He settled her in the backseat. "Buckle up. I'll be right back."

"If there are any leftover doughnuts, can we take them home? You told me you paid for them this time."

"We'll see." Sam hurried back into the building. The mayor would be the last one out. He would turn off the lights and lock the doors. Since he hadn't come outside to his car, and the lights were on inside, finding Maggie's books shouldn't be a problem.

Sam strode down the hall to the conference room at the far end. He found the mayor and his wife still tidying up after the meeting. One box of doughnuts, two-thirds full, sat open on the table. The mayor closed it and tucked it under his arm. So much for Maggie's request. Sam wasn't about to do battle over a few doughnuts. But something else needed to be aired.

"Is there something you need, Sam?" the mayor asked.

"Just picking up the books Maggie left." Sam found the books on the chair and took them.

"Well, since you're here," the mayor said, "I wanted to thank you for volunteering to play Santa at the party."

Sam turned to face the small, balding man. "I can't claim to have volunteered, Rulon. It was more like I was commandeered. And I didn't appreciate your comment about the next election. It came close to sounding like a threat, and it put me in a bad light. For the record, my decision didn't have anything to do with the damned election. I only agreed to play Santa for the sake of the kids."

"Of course you did, Sam." The mayor's voice had taken on the oily tone he used in his public speeches. "And what I said—I certainly didn't mean it as a threat. You've done a great job as sheriff. Everybody knows that."

Alice, the mayor's wife, finished dusting off the long table. "Well, Sam, as long as we're speaking frankly, that little girl of yours really upset the applecart tonight. Everything was on track until she made her suggestion. Now we're faced with a plan that could turn out to be a disaster, to say nothing of the extra work involved."

"I'm sorry you feel that way, Alice," Sam said. "Actually, I liked Maggie's idea. I was proud of her for speaking up."

"She was out of order." Alice lifted her fur coat off the back of the chair. At her nod, the mayor took the coat and held it while she slipped her ample arms into the sleeves and shrugged it onto her shoulders. "Your daughter wasn't even supposed to be in the meeting. I'd appreciate it if you wouldn't bring her again."

"I'd say that's up to the committee." Actually, Sam had no plans to bring Maggie to the next meeting, but Alice's high-handed tone rankled him. "Right now I need to get Maggie home. I'll see you at work tomorrow, Rulon. Alice." He gave the mayor's wife a nod before he walked out of the room.

In the hallway, he lengthened his stride toward the front

door. Through the glass, the fog was so dense that he could barely see his vehicle. Maggie would be getting cold. He shouldn't have wasted so much time in pointless talking.

"Did you bring the doughnuts?" Maggie's teeth were chattering as Sam climbed into the driver's seat.

"Sorry, they were all taken." Sam started the engine and drove down Main Street with the heater on and defroster blasting. The modest, bungalow-style house where he'd lived since his marriage was only a few minutes away, but the fog was like a thick, white wall, and the night was cold enough to freeze the moisture on the windshield. He thought of Grace, driving that VW bug with her windows down. Maybe he should have offered her a ride home.

"I think Miss Chapman likes you." Maggie spoke from the backseat. "And I think you like her, too."

"Give it a rest, Maggie." Sam was tired after the long day. "Miss Chapman and I barely know each other."

"But I saw the way she smiled at you. And you smiled back. I'm not stupid, Daddy. I can tell things."

No, she definitely wasn't stupid, Sam thought. And he did like Grace. But that was as far as it went. "All you saw was two people trying to be nice," he said. "We're friends, maybe. Barely that."

"But being friends is a good start."

"That's enough, Maggie. It's late, and you've got school in the morning. When we get home you're to brush your teeth and go straight to bed. Understand?" Sam signaled a left turn at the side street that led to their house.

"Uh-huh." She made a little yawning sound that ended in a sudden gasp. "Down the street, Daddy! I think I see something, maybe a car, off to the side."

Sam braked, checked his rearview mirror, and pulled out of the turn to head on down Main Street. After dimming the headlights to cut the glare against the fog, he could make out a small car pulled to the curb at an odd

angle. There could be no mistaking the lime green Volkswagen.

He pulled up behind the car, leaving his lights on. From
the rear, the small vehicle looked empty. Worry gnawing at
him, he unbuckled his seat belt and opened the door of the
Jeep. "Stay here," he told Maggie. "I'll be right back."

Armed with a flashlight and his service revolver, he
locked the door behind him to keep his daughter safe, then
walked down to the car. Through the side window he
could see that there was no one inside. The key to the car
was gone, as was Grace's purse.

There was no sign of foul play. Most likely the Volkswagen had stalled. Unable to start it, and with no help in
sight, she'd probably decided to walk home.

But her house was at least six blocks away. And, as he
remembered, she'd been wearing nothing more for warmth
than a fleece jacket over her sweater.

Blast it, if he hadn't taken time to talk to the mayor, he
might have seen her sooner. He strode back to the Jeep
and climbed into the driver's seat.

"Where's Miss Chapman?" Maggie asked anxiously.

"That's what we need to find out." Sam started the engine. "Help me with your sharp eyes. We can't go home
until we know she's safe."

He switched on the headlights, pulled away from the
curb, and headed in the direction the Volkswagen had
been going when it had stopped. He'd watched Grace
drive out of the parking lot, and he knew where she lived.
Unless she was a track star, she wouldn't have made it
home yet. He would follow the shortest route from here.
With luck, he would find her on the way.

With luck. But what if something had gone wrong—an
accident, or even a crime? Or what if she was simply lost?
That could happen in weather like this. He'd heard reports

of people who'd wandered aimlessly through fog and cold until they froze.

Worry wove a knot in the pit of his stomach as he made a right turn at the next street and headed in the direction of Grace's home.

Shivering under her light fleece jacket, with her purse slung over one shoulder, Grace wandered through the blinding fog. When the Volkswagen had stalled and refused to start, she'd been annoyed, but not worried. She knew the way home—had driven it countless times. A brisk pace would get her there in about fifteen minutes. It would also help keep her warm.

Walking with long strides, she'd turned off Main Street in the usual place, made another turn at the next corner, then the next, before she realized that she'd lost all sense of direction. The dingy gray fog was so thick that even the street signs were hidden. Lights from houses along the road glowed through the murk, but it was impossible to tell one place from another. Here and there, Christmas lights, their colors fog-blurred, gleamed like muted rainbows, lending a sense of unreality to the night, like the setting for a science fiction movie.

She could go to a house, knock, and ask directions, Grace thought. But she'd been a city girl too long to trust what lay behind unknown doors. The car that passed her on the street stirred the same wariness in her. Anybody could be behind that wheel.

As the red taillights faded, Grace told herself not to worry. She couldn't be more than a few blocks from her house. Any minute now, she would turn a corner and see, faintly, the bare branches of the old tree rising out of the fog, and she would laugh at herself for having been so nervous.

But the cold was creeping through her jacket and into her bones. Her face had gone numb. Through the thin hood, her ears felt frozen stiff. Her feet, in thin, casual boots, were like aching lumps of ice. She blew on her hands in a vain effort to warm them, then thrust them back into her pockets. How long, she wondered, could she be out here before the cold became damaging? Words like *frostbite* and *hypothermia* invaded her thoughts.

She couldn't be far from home, Grace told herself. But what if she had been traveling in the wrong direction, or going in a circle? She could be farther away than ever.

With the stars blocked by clouds, and the fog shrouding her vision, she couldn't even tell which way she was headed. Panic stirred inside her. She fought to control it, fought the urge to break into an aimless run.

She was lost, scared, and freezing. But she mustn't give in to fear. All she could do was remain calm and keep moving. Sooner or later, she would see something she recognized.

Pain shot up her leg as her toe stubbed a section of broken sidewalk. She stumbled, lost her balance, and went down hard. Her glasses flew off her face and vanished in the fog. Fear rose as she groped for them on the frozen ground. Finding her way in the fog and darkness had already been a challenge. Now, anything beyond the reach of her arms was just a blur in the fog.

With her hands skimming the ground in an ever-widening circle around her, she willed herself to stay calm. Glasses didn't have wings. They couldn't have fallen far. Maybe they'd caught on a bush or fallen into a patch of dry weeds.

Only one thing was certain. Without her eyeglasses, she wouldn't be going anywhere. And it wasn't just because she couldn't see. Those glasses, her only good pair, had been expensive. If she were to leave them behind, she might never find her way back here, even by daylight. They'd be lost for good.

At least she still had her purse, with a couple of twenty-dollar bills in it. Maybe she could find a house and offer somebody money to find her glasses and take her home.

But she could see no lights through the fog. If there were any houses on this street, they had all gone dark. There was no place she dared go for help; no one who would hear if she shouted. All she could do was huddle in place and wait, do her best to keep warm, and pray that either the fog would clear or someone would find her.

Driving slowly, with the light bar flashing and a spot-light scanning the sidewalks, Sam had arrived at Grace's house without having seen her on the way. Leaving Maggie in the Jeep, he climbed out and strode up the walk to the door. He didn't like upsetting her roommates, but he had to know whether Grace had made it home.

He was acquainted with both women, though not well. He'd spoken with Jess Graver about some troubled kids he'd encountered. And Wynette was a local girl, from a farm family on the outskirts of town.

As soon as the door opened, their worried reaction told Sam that Grace hadn't come home. Standing on the porch, he told them in a few words what had happened.

"I'll get my car and help you look," Jess offered.

"Driving in this fog wouldn't be safe for you," Sam said. "Stay here and wait. If you hear from her, or if she shows up, call the dispatcher. They'll let me know."

He returned to the vehicle to find Maggie restless and complaining. "Daddy, I'm really tired, and I need to go to the bathroom. How close are we to our house?"

"Not far, but I need to look for Grace. Come on." Opening her door, he boosted her out, carried her back to the porch, and rang the doorbell again. "Sorry," he said to Wynette, who answered. "Could I impose on you to take Maggie while I search? She needs a bathroom. Then with luck, she'll go to sleep wherever you want to put her."

"Sure. Come on in, Maggie." Wynette took the little girl's hand. "Don't worry—she'll be fine," she told Sam.

"Thanks." He hurried back to the Jeep. If Grace had taken a wrong turn somewhere and become disoriented, she could have wandered in any direction. There was always a chance she'd knock on some door and ask for help. But he'd seen enough of Grace to know that she was stubborn and independent. Since she hadn't called her roommates from somebody's home, Sam could only assume that she was still out there, wandering in the fog and the dangerous cold.

He knew the town well enough to have a mental map of the streets in his head. As he drove, he plotted out a route that would take him in a widening grid, with the house at its center. The pattern would cover every possible street that Grace might have taken. He could only pray that he'd find her before the cold began to take its toll on her body.

Fifteen minutes later, headlights on low to optimize visibility in the fog, he was still driving. So far, there'd been no sign of her. What if he couldn't find her? What if something had gone wrong?

It didn't help to know that Grace was in trouble because of him. If he hadn't hit her car, if he'd insisted on inspecting the vehicle the rental agency delivered, or if he'd spent less time talking to the mayor tonight, she would be safe at home now. But there'd be time for blame later. For now, the only thing that mattered was finding her.

What if he'd missed seeing her in the fog? He could easily have looked the wrong way at the moment he was passing her. Maybe he should go back and retrace the way he'd come. But no, as sheriff, he'd conducted enough searches to know that the entire area needed to be covered. He would finish the route he'd mapped out before he turned around.

As he drove, remembered images of Grace drifted through his mind—her beautiful dark eyes, shining with intelligence behind those funky John Lennon glasses; her flowing, willowy walk; the generous mouth that could frown one instant, and laugh the next—a mouth that made him wonder what it might be like to kiss her.

But where had that thought come from? In spite of Maggie's well-meant efforts, he had no plan to romance the woman, especially since she didn't seem the least bit interested. He was concerned for her safety tonight. He was doing his job. That was all.

He swore at the fog, which obscured everything in shrouds of ghostly gray. Even with the spotlight, he couldn't see more than twenty feet ahead. Grace could be anywhere.

He was coming to the last street on the outskirts of town, a row of weedy vacant lots, run-down trailers, and clapboard houses with junk-strewn yards. There were no streetlights here. The town hadn't bothered to spend money on them. Some unsavory folks lived along this road, as well as others like Hank Miller who were just poor and down on their luck. He couldn't believe that Grace would wander this far, but if she were to ask for help at one of these places, she could be taking a risk.

His hands tightened on the steering wheel as he turned the corner. There were no Christmas lights here, nothing in the headlight beams but a solid bank of fog. Heaven help him, where was she? He imagined her lost, and alone, maybe injured and so cold that she might not survive the night. Right now, all he wanted in this world was to see her safe.

Even with the spotlight, he could barely see as far as the

sidewalk. His best hope, wherever she might be, was that she would hear the vehicle, see the flashing red and blue lights, and come to him. Otherwise, she could be just a few feet away, and he could still miss seeing her. Sick with worry, he drove slowly along the dark street, already planning to turn around and retrace his path after he failed to find her here.

It was by purest chance that he saw the huddled form at the edge of the sidewalk, barely visible through the fog. His pulse leapt as the spotlight caught a flash of red, the color of the fleece jacket Grace had been wearing. Heart pounding, he stopped, plunged out of the vehicle, and raced across the road.

She raised her head. With a little whimpering sound, she stumbled to her feet, took a step toward him, and half fell. He caught her, pulling her into the warmth of his open sheepskin coat and wrapping her against him. "Thank God," he muttered, his lips moving against her hair.

She was cold—so cold that her jacket was stiff with frost. Her body shivered in his arms. Her teeth chattered as she tried to speak. "My . . . my . . ."

"Don't try to talk. Not till you're warmer." His clasp tightened around her. He knew he needed to get her into the heated Jeep, call Dispatch on the radio, and have them phone her roommates. But right now, just for the moment, he needed to hold her, to feel her in his arms, alive and real—to hold her until his heart stopped bucking like a wild steer. She had scared him badly. If he let her go now, his knees would give way, and he would sink to the ground in relief. He needed her—perhaps more than she needed him.

Her lips would be cold. He could warm them . . .

What was he thinking? Sam jerked himself back to reality. He had a job to do. Releasing her, he slipped out of his coat and wrapped it around her shoulders. Again she tried to speak, her chilled mouth trying to form words.

"We need to get you into the Jeep," he said. "We can talk then." He put a hand on her shoulder to guide her over the rough sidewalk, but she resisted.

"My . . . glasses." She gestured toward her eyes.

"You lost them? Here?"

She nodded, her hand sweeping back toward the spot where he'd found her.

"Get in," he ordered, guiding her toward the Jeep. "While you get warm, I'll look for them."

He helped her into the Jeep. He'd left the engine running and the heat on, so it was warm inside, but Grace was still shivering. She settled into the passenger seat with a broken sigh that was almost a sob.

A powerful flashlight was attached to the dashboard. Using it to search for Grace's glasses, Sam soon found them where they'd fallen into a clump of tall weeds. When he climbed back into the Jeep and handed them to her, he saw that she was quietly weeping.

"It's all right, Grace." He reached across the console and circled her shoulders with one arm. Still shivering, she let him. The urge to pull her close and kiss her was almost more than Sam could stand. But that would be a bad move. "You're one brave lady," he said, releasing her.

"But I'm not brave at all, or even smart." Her voice shook as she cleaned her glasses with the hem of her jacket and put them on. "When I realized I was lost, I was scared to death. I'm not cut out for risk-taking, Sam. What made me think I could find my way home in that fog? I could've died out there. I should've stayed in the blasted car when it broke down."

"If you had, I'd have found you a few minutes later. But we can't go back. I've learned that the hard way. Anyhow, everything's all right." He ached to hold her again, but he'd already crossed that line once. He couldn't risk it a second time. "Now, if you'll give me a minute, I need to let folks know you're safe. Then I'll drive you home."

He radioed the dispatcher, who promised to call Grace's roommates. Then he put the Jeep in gear and turned around at the end of the street. Grace was calm now; she sat quietly, warming her hands in the heat that blew from the vents.

"I feel like I'm the one to blame here," he said. "If I hadn't run into your car, or if I'd done a better job of following up on the rental, none of this would have happened."

"It was just as much my fault for getting out of the car," she said. "Or maybe it was even Maggie's fault for pulling the stunt that got you to come to school. Blaming is a waste of time, Sam."

"Good point." He chuckled. They were back on Main Street now, the Christmas lights reflecting rainbows through the windshield.

"How did you find me?" she asked. "It couldn't have been easy."

He managed a chuckle. "It wasn't. But I've always said that I could find my way around Branding Iron blindfolded. Tonight I pretty well proved it. I drove every street you might have taken, all the way to the last street in town. I was beginning to worry that I'd missed you when, all of a sudden, there you were. I still can't believe you wandered that far in the fog."

"You'd believe it if you knew me. I can get lost in parking lots and shopping malls. Tonight I took one wrong turn and my sense of direction was gone. I barely knew which way was up. After I fell and lost my glasses, it was all over." She paused, gazing out the side window at the fog. "What if you had missed me? Would you have given up?"

Sam shook his head. "I'd have finished the last street, turned around, and retraced every inch of the way I'd come. Then I'd have looked for other ways you might have gone. I wouldn't have stopped searching until I found you. I would never have given up on you, Grace."

I would never have given up on you. Sam's words lingered in Grace's mind. No, Sam wouldn't have given up. She hadn't known him long, but she could already recognize the kind of man he was. He was as steadfast as the flow of a river, or the rising of the sun, the kind of man who would never give up on a friend or someone in need— the kind of man who loved once in his life and never again.

And she was the kind of woman who fled like a startled bird at the first sign of doubt—a woman who expected that every man she tried to love would betray her, just as her father had betrayed his family.

She studied Sam's profile in the darkness of the cab, the rugged features, the dark hair in need of a trim, curling over the edge of his collar, the big, powerful hands, resting on the steering wheel. She remembered how safe she'd felt when he'd wrapped her in his coat and held her against him. She'd been numb with cold; but for that moment, snuggling into his solid warmth had been almost like coming to a new place and knowing it was home.

But even then she'd known better than to trust a fleeting rush of emotion. This was reality. He was taking her home. She would thank him. He would see that her car problem was fixed. Then, except for the Christmas party committee and a few routine parent-teacher conferences, they would become strangers again. End of story.

Chapter Seven

After delivering Grace safely home, Sam thanked her roommates for babysitting, loaded his daughter into the Jeep, and started for home. Maggie, who clearly hadn't slept a wink, chattered all the way.

"Daddy, I had so much fun! Wynette let me help make chocolate chip cookies." She held up a plastic container with cookies in it. "She even wrote down the recipe so I can make them at home. You'll just need to buy me some chocolate chips. Wynette's nice, and pretty, too. But I think she's too young for you. And Jess might be a little too old. But Miss Chapman is just the right age. Are you listening, Daddy?"

Sam stifled a groan. "I told you, Maggie, Miss Chapman and I are just friends."

"But you saved her tonight. I bet she'll really like you now."

"That's not the way things work." Sam remembered wrapping Grace in his coat and holding her close to warm her—the way her slim body fit against his, the subtle curves in all the right places, the soft fragrance of her hair, the way she trembled as she clung to him. He'd liked it— liked it too much. If he hadn't let her go, he could've been in serious trouble.

"Can we put the tree up tomorrow night?" Maggie asked.

"Maybe, if I don't get a call to work. We'll see how it goes." That was the trouble, balancing his job with being a single dad. He had to be available for emergency calls twenty-four seven. That made it hard to plan for family time.

"Maybe we could invite Miss Chapman over to decorate the tree with us. We could even get pizza from Bucka-roo's."

"Maggie, remember what we talked about? Miss Chapman is just your teacher. She's not family, and she's not my girlfriend. Inviting her over would be awkward. She probably wouldn't even want to come."

"Well, then, we could invite her roommates, too. It would be fun. Like a party."

"Maggie, that's enough. Stop pushing this."

"But it won't be as much fun, doing it by ourselves."

"I said that's enough. We're almost home, and when we get there you're to go straight to bed."

Maggie didn't answer. Sam could tell she was pouting. Not that he blamed her. Any little girl deserved a festive holiday. But the thought of bringing Bethany's beloved ornaments down from the attic and hanging them on the tree was almost more than he could stand. His wife had loved Christmas—every silly tradition, every sappy movie, every song, every ornament, advent calendar, and manger scene. Sam had loved teasing her, calling her his Christmas angel. Now, for their daughter's sake, he was duty bound to break out the trimmings, paste a fake smile on his face, and go through the whole damned rigamarole without her.

After Maggie had left with Sam, Grace's roommates took charge. While Jess inspected Grace's chilled fingers and toes for signs of frostbite, Wynette made her a giant mug of steaming hot chocolate with marshmallows. Grace had never cared for marshmallows, but this was no time to say so. Her friends were doing their best to show they cared. And at least the hot liquid flowing into her body was helping to warm her—though all she really wanted was a hot shower and a cozy bed.

"Heavens, Grace," Jess scolded. "You could have frozen to death out there. How did you manage to get so lost?"

Grace shivered under the blanket they'd used to wrap her. "When the car died, I thought I could leave it and walk home. But I couldn't even see the street signs. I took a wrong turn somewhere and just kept going. Then I fell and lost my glasses. It was like being blind. All I could do was hunker down and pray somebody would come and find me."

"So Sam was the answer to your prayers." Wynette took the empty mug from Grace's hands. "Now, that's what I call romance material. Did he sweep you off your feet?" Her blue eyes widened. "Did he kiss you?"

"Oh, for Pete's sake, Wynette," Grace said. "Sam was just doing his job. He got me on my feet, put me in the Jeep, and drove me home." No need to mention how Sam had held her, or how she'd wanted to melt in his arms and just flow into him.

"Well, we had our own entertainment," Jess said. "That little Maggie is a talker. She says that her dad really likes you."

"That's just wishful thinking on her part," Grace said. "Maggie's been pushing to get us together, but Sam's still in love with his late wife. I know the signs, and I don't need that kind of competition."

Grace rose from the couch and gathered up her purse, along with her boots and socks, which Jess had removed to check her feet. "Now that the excitement's over, I'm going to shower and go to bed. I've got a big day planned with my class tomorrow."

"How can you even think of going to work, Grace?" Jess demanded. "After what you've been through, you need a day off to rest. Let me call the district hotline and let them know you'll need a substitute."

"No, I need to be at school," Grace said. "I promised the class we'd put up our tree and make decorations. I'm also going to need their help brainstorming for kids' activities at the Christmas ball. Don't worry, I'll be fine."

"The Christmas party's going to be a ball?" Wynette's eyes brightened. "Wow, what great news! That'll be so much fun! There's no place to dance around here unless you want to go to Rowdy's Roost and fight off the drunks."

"Actually, Wynette has her own good news, too," Jess said. "Don't you, Wynette?"

Wynette's grin broadened. "I've got a job, for now at least. Starting tomorrow, I'll be helping out at Stella's Bakery over the holidays."

"That's great," Grace said. "You're a fabulous baker. I've probably gained ten pounds since we moved in together."

"Sure, you have. So where did you put it?" Wynette laughed. "Seriously, I'll learn a lot from Stella. Since she plans on getting married, and will want more free time, I'm hoping she'll keep me on. If things work out, I could even end up managing the place. Meanwhile, I can still keep my Mirabella Beauty clients and take orders. Ladies, I'm coming up in the world!"

"You were never down." Grace hugged her friend with her free arm. "Just promise you'll bring home some leftovers for us."

"You got it!" Wynette breezed into the kitchen to clean

up the remains of the cookies she'd made with Maggie. Grace made her way to her room, dropped her boots and purse, and stripped down for her shower. She was feeling stronger, but the cold still lingered in her limbs, as if it had frozen the marrow of her bones. Tomorrow was bound to be one more day of the Christmas crazies at school. Staying ahead of her students would demand all her energy and focus. She would put tonight behind her, Grace resolved, and concentrate on the day ahead.

But later, as she drifted into sleep, it was the memory of Sam's arms, holding her close, that carried her into dreams.

The next day, Maggie was on her best behavior. She listened to every word the teacher said and raised her hand to be called on. Not once did she appear to want extra attention from Miss Chapman because of last night. She didn't even tell Brenda that she'd stayed at Miss Chapman's house and had a wonderful time with her roommates, or that Sam had agreed to play Santa. Maggie disliked keeping things from her best friend. But Brenda liked to talk, and no secret was safe with her.

She played dodgeball in the gym and didn't complain once, not even when the ball slammed her hard in the ribs. She didn't want to do anything to change the good luck she was having with her father and Miss Chapman. True, her strike had led to their meeting. But the events that had followed—the damage to her car, the bad replacement, the Christmas party meeting, the fog, and Sam's rescue of Miss Chapman—had been nothing but luck and fate. Surely the two of them were meant to be together. How else could she explain the way everything had fallen into place?

In the morning, after math practice, Miss Chapman told the class about the Christmas ball and the need for some children's activities. The students came up with a great list of videos, board games, and crafts that younger children would enjoy. Some of them even offered to bring games and videos from home and help make craft materials.

After lunch, two sixth grade boys helped Miss Chapman bring the Christmas tree inside and set it up on a stand. The heavenly smell of pine filled the classroom. While Christmas music played, the students had made paper chains and cut snowflakes and stars, sparkling with glued-on glitter, to hang on the tree.

It was one of her favorite school days ever, Maggie thought as she walked down the hall toward the front door. The only thing better would've been going home to tell her mom all about it, then planning how they would decorate their own Christmas tree. Her mother had loved everything about Christmas. Celebrating without her this year was going to be hard. But Maggie was determined to give Sam a reason to smile. That was what her mother would want.

Sam would be picking her up today. Their house wasn't far. Some days, when he couldn't make it, she walked home and went to the neighbors until he got off work. But she liked it when they could go home together—especially today. Maybe after supper, he would feel like getting their Christmas tree up.

He was waiting in the Jeep when Maggie came outside. Something else was waiting, too. There in Miss Chapman's parking place was a big, shiny, bright red car. Maggie could tell by the fancy emblem on the trunk that it was a Cadillac.

"Wow!" she said as Sam climbed out of the Jeep to lift her into the rear seat. "Miss Chapman will be so surprised. Is that the car you ordered for her?"

"It is. She was supposed to get it yesterday, but the rental agency made a mistake, and you know what that led to. I called them this morning and threatened to take them to court if they didn't make it right. It looks like they did."

"Miss Chapman is still in the building," Maggie said. "Do you want to wait for her to come out?"

Sam shook his head. "I think the surprise will be better if we're not here. Let's go home. I think I can find the makings for spaghetti. How does that sound?"

"Good. Let's go." Maggie wanted to mention the Christmas tree, but maybe she'd have better luck waiting until after supper. She knew it wouldn't be easy for Sam, getting her mom's decorations out and hanging them up. But if she didn't push him, he might put it off forever. She couldn't let that happen.

Grace stayed an extra forty-five minutes after school to tidy up the classroom and arrange her lesson materials for the next day. On her way out of the building, she stopped at the office, hoping to find the paperwork and the key to the rental car Sam had promised to leave. The secretary had left for the day, but Grace found what she needed in her mailbox. She tucked the papers in her briefcase without looking at them. The car could be a surprise. She didn't know what to expect, but anything would be better than the tiny green Volkswagen she'd left broken down on Main Street.

She'd almost reached the back door that opened on the parking lot when she heard a voice from the hallway behind her, calling her name.

"Miss Chapman. I'd like a word with you." It was her principal, Ed Judkins.

What now? All Grace wanted to do was go home. She was tempted to pretend she hadn't heard him. But this was her job and he was her boss. She turned around.

"Yes, Mr. Judkins, what is it you need?"

"Just to talk. We can do it in my office." He waited for her to catch up before he spoke again. "By the way, you can call me Ed outside of school hours."

Great.

At least it didn't appear that she was going to get repri-
manded or fired. But as she walked beside him, back the
way she'd come, Grace felt a prickle of unease.

They passed through the empty outer office and into the
principal's private space in the rear. After opening the door
for her, he closed it behind them and motioned her to a
seat on the padded chair that faced his desk. Grace had expected him to sit behind the desk, but he remained on his
feet, prowling the room as he talked.

"I just wanted to ask you how the meeting went last
night," he said. "It's always good to keep abreast of what's
happening in the community. Don't you agree?"

"Yes, of course." She could have answered that question outside, in the hall, Grace thought. "It was an interesting meeting. The committee decided to change the holiday
party to a ball."

"Oh? And did you make a contribution?"

"Actually, I did. I've been put in charge of setting up
some activities for the children. I asked my students for
suggestions this morning. They gave me some great ideas.
Is there something you need from me, Mr. Judkins?"

"As I said, it's Ed for now. And I hope you don't mind
my calling you Grace."

He moved to the bulletin board behind his desk, then
turned around to fix his gaze on her, an odd expression in
his washed-out blue eyes. Grace stirred nervously. Was he
coming on to her? Surely not. She knew for a fact that Ed
Judkins was a married man. She'd even met his wife and
heard mention of their two children.

"Have I done something wrong?" she ventured.

"Not at all." He gave her a smile. "I've heard nothing
but good things about you. But since you're new, I just
want to make sure you're happy here. I do care about
you—I care about all my teachers. But you have special

qualities, Grace. I sense that you're a very understanding woman."

Something was going on, and it wasn't good. Grace shifted in the chair, her mind groping for some excuse to leave. "I really need to be going," she said, lying out of desperation. "I promised to meet a friend for coffee after school."

He ignored her obvious discomfort. "I won't keep you long. But I'm going through something, and sometimes I just need to talk," he said. "Sharon, my wife, wants me out of the house. She promised I could stay through Christmas, but after that . . ." He shrugged. "I'm looking for a place to rent. If I find one, I'll move sooner. We're calling it a trial separation, but something tells me it's going to be permanent."

"That's too bad," Grace said. "I'm sorry."

"I've forgotten what being alone is like. As I say, I need someone, just to listen to me. And you strike me as a good listener, Grace."

Moving behind her, he laid a hand on her shoulder. His touch sent a cold shock through her body. She needed to get out of here.

"This isn't a good idea," she said, twisting free, rising from her chair, and turning to face him. "If you need to talk, maybe you should get some counseling, Mr. Judkins. Right now, I have to go."

Stepping around the chair, she maneuvered her way out of the principal's office and strode down the hall toward the door. She knew Judkins was watching her. Otherwise, she'd have broken into a run.

Her heart was racing, stomach churning below her ribs. Judkins had power over her. If she wouldn't go along with what he wanted, he could fire her from her job and smear her reputation so badly that no school would ever hire her again.

He had done nothing—only talked and laid a hand on her shoulder. But the implication had been there in twenty-point capital letters. Maybe she should have been more sympathetic, pretended to play along until she could make a graceful exit. But that would only have left the door open for the next time. She could only hope that she had made herself clear and that there would be no repercussions.

Her hand was still clutching the key to the new rental car. As she stepped out of the building, she saw the car on the far side of the parking lot. Her breath caught. Sam had outdone himself this time. The dark red Cadillac was the kind of car a visiting celebrity would drive.

Almost disbelieving, she hurried across the lot. The flashy, expensive car was bound to attract a lot of attention—maybe too much. But as long as she had it, she'd be a fool not to glean a little enjoyment from driving it. At least it might take her mind off the encounter with Ed Judkins.

The door unlocked remotely, with a click of the key fob. Grace opened it and slipped behind the wheel. The seats were upholstered in tan leather as supple as a baby's skin. She locked the door, closing her eyes to rest them a moment as she sank into its softness. The car's aroma seeped into her senses—a rich blend of fragrances that Grace couldn't identify—leather, sage, some kind of expensive men's cologne . . . Maybe this was the smell of money. Whatever it was, she could get used to it.

Opening her eyes, she saw Ed Judkins coming out of the building. Her pulse slammed. He was staring at the car from across the parking lot, staring at her, as if he were about to come over. He was bound to have questions, but she was in no frame of mind to answer them.

As he started toward her, she turned the key in the ignition. The engine purred to life. The car all but sprang forward as she shifted, touched the gas pedal, and zoomed out of the lot. After slowing down, she drove aimlessly through the back streets, fighting her emotions. This was ridiculous. The man wasn't dangerous. He only wanted to intimidate her. But his words and his touch had triggered responses that she'd struggled to bury for years. She was angry, scared, and on the edge of losing control.

By the time she pulled onto a side street and stopped in front of an empty house with a realty sign out front, she was shaking.

Clutching the top of the steering wheel, she rested her forehead on the backs of her hands. She could feel her heart pounding inside her rib cage. She'd come to Branding Iron for a new start—to heal from the anxieties that had plagued her life and to find her own strengths. Until today, she'd believed she was making progress. She had a job she loved, good friends, and the chance to become a part of this close-knit community.

But all it had taken was a word and a touch from a man in power to reduce her to a bundle of raw, quivering nerves. The encounter had carried her back to the moment she'd come home from school and heard those sounds behind the bedroom door—the moment she'd learned that no man—not even her beloved father—could be trusted.

And her boss was no different from the others.

She couldn't let it happen again. But something told her that Judkins hadn't given up. Maybe she should just confront him. But Judkins had an ego. Challenging his power could put her job in jeopardy. It might be easier, and smarter, to lie and say that she had a boyfriend. Sam was a friend. Maybe he'd be willing to help her out with some role-playing.

But what was she thinking? This was *her* problem, and she mustn't depend on a man to rescue her. Whatever it took, she would handle this issue herself.

Right now it was time to take deep breaths and think about something else. As she started the car and headed back toward Main Street, Sam came easily to mind—Sam, with his gentle gray eyes, his big, strong hands, and his way of making her feel safe when he was around.

Last night, the sheriff had literally saved her life. And today he'd taken extra pains—and surely paid more than his insurance would cover—to make sure she had a first-class car to drive.

She hadn't even thanked him properly. Maybe it was time she did.

Stella's Bakery was on Main Street. Wynette had mentioned that she'd be starting work there today. It wouldn't be a bad idea to stop by and give her some support—and to pick up some thank-you treats. Grace parked at the curb and climbed out of the car. The red Cadillac drew stares from passersby, who probably thought she'd won the lottery.

By now, the sun was going down. Christmas lights glowed through the wintry twilight. Shoppers hurried to their cars. The stores, including the bakery, closed at six. Grace had arrived just in time.

Wynette gave her a smile from behind the glass-fronted counter. Wearing a pink smock, she looked tired but happy after what must've been a long day. "Heavens, Grace," she said, staring through the front window at the car. "Did you rob a bank or something?"

Grace laughed. "It's the sheriff's replacement for the green bug. Mine to drive until the Honda's fixed."

"Wow!" Wynette brushed a smear of flour off her cheek. "I know what you keep telling us, but I think that man has got it bad for you."

Grace shook her head. "I'm sure he was just feeling guilty. But I wanted to thank him by dropping off some treats. Have you got anything left?"

"Just doughnuts, but you know they're good. I can give you a dozen assorted. We box them at the end of the day, but they're still fresh."

"Great. I'll take a box." Grace slipped a bill out of the wallet in her purse. "How has your first day gone, Wynette?"

"Awesome." Wynette handed Grace her change and a pink cardboard bakery box. "My feet are killing me, and I've got a lot to learn, but I can tell I'm going to love this job. I'm really hoping Stella will keep me on."

Just then, Wynette's new boss, Stella Galanos, walked out of the back. A stunning, dark-eyed brunette of about thirty, she was dressed in a pink smock similar to Wynette's. An impressive diamond engagement ring dangled from a chain around her neck, most likely to keep it safe while Stella baked. Wynette had mentioned earlier that Stella's fiancé owned a fancy Greek restaurant in Cottonwood Springs. If the size of the diamond was any indication, the man must be doing all right.

After greeting Grace with a dazzling smile, Stella turned to Wynette. "Great job today," she said. "When you're free, I need to show you how we close up the shop."

"I was just leaving." Grace said good-bye and walked back outside to the car. Ignoring the curious stares, she climbed inside and drove away.

Grace knew where the sheriff lived. She'd been given a list of contact information for all her students, and his address had stuck in her mind. As she turned onto the street, which wasn't far from the school, she could see the big tan Jeep in the driveway. The older pickup truck he drove when he was off duty was parked next to it.

Hesitation almost overcame her as she climbed out of the car. What if Sam felt uncomfortable, having her stop by his house uninvited? What if he thought she was pushing for a relationship? For a moment she was tempted to leave the box on the doorstep, ring the bell, and leave. But the porch light had just come on. Someone in the house must've seen her drive up. They'd expect her to be standing there when the door opened.

But she wouldn't have to stay. She could just hand over the doughnuts, explain why she'd brought them, and flee back to the car. Yes, that would work.

Clutching the pink cardboard box, Grace mounted the porch and rang the bell.

Chapter Eight

It was Maggie who opened the door. The grin on her small face would have lit up the gloomiest winter twilight. "I saw you drive up," she said. "Come on in, Miss Chapman. I'll tell Daddy you're here."

The little girl danced through an open archway and vanished into the kitchen. Grace had a moment to take in the cozy living room, the worn but comfortable leather furniture and the bookshelves along one wall. Unlit logs were stacked in the brick fireplace. The crooked tree, still untrimmed, stood in one corner. Three taped cardboard boxes were piled next to it.

"Hi." Sam appeared in the archway, the kitchen light bright behind him. He was wearing jeans and a plaid shirt, the sleeves rolled up to show his muscular forearms. "I just set another place at the table. I hope you like spaghetti."

Grace had prepared herself for something like this and had a ready response. "Oh, thanks, but I can't stay. I just dropped by to bring you these." She held up the box of doughnuts. "I wanted to thank you for finding me last night, and for the car. I don't know what you said to that rental agency, but it worked."

"I tried to put a little fear into them. But if you really want to thank me, you can stay for supper. Maggie will be downhearted for the rest of the night if you leave."

Grace felt her guilt buttons being pushed, but there was no gracious way to refuse. "Well, at least I brought dessert," she said, thrusting the box toward him. "What can I do to help?"

"Nothing." He set the box on the countertop. "It's all ready. Just have a seat. I hope you don't mind store-bought sauce. Maggie will tell you that I'm not much of a cook."

"He's not." Maggie added a set of tongs to the bowl of pasta and put a shaker of dried parmesan on the table. "That's why I'm going to learn. Everything I need to know is right in that big book." She nodded toward the large, red checkered *Better Homes and Gardens* cookbook that lay on the far end of the table, next to her homework. "All I have to do is read it and do what it tells me."

Grace glanced at Sam and saw the gleam of pride in his eyes. Teaching herself to cook might prove too much for a child as young as Maggie, but no one could fault her ambition. "My mom had that same cookbook," Grace said. "I wish I'd kept it. It would come in handy now."

"Dinner is served." Sam pulled out a chair for Grace, then did the same for Maggie, who giggled. "I can get my own chair, Daddy."

"I know. But sometimes I like to remind myself that my best girl is a lady."

"Who's your best girl, me or Miss Chapman?"

Sam took his seat. "Tonight I'm extra lucky. I get to have two best girls. So, let's bless the food and eat."

Grace had skipped lunch, so she was hungry; the spaghetti with meat sauce tasted good. Even the bagged salad with bottled dressing and the warmed-over garlic bread were edible. She was grateful for the invitation. After all, Sam and his daughter hadn't been expecting company when the meal was prepared.

"We're going to decorate our tree after supper," Maggie said. "Can you stay and help us, Miss Chapman?"

Grace glanced at Sam. His expression revealed nothing.

"Thank you for asking, Maggie," she said, "but I really need to go. I have things to do at home."

"Oh, please!" Maggie begged. "We could decorate the tree and have hot cocoa with the doughnuts you brought. It would be so much more fun with you here than just Daddy and me. Wouldn't it, Daddy?"

Sensing Sam's discomfort, Grace spoke up before he could reply. "I'm sorry, Maggie. I know I'd enjoy it, but I really should leave. I'll stay long enough to help clean up in here. Then I'll be on my way."

"But the tree wouldn't take long." Maggie's expression would have melted the coldest heart. "Daddy already got the boxes down from the attic. And I'll do most of the work. You can just hand me things, and Daddy can lift me up to put the star on top." She turned to her father. "Please, Daddy. Tell Miss Chapman we want her to stay."

"Of course we do." Sam's smile was forced. He'd been dreading this night for weeks, taking out Bethany's cherished ornaments, each one holding a memory, and hanging them on the tree, where he'd have to look at them for the rest of the holiday season. And having Grace here wouldn't make the ordeal any easier. It just meant he would have to keep an even tighter rein on his emotions.

Grace, he sensed, wasn't keen on the idea either. She seemed anxious, as if she couldn't wait to rush out to her car and drive away. But there was no way he could tell her that she wasn't welcome.

And after all, this wasn't about him, or even about

Grace. It was about making a warm Christmas memory for his little girl. If Maggie wanted Grace to be here, and if she could talk Grace into staying, he would make the best of it.

"Please stay, Miss Chapman," Maggie pleaded. "It would make me so happy."

Grace glanced at Sam. He gave her a smile and a nod. She sighed. "All right, Maggie. But I can't stay long. What do you say we clear the table and put everything away in the kitchen? Then we can go in and decorate your tree."

"Yes!" Maggie clapped her hands, jumping up and down.

They made short work of cleaning up the kitchen. Sam set three mugs on the counter and spooned instant cocoa mix into each one. When the tree was done, he could heat some water for the hot chocolate Maggie had promised. Maybe everything would be all right, he told himself. Maybe the holiday ritual he'd been dreading wouldn't be so bad after all.

They gathered in the living room, Grace taking a seat on the ottoman next to the tree, Maggie already flitting to the boxes to tear away the masking tape that had held them closed for almost two years. Tearing away at memories that were still raw—maybe too raw for Sam to handle.

But for Maggie's sake, maybe it was time he tried.

Sam touched a match to the newspaper he'd stuffed under the stacked wood in the fireplace. Kindling crackled as the fire caught. By the time the logs began to blaze, Maggie had all three of the boxes opened.

Sam settled on the arm of the sofa, close to the tree and close to Grace. "All right, Miss Maggie, you're in charge," he said.

"First the lights." Maggie pulled the carefully wound string of lights out of the first box. "I need both of you to help me."

Lights, at least, were just lights. Sam and Grace stood on either side of the lopsided tree, guiding the string of lights where Maggie directed. Once Sam wound the last few feet of the string around the upper part of the tree, the job was done.

"I see an outlet behind the tree," Grace said. "Do you want me to plug the lights in?"

"Not yet," Maggie said. "We have to wait till the tree's all decorated. Then we plug in the lights. That's how Mom liked to do it."

Sam glanced at Grace, wondering if Maggie's mention of her mother had bothered her. But then, why should it? Grace was here as a friend. She was only staying because Maggie had begged her to.

Maggie pushed the second box toward Grace. "You can hand me the ornaments, Miss Chapman, and I'll hang them on the tree. Daddy, you can watch until we're ready to hang the ones that go up high. Okay?"

"Okay." Sam settled back onto the couch. Maggie had been just four years old the last time her family had decorated a Christmas tree. But he knew his little girl. She would remember every detail. The memories would hurt, and he would let them. Maybe he'd been holding them back for too long. Maybe this was what they both needed.

Grace sat with her ankles crossed, reflected firelight glowing on her skin. She was smiling at something Maggie had said, her lips soft, her expression tender. She hadn't meant to stay and probably felt out of place, but she was making an effort to fit in. Sam liked her for that.

The porcelain ornaments in the box were protected by layers of bubble wrap, each one lovingly packed away by Bethany's hands. She had bought them at specialty stores, and had even ordered some of them custom-made. Each one had its own special meaning. Her plan had been to buy one to commemorate each important memory in their lives as the years passed, so that each Christmas, the tree would tell the story of their family. That plan had ended last November, on a storm-slicked road coming home from Cottonwood Springs, where she'd gone to do some early Christmas shopping.

But he wouldn't think about that now. This year's tree, with its tokens of memory, would be for Maggie.

The first ornament Grace unwrapped and handed to Maggie was a miniature wedding cake, complete with a bride and groom on top. "Mom bought this to remember when she and Daddy got married," Maggie said. "She hung it on their very first Christmas tree."

Sam watched his daughter hang the wedding ornament on one of the lower branches. The feeling that came over him was bittersweet. Bethany was gone, but they'd made good memories together. There was a rightness about keeping those memories alive. Even so, Maggie had been right. Bethany would have wanted him to be happy. She would have wanted him to move on.

For the first time in more than a year, Sam realized that he was going to be all right.

Next, Grace unwrapped a pretty little porcelain house. "This one is to remember when Mom and Daddy got this house. Mom told me that Daddy worked really hard to buy it." Maggie hung the ornament on the tree.

"And this?" Grace had unwrapped the figure of an angel with wings—but not a traditional Christmas angel. This one appeared to be an elderly woman with short, white hair and glasses. It must have been custom-made. Grace had never seen anything like it for sale.

"That's my grandma. Her name was Maggie, too, same as mine." Maggie took the angel from Grace's hand and hung it as high on the tree as she could reach. "She's an angel in heaven. So's my grandpa. Mom had her friend make angels to remember them. I've still got my other grandma and grandpa. They live in Arizona now, where it doesn't get cold."

As Grace unwrapped other memory ornaments and watched Maggie hang them on the tree, her heart crept into her throat. When she'd agreed to stay and help with the tree, she'd expected to hang a few pretty glass balls and some tinsel and be done. But this was personal. This was family—a family she couldn't let herself care about. She didn't belong here.

She glanced at Sam. He was watching his daughter and seemed oblivious to her own discomfort. Maybe she should leave now, Grace thought. But that would upset Maggie. And now, except for two small ornaments, this box was almost empty. The third box, which was already open, appeared to hold mostly tinsel and glittery balls. She'd stayed this long. She could hold out a little longer.

There were two ornaments left in the box, both of them well padded. Grace chose one at random and carefully unwound the layers of bubble wrap. The porcelain ornament underneath was a small cradle with a baby in it—a baby with red hair.

Grace smiled as she handed it to Maggie. "This is you, isn't it?"

"Uh-huh. Mom always said it was her favorite." Maggie hung the cradle partway up the tree. One angel was missing—Maggie's mother, who'd clearly loved these little ornaments, just as she'd loved her family. Grace glanced at Sam. She could imagine how much he must be missing his wife, and how painful it must be for him to see these precious tokens of their life together.

It was all Grace could do to keep a smile on her face. Everything about the situation was wrong. She shouldn't be here, sharing this private grief with a man she barely knew. *A man who could, in no way, ever be hers.*

There was one ornament left in the box. As Grace unwrapped it, she could feel wings through the wrapping—
another angel, but smaller than the others. A baby angel,
she realized as the wrapping fell away. Her heart con-
tracted as she guessed what it might represent.

"This little angel is my brother," Maggie said, taking it
from Grace's hand. "He went back to heaven before I was
born. He was only here for a day. But Mom wanted us to
remember him. His name was Michael."

Grace's heart seemed to stop.

Oh, Sam . . . Sam. She couldn't meet his eyes. She felt
herself breaking apart inside. She had to get out of here
before she fell to pieces.

"I'm sorry, I've got to go." She pushed to her feet and
rushed blindly toward the front door. Her keys were in the
pocket of her blazer, and she'd left her purse and warm
coat in the car. There was nothing to take. All she needed
to do was leave.

"Grace—" Sam was on his feet striding after her, but
she reached the door ahead of him and flung it open.
"Thank you for . . . everything." She stammered out the
words before she plunged out the door and closed it behind her. Then she was running down the steps, her way
barely lit by the porch light, her tears breaking like a
storm.

Behind her, she heard the door open and close again,
and the sound of Sam's footsteps, but she didn't stop or
even look back. All she wanted was to get away.

She had reached her car and was fumbling in her pocket
for the keys when he caught up with her.

"You don't have to go, Grace." He turned her toward
him with a light hand on her shoulder.

She kept her face lowered to hide her tears. "Yes, I do. I
don't want to hurt Maggie, but I don't belong here. I'm

not part of your family. I can't be part of what you must be feeling."

"Listen to me," he said. "I can imagine what you're thinking. But I needed you in there. I've been dreading the sight of those ornaments. But having you to share it with us—it made a difference, Grace. It helped me, and I think it helped Maggie, too."

Grace shook her head. "It doesn't matter. I feel like I've been run through a wringer, and every drop of emotion's been squeezed out of me. I've got enough troubles of my own. I don't want to care about you and Maggie. But I do. It hurts, and I've had all I can take tonight. That's why I have to go."

"But don't go like this." He lifted her chin, forcing her to look up at him. The faint light from the porch shone on her tear-streaked face.

His gaze softened. "Grace . . ." he murmured. "Oh, damn it, Grace."

He kissed her, his lips tender but hungrily seeking, rousing a flood of sweet sensations in her. One hand, cupping her face, was his only hold on her, but she was powerless to resist. Heart pounding, she stretched on tiptoe to deepen the kiss. Only now did she realize how much she'd wanted this—his mouth molding hers, the light brush of stubble against her skin, the aromas of woodsmoke and clean soap swirling in her senses, the feel of him, the taste of him, the waves of delicious response that shimmered through her body. Heaven help her, she couldn't get enough.

But it had to end; and even before he released her, trembling and breathless, she knew the kiss had been nothing but a reckless impulse. Neither of them was ready for a fling, let alone any kind of lasting relationship.

She looked up at him. Sam's face was in shadow, hiding his expression, but his silence was a sure sign that he felt the same way.

Grace took a breath, struggling to compose herself. "I'm going to forget this ever happened," she said. "And I'm sure you'll do the same. Now—" Her voice quivered and broke. She tried again. "Now I have to go. Please explain to Maggie—make up any story you like. Tell her I'll see her at school."

Without giving Sam a chance to reply, she climbed into the car, started the engine, switched on the headlights, and hit the gas pedal. The tires spat gravel as she pulled away from the curb. When she glanced in the rearview mirror, Sam was no longer in sight.

By the time Grace turned onto her street, she'd developed a pounding headache. The day had been like a runaway roller coaster—the busy time in class, Ed Judkins's nasty surprise, the car, the visit to Sam's house, with its heart-twisting revelations . . . and finally the kiss that had shaken her to the roots of her soul.

Why had Sam kissed her? And why had she let him? Grace had no answers to those questions. She'd come to Branding Iron to pull herself together after her broken engagement and take a break from men. It was cruel fate that she should meet the most appealing man who'd ever walked into her life.

Falling in love with Sam could be the easiest thing she'd ever done. But letting it happen would only end in one more emotional train wreck. Sam and Maggie deserved better than that. They deserved a happily ever after, like the endings in Wynette's romance novels—something Grace was too badly broken to offer them.

Maybe she should just chalk the whole day up to the Christmas crazies.

A few minutes later, she pulled into the driveway. In the house, her roommates were watching the end of a Christmas movie on TV. "We saved you a plate of enchiladas and beans," Jess said. "It's in the fridge. You can micro-wave it if you're hungry."

"I've eaten, thanks." Grace tossed her coat onto the rack. "All I want to do is get ready for bed and sleep off this headache. I've had a day of it."

"Oh, Grace!" Wynette was staring at her over the back of the couch. "You look like you've been crying. What's wrong?"

Grace managed a feeble smile. "Nothing serious. Like I say, it's been a long day."

"But what happened? You were fine when I saw you at the bakery."

Grace shook her head. "Oh, no, you don't. You're not getting a story tonight. I'll be fine, but right now I'm too tired to talk."

"Oh—that reminds me," Jess said. "You had a phone call about twenty minutes ago. Someone named Nicky. He said he'd call back. I hope it's not bad news. It looks like that's the last thing you need tonight."

Nicky. Grace's headache throbbed. Nicky Treadwell, who served as an assistant principal in the school district where Grace formerly worked, had never come to terms with her leaving him virtually at the altar. She'd learned to expect a call from him every few weeks, usually late at night when he'd been drinking. She certainly hadn't given him her number here, but it would have been easy enough to get it from one of their mutual friends.

Grace knew she'd hurt him—or at least hurt his pride. Nicky's constant neediness had made her feel loved. But as the wedding date neared, his growing demands for atten-tion and control had begun to worry her. Days before her planned walk down the aisle, she'd given his ring back.

Time and distance had convinced her that she'd made a wise choice. But had the problem been with Nicky or with her own insecurities about her father? Grace was still struggling with the answer to that question.

"You look exhausted, Grace," Jess said. "Go on to bed. If he calls again, I can just ask him to leave a message."

"Thanks, but I don't think he'll be satisfied with that." Grace had never told her roommates about her past. Now wasn't the time. "I'll give him a few minutes. Maybe he won't call."

Just then the phone rang. Jess gave Grace a questioning look.

"No, I'll get it." Grace reached for the phone. Nicky's number showed on the caller ID.

"What do you want, Nicky?" she asked. "I can't talk long. I need my sleep."

"I just want to remind you that you ruined my life." He sounded drunk. "I'll never get over this, Grace, and I'll never forgive you. If you hear that I jumped off a bridge, I want you to know that it was your fault."

He made the same threat almost every time he called. Unlikely as it probably was, it still worried her. "Get some help, Nicky," she said. "Find a therapist or a support group. Or get yourself a girlfriend. I can't help you from here."

"You're a heartless bitch, Grace." He slurred the words. "One day I'll make you pay for what you did."

"As I said, get some help, Nicky. And don't call me again." She hung up the phone before he could say more.

Jess had busied herself with cleaning up the popcorn bowl and soda cans from the coffee table. But Wynette was staring at Grace. "What's going on, girl? Are you all right?"

Grace gave her friend a faint smile, knowing that her concern was well meant. "I'll be fine," she said. "As for what's going on, that story's best saved for another time."

Just getting ready for bed drained what was left of her energy. But settling into sleep was harder than she'd hoped. Time crawled as she tossed and turned, the day's events replaying in her mind like scenes from a B-grade movie.

At last, exhaustion won out and she drifted into a dream. She was in Sam's arms, his tender, passionate kisses sending ripples of desire through her body. She wanted him. She loved him, and for the first time, everything felt right.

Then, suddenly, his hands tightened on her shoulders, hard enough to hurt as he thrust her away from him. His handsome features twisted in anger. *You're a heartless bitch, Grace Chapman,* he railed at her. *You've ruined our lives, mine and Maggie's. We'll never forgive you.*

Sam tucked his daughter into her bed and brushed a good-night kiss on her forehead. "Sleep tight," he whispered, wishing he could give her more than a lonely Christmas with a busy father.

"Thanks for finishing the tree with me, Daddy," she said. "And thanks for making the cocoa. I just wish Miss Chapman hadn't had to go. Was she sick?"

"Just really tired, I think." At least Maggie had been busy with the tree and hadn't seen him kissing her teacher. That would have complicated everything.

"I can tell she really likes you," Maggie said. "And I think you like her, too. Maybe we can invite her back soon."

"I don't know if that's such a good idea, honey."

"Why not?" Maggie lifted her head off the pillow, eyes wide with dismay. "Didn't she have a good time?"

"It's not that." Sam groped for an explanation that Maggie would accept. "Remember what we talked about— that Miss Chapman wants to treat all her students the same? Coming to our house and being our friend would make that hard to do."

"Well, you could still ask her out. I wouldn't have to come with. Take her to dinner or to a movie. I know you like her, Daddy."

With a weary sigh, Sam eased her back onto the pillow. "I'm sorry, Maggie, but things aren't going to work out between Miss Chapman and me. There are too many complications."

"Like what?"

"Things you wouldn't understand. Now go to sleep, all right?"

"All *right*." With a little huff of displeasure, Maggie closed her eyes. Sam walked softly out into the hall, leaving the door ajar, the way she liked it.

In the living room, he unplugged the glowing Christmas tree lights. Even in the afterglow of the dying fire, he could see the precious ornaments that Bethany had chosen and loved. No doubt they would become family heirlooms, part of Maggie's Christmas for the rest of her childhood, if not her life.

But how could memories hung on a tree ever be enough—for Maggie or for him?

Chapter Nine

Three days, including the weekend, had passed without any word from Grace. Maggie had mentioned to Sam that her teacher was helping the class get ready for the holidays. The students were practicing songs for the school Christmas program, which would be held for parents on the last day before vacation.

At least Sam knew that Grace was all right. But it surprised him how much he missed seeing her.

Grace's silence came as no surprise. After that sizzling kiss, she'd made it clear that she wanted to keep her distance. Sam could understand why—in fact, he had his own misgivings. But he knew better than to think they'd seen the last of each other. In a small town like Branding Iron their paths were bound to cross again.

Sam had heard from the body shop in Cottonwood Springs. The new fender for Grace's Honda had been ordered, but holiday shipping tended to run at a crawl. The car wouldn't be ready until after Christmas. He needed to pass the news on to Grace. A phone call would be awkward, and he had no wish to use Maggie as a messenger. But he'd be seeing Grace on Monday at the meeting to follow up on the Christmas ball plans. He could tell her about her car then.

How would she react to seeing him again? Sam had worried some about that. But they were both civilized adults. They'd be fine. Meanwhile, his job alone was enough to keep him occupied.

With Christmas approaching, crime and domestic stress tended to go up. Winter roads, coupled with holiday traffic, raised the number of accidents. Then there were the people who just needed extra looking after—people like Hank Miller.

Monday morning, finding himself with some free time, Sam drove across town to the weedy lot where Hank's trailer stood. Checking on the town's hard-luck cases wasn't part of Sam's job. But somebody needed to do it, and there was no one else. Sam had suggested to the mayor that the city arrange with Cottonwood Springs for a part-time social worker, or at least pay some local person to see to their welfare. But Mayor Wilkins had dismissed the idea as too expensive and shooed Sam out of his newly refurbished office with its massive walnut desk, oak paneling, and designer curtains.

Rulon Wilkins had also used public money to fly himself and his wife to a national mayor's convention in New York City. According to Helen, who was friends with the mayor's secretary, the trip had included shopping, lavish dinners, and Broadway shows. Too bad the man was a shoo-in for reelection next November. He was a likable glad-hander, and people gave him their votes. But they didn't seem to be getting much in return.

The street where Hank lived was peppered with potholes and lined with cracked, broken sidewalks. Most of the people who lived here were either on disability or worked at low-paying, menial jobs in town. Some were addicted to alcohol and drugs. Nobody seemed to care about them except Sam. He knew all their names, even the names of the children, and he tried to make sure they were all right, even if it meant buying groceries out of his own pocket.

He parked at the curb and followed the worn dirt path to the trailer. The beat-up Ford coupe Hank drove was parked out front. But the place was quiet. Maybe too quiet. What if something was wrong? Maybe he should have come around sooner.

Sam rapped on the door. There was no answer, but the door was unlocked. He rapped one more time, then opened it and stepped inside.

The trailer was frigid, even colder inside than the sunlit air outdoors. In the dim light, Sam could see the electric space heater where he'd left it earlier. It was plugged in and turned on, but it wasn't running. A flip of the light switch confirmed that the power was off.

"Hank?" There was no answer. Sick with dread, Sam moved through the kitchenette toward the bedroom in the back. An empty whiskey bottle sat on the counter next to the kitchen sink. Not a good sign. In cold weather like this, with no heat, a man could drink himself into a stupor and die of hypothermia.

The bedroom door was ajar but not far enough for Sam to see inside. He was about to open it, bracing himself for what he might find on the other side, when a familiar sound reached his ears.

It was the deep, rumbling wheeze of Hank's snoring.
Thank God!

Sam's knees sagged with relief. He leaned against the wall for a moment to steady himself before opening the door.

In the dim light that filtered through the tightly drawn blinds, he could make out a heap of blankets, coats, even a bathroom rug. It appeared that Hank, who was still snoring, had piled everything he could find on the bed and crawled underneath.

The air in the room reeked of whiskey—an odor that worsened as Sam pawed through the mountain of covers to find Hank and rouse him.

"Wake up, Hank." Sam shook his shoulder. "Come on, we've got to get you moving."

Hank swore. "Go 'way. Damn head feels like it got pounded with a sledgehammer. Lemme sleep it off."

"Come on. We need to get some coffee and hot food down you. I'm taking you to Buckaroo's."

Muttering curses, Hank crawled out of bed. He looked bad, but Sam had seen him worse. He'd slept in his clothes, which were rumpled but not too dirty. After some help with his prosthetic leg and a quick cleanup in the bathroom, Sam was able to get him into his coat and out the door.

Sam helped him into the Jeep and turned the heater on full blast before heading back downtown. Hank's eyes were red, as if he'd been crying before he went to sleep.

"What happened to the power in your trailer?" Sam steered around a crater-sized pothole in the street. "You could've frozen to death in there, Hank. I was afraid you had."

"Damn power company shut me off." Hank blew his nose on a tissue he'd found in his pocket. "I was gonna pay them yesterday. I'd cashed my disability check and had the money. But then somethin' happened and I forgot. Bastards didn't even give me an extra few hours before they pulled the plug."

Sam turned into the parking lot at Buckaroo's. If he was to help the man, he needed to know what had kept Hank from paying his power bill and maybe caused him to get drunk again. But he would get some hot coffee in him before asking.

Buckaroo's was open for breakfast. Sam found a quiet

booth and ordered bacon, eggs, hash browns, and pan-cakes for Hank and coffee for them both.

"Better?" he asked as Sam emptied his mug and got a refill from the waitress.

"Head's startin' to clear some," Hank muttered. "But no. Nothin's better. Reckon it never will be."

"Want to tell me about it? It might help to talk."

"Won't help. But I'll tell you anyway. You always were a good listener, Sam."

"I'm listening now."

Hank stirred a packet of sugar into his coffee. "Like I said, I got my disability check. Cashed it at the bank. Felt good to have some money in my hands."

"Always does."

"I knew I needed to pay the power bill today. But on the way, I got to thinking. This would be my last check before Christmas. I wanted to send a little something to my boy, Travis, just so he'd know I was thinking about him."

Tears welled in Hank's bloodshot eyes. Sam already knew that he'd given up parental rights and allowed his son, who was a little older than Maggie, to be adopted by his ex-wife's new husband. He'd done it out of love, even though it broke his heart.

"I already had the phone number and the address," Hank continued. "But I found a pay phone and made a call to ask if there was anything special he might like.

"It was Marilyn who answered the phone. She—" He wiped his eyes on his sleeve. "She said that since I'd signed away my rights, Travis was no longer my son. She'd told him that I didn't want him anymore—a lie, you know that, Sam. She said that if I tried to contact Travis again, she'd take out a restraining order and have me arrested if I violated it."

"Oh, God, Hank, I'm sorry." Sam could imagine how

he'd feel if someone took Maggie away. "But Marilyn's within her legal right to do that. It's the law."

"I know. But when I signed the papers, I thought, at least, I'd be able to stay in touch with the boy. It's like I'm dead to him. Dead is how I feel."

Sam could guess the rest of the story. Instead of paying his overdue power bill, Hank had bought a bottle of cheap whiskey and taken it home to drown his sorrows. At least he'd made it to bed and covered up. Otherwise he might not be here.

The waitress had brought Hank's breakfast. He looked at it but made no move to pick up his fork.

"I know you don't feel like eating," Sam said. "But you won't survive on an empty stomach. Give it a try."

Hank nibbled a slice of crisp bacon, then, with a sigh, he forked a bite of pancake and managed to get it down. "It's not that I don't appreciate this, Sam. But right now, I don't much care whether I live or die."

"I take it you haven't made it to the AA meetings. They can do a world of good. I know people who've literally been saved by following the program."

"Forget that. I don't need hard-luck stories and platitudes."

"Then what do you need, Hank? Your family's gone. What else could make a difference for you? Think about it."

Hank took his time, squirting ketchup on his hash browns and taking a couple of bites before he answered.

"I need a job, Sam—something better to do than sit around, drink, and feel sorry for myself. I know plenty about farming and how to fix most machines and take care of stock. I can't do the physical work with my leg gone, but what's in my head and hands has to be worth something." He shrugged. "Never mind. Who's going to hire a one-legged drunk, eh?"

"Nobody wants to hire even a two-legged drunk. Sober up, and you might have a decent chance." Sam finished his coffee. As he set the mug on the table, an idea struck him.

"I'll tell you what. Let's make a deal. If you'll start going to AA meetings and making an honest effort to sober up, I'll help you find a job."

"You'll *help* me?" Hank raised an eyebrow. "That doesn't sound like much of a deal to me. What if I do all the work and sit through those damned meetings, and you can't even find me an interview?"

"All right, how's this?" Sam signaled the waitress for the check. "Sober up for real, and if we haven't found you a job, I'll hire you myself."

"Doing what?"

"I don't know, but it's the best offer you're going to get. So, what do you say?"

Hank sighed, then nodded. "All right. What've I got to lose? I'll give it a try."

"Fine. But if you don't do your part, the deal is off." Sam fished his credit card out of his wallet. "Finish your breakfast. Then we'll go and see about getting your power back on—and check the schedule for the next AA meeting."

The follow-up meeting for the Christmas ball committee was set for that night. Maggie had begged to be included again. "Please, Daddy. Remember how much help I was last time? The Christmas ball was my idea."

"I know, honey," Sam had said. "But the meeting's for grown-ups. You can go next door and stay with the McDermotts. They'll be putting up their Christmas tree tonight. Mrs. McDermott told me they could really use your help."

"Really?" Maggie's green eyes had sparkled. Like her mother, she was a Christmas girl through and through.

She'd skipped and danced all the way to the house next door, leaving Sam to drive to his meeting alone.

Sam felt lucky to have good neighbors who liked Maggie and were willing to take her on short notice. The money he insisted on paying the retired couple was a bargain. But he knew that Maggie needed more of him than he had time to give her. He felt the guilt every time they had to cancel fun plans because of his work, and every time he was called away on some emergency in the night. Serving his community was important. But so was being a father to his motherless little girl.

He drove into the parking lot at the city and county building and parked next to Grace's red Cadillac. If he didn't get a chance to talk to her in the meeting, he could at least catch her at her car.

The night was cold and diamond clear, the sky a spectacle of stars, like glitter spilled across dark velvet. As he crossed the parking lot to the building entrance, Sam remembered kissing Grace, the feel of her responsive mouth like warm satin against his. He'd yearned to wrap her in his arms and mold her slender curves to his body. But that would have been going too far. At least he'd had the wisdom to hold back. But he knew that when he saw Grace in the meeting, whether he wanted to or not, he'd be remembering that kiss. And something told him so would she.

He'd hoped to arrive early, but at the last minute, before leaving home, he'd misplaced his keys. The search, which ended when he found them in his jacket, had delayed him by about ten minutes. He walked into the meeting just as it was starting.

The mayor frowned as Sam entered and took the only empty seat which, as luck would have it, was across the table from Grace. She gave him a faint smile and looked away.

"Well, Sam, we're grateful you decided to join us," the mayor said. "We were about to start without you. I take it you didn't bring your lovely daughter tonight."

Sam replied with a shake of his head and poured himself some coffee from the carafe on the table. If Rulon Wilkins was waiting for an apology, he was out of luck.

"Alice, do you have the minutes from the last meeting?" the mayor asked.

"I do." The mayor's wife stood and read the notes in her high-pitched voice. "Mr. Chairman," she concluded, addressing her husband, "I move that the minutes be added to the city record."

Someone mumbled a second, and the motion was voted in. Sam helped himself to a doughnut from the box on the table. It was going to be a long evening.

Next it was time for follow-up reports from last week's assignments. At least this might be interesting. Sam, whose only contribution had been agreeing to play Santa, had nothing to report. He settled back to listen to the others, doing his best to keep his eyes off Grace. The last thing he wanted was to make her uncomfortable.

Buffy, the gym teacher, was enthusiastic. "My students love the idea of a dance. I've got offers to make CDs of the best country songs. And the girls who know the dances are teaching the ones who don't know—even the boys. It's going to be great fun."

Alice looked up from scribbling notes. "I'm still not sure this is a good idea. A bunch of out-of-control teenagers taking over the dance floor. All those raging hormones. Anything could happen." She clicked her tongue and shook her head, but no one else paid her much attention.

Doris Cullimore, who ran the feed and hardware store with her husband, promised that they'd pick up the large Christmas tree in Cottonwood Springs and truck it to the gym in time for it to be decorated. "We'd planned to get the tree sooner," she said. "But things have been so busy at the store, it's hard to get away. We've talked about hiring extra help, but the kids who want to work over the holidays don't know a socket wrench from a pitchfork. We'd hoped to cut back our hours as we get close to retirement. That's our problem, not yours. But for sure, the tree will be there for you."

Sam listened with interest, resolving to find out more later. He might have the perfect employee for the store—if he could get him sober and keep him that way.

There was a report from the dinner committee. Since the families in town had been bringing in food for years, and this hadn't changed, there was little to be discussed.

Then it was Grace's turn. She stood, giving Sam the chance to devour her with his eyes and drown in her voice. She was so damned beautiful. He hadn't realized how beautiful she was until he'd tasted her lips.

Too bad it wasn't likely to happen again.

"My first graders really came through for me," Grace said. "They came up with some great ideas for games. They'll also be lending us videos and board games and helping with crafts. All I need from the committee is to make sure we have a room with tables and chairs and a TV with a video player."

"I can check into that for you," Buffy offered. "I'll talk to the people in charge at the high school."

"And don't forget that I offered to bring some books from the library and read stories," Clara Marsden said.

"That would be wonderful. I guess that's all for now." Grace took her seat again. For an instant her gaze locked with Sam's. He gave her a smile and a thumbs-up sign, then wondered if that show of support had been a mistake. Maybe she'd think he was flirting with her. Maybe he was.

The mayor turned to the woman who had a beauty salon in her home. "Lois, where are we on promotion?"

Lois Harper stood and lifted several posters from behind her chair. "I called the radio station. And my daughter made these posters for us. She did a great job if I say so myself."

The posters, done with Magic Marker on sheets of poster board, weren't professional, but they were cute and clever. Sam could tell how proud Lois was of her twelve-year-old daughter.

"Oh, no! Oh, dear!" Alice Wilkins gasped. "These won't do at all. Look, she's called it The *Cowboy* Christmas Ball. According to the minutes, the posters need to say The *Cowboys'* Christmas Ball, with an *s* and an apostrophe." She stressed the *s* sound, like a hiss. "They need to be done over and done correctly."

Lois looked stricken. Grace raised her hand for permission to speak. "Excuse me, but I don't see a problem with these great posters. If they don't match what's written in the minutes, there's a simple solution. I move we call our event The Cowboy Christmas Ball—with no *s*."

"Seconded," Sam said.

Scowling his disapproval, the mayor called for the vote. The only dissenter was his wife, who looked as if she'd just swallowed a pickle. "The minutes are inviolate," she protested, "like the Constitution."

"Motion carried." The mayor didn't look much happier than his wife did. Sam and Grace exchanged glances. She gave him a fleeting smile and the lift of an eyebrow. It was a small victory, but a sweet one. He was proud of her. Better yet, the incident might have thawed the ice between them.

The meeting ended a few minutes later, with a reminder that they'd be getting together again at their regular time on Wednesday, the eleventh. Grace left first, but Sam caught up with her in the hall. He liked to think she'd slowed her steps for him. But he couldn't be sure.

"That was a good move, suggesting we change the name of the party to match the posters," he said, making conversation.

"It was the only thing that made sense." She still sounded distant. "How could we ask Lois's daughter to do them over? That would be mean-spirited. Her mother was so proud, and those posters were so cute."

"I got a phone call about your car today," Sam said. "The folks at the body shop have found a replacement for the fender on your Honda, but it won't be here for several weeks. You probably won't get your car back until after the holidays."

Grace laughed. "Tell them they can keep it all winter if they want. I'm getting accustomed to those lovely, heated leather seats."

"Good."

They were approaching the exit that opened onto the parking lot. Sam found himself scrambling for an excuse to keep her with him. But he'd given her the news about the car, and now he was strangely tongue-tied. What could he say next?

You know, Grace, I really enjoyed that kiss. What do you think about trying it again?

No way.

I've been missing you, Grace. Maybe we could get together over coffee sometime after work.

Better. But she was still likely to say no.

He opened the door for her, and they stepped outside, into the chilly night. In a moment she'd be gone, and he'd have no reason to see her again until next week's committee meeting.

Blast it! What could he do to get more time with her?

* * *

Grace could sense the tension that hung between them, crackling like the air before a thunderstorm. She'd felt it from the moment he walked into the meeting tonight. The chemistry was there, all right. But that didn't mean it was a good thing—not given her history with men and the potential for damage.

It was time to throw cold water on any chance of involvement with this sexy, gentle, compelling man who was in danger of capturing her heart. And Grace knew of just one sure way to do that—tell him the truth.

"Walk me to my car, Sam," she said. "I need to talk to you."

"This sounds serious." He kept pace with her as they crossed the parking lot.

"It is." She shivered as a gust of cold wind pierced her jacket. "But if you need to get right home to Maggie—"

"Maggie's fine. She's at the neighbors'."

"Then maybe we should get in the car. It's freezing out here."

"Sounds like a good idea." He opened the door for her, then went around the car and climbed into the passenger seat.

"I can warm it up," she said.

"No need." His tone was cautious. "I'm listening."

She turned in the seat to face him. "Thanks, Sam. You're a decent man. That's why I want to be honest with you."

"Go on. Whatever you've got to say, I can handle it."

Grace took a deep breath. Why did this have to be so hard? "That kiss—it was the real thing," she said. "You're a wonderful man. I could fall for you in a heartbeat."

"But?"

"I'm a train wreck, Sam. I tend to mess up every life I

touch, and I don't want to mess up your life or Maggie's. You deserve better."

Sam didn't reply. But his face, lit by the parking lot's security lamp, showed nothing but kindness and patience. As sheriff, he'd probably heard every hard-luck story in the book. But he hadn't heard this one.

"I've been engaged twice," she said. "Both times I got cold feet and gave the rings back. The last time was just a few days before the wedding. I had my dress, the venue was reserved, the invitations mailed, the food ordered, my brother had flown in to walk me down the aisle—and suddenly I knew I couldn't go through with it. My ex-fiancé still phones me and accuses me of ruining his life."

"It sounds like you made the right decision."

"I know that now. But the other engagement was to a perfectly nice guy. I just couldn't go through with it. And before that—"

"Before that?" Was he dismayed or just curious?

"Sam, every relationship I've ever had with a man ended when I got scared and broke it off."

Sam was silent, as if weighing his words before he spoke. "So, you're concerned that the same thing would happen with me?"

"It's not just you I'm concerned about. It's Maggie. I love that little girl of yours, Sam. If I were to get her expectations up and then break her heart, I'd never forgive myself."

"I understand."

And he did understand, Grace was sure. He might take a chance with his own feelings, but he would never risk hurting Maggie.

So maybe now he would say good-bye and get out of the car. Maybe after this she would only see him at school and city functions. Wasn't that what she'd set out to do?

"You mentioned being scared, Grace," he said. "Have you talked to a therapist?"

"I have. It helped me to understand the problem. But it didn't fix it."

She told him then, about the childhood incident that had triggered it all—coming home from school in the middle of the day to discover her father in bed with his girlfriend.

"I never told anyone about it except the therapist, and now you. But I adored my dad, the way Maggie loves you. I was his best girl, his little princess. When he left our family to marry that woman, it destroyed my mother and left me afraid to trust any man in a relationship."

"Are you in touch with your father?"

"I haven't spoken to him since he left. He tried for a while—phone calls, birthday cards, and gifts. My mother sent them all back. After a while they stopped coming. My brother keeps track of him. But Cooper was in high school when our family came apart. He was on the football team, had a girlfriend, lived in his own world. Dad's betrayal didn't hurt him the way it hurt me."

Grace released a ragged breath. "I'm sorry for unloading on you like this, Sam. I just wanted you to understand my craziness, and to know that if I push you away, it isn't your fault. Before I get involved again, I need time and space to work things out. Otherwise, I'll only risk hurting people I care about."

"It's all right." He didn't reach for her, even though Grace found herself wishing he would. Those big, strong arms would feel comforting right now. But she had drawn a line, and she knew that Sam wouldn't cross it. He had too much integrity and too much pride.

"Thanks for being honest," he said. "I care about you, Grace—enough to take this as far as you'll let me. But if you need time and space, I won't reach out to you or push you in any way. If and when you feel ready to take a chance, you know where to find me. Got it?"

"Got it." What she really wanted was for him to take her in his arms and kiss her until stars exploded in her head. But that would only complicate things. "Don't think I expect you to wait around for me," she said. "If you happen to meet somebody else—"

"We'll cross that bridge when we come to it." He gave her hand a quick squeeze and withdrew. "I'll be going now. Maggie will be wondering where her father is. Take care, Grace."

When he'd gone, she started the car and drove home. Sam was right. If anything good and lasting was to happen between them, she had to get past her fears. But that could take time, and she was already missing him—his gentle smile, his strength, his patience, his ability to thrill her with a touch . . .

Had she been fool enough to fall in love with him?

Chapter Ten

The window of Grace's classroom gave her a partial view of the circular driveway where parents could let off their students and pick them up after school. From where she stood, waiting for the day to begin, she watched the sheriff's Jeep stop at the curb. Sam came around the vehicle to help his daughter to the ground. After passing down her schoolbag and accepting a quick hug, he stood watching her run into the building. Only after she'd gone inside did he climb back into the Jeep and pull out of sight.

As she turned away from the window, Grace felt a familiar ache in her throat. Sam cared for everyone—his daughter, his town, and even her. He deserved a woman with a heart as big as his own—not a scarred victim of childhood trauma, unable to trust. Grace knew she was broken. She wanted desperately to heal, not only for Sam but for herself. But she didn't know how. Until she could find a way, she had little choice except to keep her distance.

She would see Sam tonight at the committee meeting. They would be polite and friendly. Maybe he would ask her how she was doing. She would answer that she was fine. But both of them would know that she didn't mean it. As they sat at the table, she would devour him with her eyes, turning her gaze away only when he looked at her. After the meeting ended, she would avoid walking out alone with him. Nothing about this arrangement felt natural. But for now, it was the way things had to be.

The first bell had rung. Her students were pouring into the classroom, eyes sparkling, voices chattering, all of them excited that the holiday was almost here. Maggie walked in with her friend Brenda. As they took their seats, the second bell rang. The P.A. came on with the Pledge of Allegiance and the daily announcements. It was time for Grace to forget her own troubles and make it a happy day for her class.

Where had her plan gone wrong? Maggie looked up from her math worksheet to study her teacher. Miss Chapman had been all cheery smiles this morning when she'd greeted the class. But now as she moved among the students, hushing some and helping others as needed, Maggie sensed that something was wrong. It was as if the light and joy had drained from her face.

Sam had been looking much the same way for most of the week. When he talked to Maggie, especially about Christmas, it was as if he'd put on a happy, smiling mask. But when he didn't think she was watching him, the mask fell away. He looked lonely, the way he had much of the time before Miss Chapman came into his life.

Had they had an argument? Had they broken up? Maggie didn't know; and she suspected that if she were to ask, neither of them would tell her the truth. She only knew that Miss Chapman hadn't come around in the past week, and Sam hadn't brought her name up even once. Something needed to be set right. And this time Maggie was out of ideas.

Tonight they'd be seeing each other at the meeting to plan the Christmas ball. If Maggie could be there, too, she might be able to move things in the right direction. She knew that Sam hadn't planned to take her. But maybe if she begged, she could change his mind. For now, all she could do was hope.

"Miss Chapman." The voice, coming from behind her in the hallway, stopped Grace in her tracks. Her heart sank. She'd hoped that Ed Judkins had given up on targeting her as a confidante. Steeling herself, she turned to face her boss.

"I was hoping to catch you before you left." He appeared flushed and slightly out of breath. "I'd like to talk to you. Would you join me in my office?"

"I'm in a hurry," Grace said. "Can't we talk right here?"

"This won't take long." He glanced at the custodian, who passed them pushing a wheeled cart. "Come on, Grace—I may call you Grace, mayn't I? We can talk on the way."

She half feared that he would take her arm or put a hand against her back. He hadn't touched her since the time he'd laid a hand on her shoulder, but the thought that he might made her want to break and run. She didn't want a nasty confrontation, but if he crossed a line, she would put him in his place—and possibly put her future job prospects in danger.

"I understand the annual town Christmas party has become a costume ball," he said.

"That's right. Although western dress is just an option. Are you about to tell me that you don't approve?"

"Not at all. I think it's a dandy idea. Maybe I'll come as a gambler."

They passed through the outer office, which was empty, and into the principal's space. As he reached behind her to close the door, she stopped him. "Please leave that open, if you don't mind."

"Are you saying you don't trust me?"

"I'm saying that I don't trust anybody who might walk past that door, see it closed, and start spreading gossip—even though there's nothing worth gossiping about."

"Very well. Have a seat." He sounded disappointed, but he left the door partway open. "I just have some news. Since it's of a personal nature, I'd like to keep it between us."

Grace mentally measured the number of steps from her seat to the door. "If it's personal, maybe you shouldn't be sharing it."

"I just need to share it with someone, and since you already know about my situation . . . I just became a free man. There are a few legal formalities left, but I've found an apartment, and the papers were signed and witnessed last night. It's done."

"Should I congratulate you?"

"I was hoping you'd do more, like join me for dinner to celebrate. I know you're busy tonight, but we can do it another time. Maybe this weekend."

Grace felt her stomach clench. "I'm sorry, but given our work relationship, I don't think that would be appropriate."

"Well, nobody has to know, do they? We can drive to Cottonwood Springs. I know a quiet place that has great prime rib and a decent wine list. So, what do you say?"

"I'm sorry, but my answer has to be no. I just don't think it's a good idea." *Also you're a troll, and I wouldn't go to a hot dog eating contest with you.* Too bad she couldn't just tell him that.

"Now that the question is settled, I need to go," she said, standing.

He sighed and stood with her. "Fine, but I haven't given

up. I have the power to make your life pretty sweet around here. Or I can make it a hell of a lot harder. Think about it. If you change your mind, let me know."

"I'm going to forget I ever heard that, Mr. Judkins. And now I'll be on my way. No need to show me out."

She strode out of the room, down the hall, and out the back exit to the parking lot.

By the time she got her car open, she was shaking so hard that her legs would barely hold her. She sank onto the seat, closed the door, and pressed her hands to her face. She had to get out of here. It wouldn't do to have Judkins come out of the building and see her still sitting in her car.

Summoning the last of her self-control, she started the car, drove out of the parking lot, and headed home. She'd done the only right thing, she told herself. There was no way she would have accepted her boss's invitation. But at what price?

His implied threat had been unethical. She could file a complaint with the school board. Maybe she should. But with no witnesses, who would believe her? He'd invited her to dinner, that was all. He'd left the door open when she'd asked, and he hadn't laid a hand on her. But he had implied, in his own subtle way, that if he chose to, he could see that she never taught school in Texas again.

She was too emotional, and too inexperienced, to think this out on her own. But there was a friend she could talk to, someone calm, wise, and sensible who might understand the situation. Maybe Jess could help her find some answers.

Jess's silver Ford Taurus was parked in the driveway. She was home. And Wynette would be working till six o'clock, so they'd be alone for now. This could be the best time to talk.

Grace found her roommate in the kitchen cutting vegetables into thin slices. A pot of rice simmered on the stove. Jess looked up and smiled. Tall and dark, with her hair pinned up in a classic twist, she was dressed in the simple gray knit pants and sweater she'd worn to work. Something about her always reminded Grace of a French fashion model, although Jess would have laughed at the comparison. She kept mostly to herself and seemed an odd fit for a small rural town. But since she'd bought a home here, it appeared that she meant to stay.

She scraped a mound of chopped onion off the cutting board and into a sizzling cast-iron pan, then added some minced garlic. "I got off early today and thought Chinese sounded good. Since there's no takeout here—" Her expression changed to one of concern. "You look stressed, Grace. Is something wrong?"

Grace set her purse on the table. "Actually, yes. I need your wisdom."

"I can't promise wisdom, but I'll be happy to listen and sympathize. What's the matter? Is it Sam or your ex—?" She caught herself. "Sorry. I didn't mean to pry."

"It's all right. And no, it isn't Sam. He and I are just friends. And Nicky is history. This problem is work related, and it's serious. Give me a minute to wash up. Then I can help you as we talk."

Over sliced carrots, mushrooms, and canned water chestnuts, Grace's story emerged. Jess listened, mostly in silence, her dark eyes warm with sympathy.

"The first time he called me into his office, I was just annoyed," Grace said. "After today, I'm scared. Ed Judkins could make up some charge and put it on my record. No one would question his word. I'd be ruined."

"You say he didn't touch you."

"Not this time. And any threats he made were just implied. I know sexual harassment when I hear it. But I have no proof. Even if I did, he could dismiss it as a misunderstanding. He's got all the power. What can I do, Jess?"

Jess stirred the freshly cut vegetables. "It sounds as if he's being careful not to give you any proof. I'm guessing he might have done something like this before. I agree that you don't have enough on him to file a complaint—or even threaten to. He might give up and decide to look elsewhere. But in case he doesn't, you need to protect yourself. First of all, as soon as possible, write down everything that's happened, exact dates and times, exactly what was said. Going forward, keep a record of everything. If he so much as looks at you, write it down. If Judkins does cross the line, at least you'll have something to back up your story."

"That makes sense." Grace found the soy sauce in the cupboard and sprinkled it over the vegetables. "But it isn't proof. It would still be my word against his."

"That's why I'm going to suggest something more theatrical. Do you happen to have a mini cassette recorder?"

"I'm not sure. Maybe somewhere—"

"Never mind, I've got one you can borrow. Keep it close, in a pocket, where you can reach it."

Grace gave a little gasp. "Oh, my stars, you're not kidding, are you? This is like something out of the movies."

Jess's lips twitched in a faint smile. "If he corners you or invites you into his office, turn it on. But be aware that you can't lead him on or encourage him in any way. What he does and says has to be his idea. Otherwise, it's entrapment. Understood?"

"Understood." Grace stared at her friend as awareness struck her. "You've done something like this before, haven't you, Jess?"

"Maybe. But that's all you're going to get from me. We're all entitled to our little secrets." Jess turned away, toward the sink, then glanced back. "I'd rather you didn't tell Wynette about this conversation. She's a darling, but maybe a little too curious. Okay?"

"Of course."

"The cassette recorder will be under your pillow when you get home tonight."

"Thanks. I'll set the table."

Grace's hands trembled slightly as she arranged three place settings. When she'd asked her roommate for advice, she'd gotten a lot more than she'd bargained for. She glanced back at Jess, who was checking the rice on the stove. Who was this woman? What was she doing in a place like Branding Iron?

For now, Grace would have to be content with not knowing.

Sam kissed Maggie good-bye and watched as she rang the McDermotts' doorbell and was warmly welcomed into the house. She had begged to go to tonight's meeting of the Christmas ball committee. But Sam had stood firm.

"The meeting is for grown-ups, Maggie," he'd said. "Besides, I need to go by Hank's place afterward and make sure he goes to his AA meeting. If he drags his heels, I might even need to go with him."

"Why do people drink, Daddy?" she'd asked.

"Lots of reasons." Sam remembered his college days, the wild parties, and later, after he'd blown out his knee, the mind-numbing effect of a few drinks. He'd never been a full-fledged alcoholic, but he'd come close.

"Some people drink because their friends do it, or because they think it's fun to get drunk and act stupid. But people like Hank drink because they're sad or hurting. Drinking helps them forget the pain. That's one reason it's so hard to quit. But Hank is trying. That's why I want to help him."

"Did you ever drink?"

"Years ago when I was young and not very smart. Then I met your mom, and she made me want to quit. So I did."

"I'll never drink, Daddy."

"Good for you. Now run along."

He drove his own truck back to the city building. Maggie was so easy now. What would she be like as a headstrong teenager? Would he still be doing his best to manage her on his own, or would they be members of a new family?

What would the years ahead be like? Would Grace be part of those years? He liked the idea. But Grace was struggling with issues of her own. He might be ready for her. But would she ever be ready for him?

Tonight he arrived ahead of her. He was pouring himself some coffee when she walked in with Buffy Burton. She looked preoccupied, he thought. Could it have something to do with him? No doubt that idea had sprung from male vanity. Grace had a busy life. There were plenty of other things she could have on her mind.

She gave him a smile and a nod as she took her seat. There was no time for the two of them to talk, which was just as well. What would they have to say to each other?

The mayor called the meeting to order. His wife, her blond hair freshly bleached and curled, stood to read the minutes. She cleared her throat, then paused to gaze around the table, her plump face beaming. "Before I begin, we have a special surprise for someone here tonight. Sam, would you please stand?"

What in hell's name . . . .? Sam rose reluctantly to his feet.

"Ta-daaa!" Turning, Alice swept her arms toward a large carboard box sitting on the credenza behind her. Sam gave her a puzzled frown.

"It's your Santa Claus suit!" she exclaimed. "All cleaned, pressed, and ready for you. Everything's there, even the beard and the boots."

Sam sighed. Why couldn't she have just dropped the damned thing off at his house?

"How about trying it on and giving us a preview?" Alice's tone suggested that this was an order, not a suggestion. "You can change in Rulon's office next door."

"Thanks, but I'll save it for when I'm home." No way was Sam going to dress up and make a fool of himself just to satisfy the mayor's wife.

"But don't you want to see if it fits?"

"Why bother with that, since it can't be altered?" Sam struggled to rein in his temper. "Don't worry, I'll make it work. Let's get on with the meeting."

With a huff of displeasure, Alice adjusted her reading glasses and started on the minutes. Sam's gaze wandered to Grace, who was sitting across from him again. For the space of a heartbeat their eyes met. Then she looked away. Sam had hoped for a secret smile or a look of understanding. But that wasn't to be.

Blast it, he was already tired of keeping his distance. He wanted to talk with her, to touch her, to kiss her. But he'd promised to respect her need for time and space. He couldn't go back on his word.

The meeting was mostly a rehash of earlier decisions and a progress report on how they were being carried out—posters up, announcements out, ticket sales arranged, food planned, Christmas tree, seating, and tables to be set up, audio equipment and music ready, and a room with video reserved for children's activities. Next Wednesday, the eighteenth, would be their final session before the party, which was traditionally held on the last Saturday before Christmas Eve. After the mayor's unnecessary lecture on the importance of everyone showing up, the meeting was adjourned.

Sam picked up the box, which was bulky but not heavy, and headed for the entrance. Glancing ahead, he saw that Grace was holding the front door open for him.

"Thanks," he muttered, passing through.

"I was really hoping to see you in that suit tonight," she joked as they walked out to the parking lot. At least she was being friendly.

"You'll see me soon enough," he said. "I'll probably be the grumpiest Santa in the history of Christmas. I'll give the little kiddies bad dreams."

"You'll be fine. I know you're just a big softie at heart."

"You think?" Sam opened the door of his pickup and laid the box on the passenger seat. "To be honest, I just want the whole blessed holiday to be over. But then there's Maggie."

"Yes, there's Maggie. And I know you'll do anything to make her Christmas a happy one. You're a good man, Sam Delaney."

"Don't be too sure of that." She might change her mind if she knew what he was thinking. If he had free rein to do as he wanted, he would pull her into the truck right now and crush her lips with kisses.

"I've got to go," he said.

"Me, too. You're coming to Maggie's Christmas program next week, aren't you?"

"Wouldn't miss it." Emotions welled as Sam stood looking down at her. He struggled against the urge to tell her he was tired of this standoff, that he wanted her in his arms and in his life, that he was falling in love with her.

But self-control won out. He watched her get into her car and drive away. There'd be other times, he told himself. Better times than tonight.

After making sure that Hank made it to his AA meeting, Sam drove home and collected Maggie from the neighbors' house. After she'd gotten herself ready for bed, he came into her room to hear her prayers and tuck her in.

Bethany's senior high school photo, framed in rosewood, sat on the nightstand. It was the only copy they had, and Sam had let Maggie keep it in her room. He didn't need a photograph to remember his wife's gentle smile. Bethany hadn't had a mean or jealous bone in her body. Maggie was right. She would want her loved ones to be happy.

"Did you talk to Miss Chapman tonight?" Maggie asked as Sam laid an extra warm blanket over her.

"I did. She reminded me about your school program next week. I said I wouldn't miss it."

"Are you still friends?"

"We are. But just friends, Maggie."

"Oh." She snuggled deeper into the bed. "But she's a good one, Daddy. If I were you, I wouldn't let her get away."

"Go to sleep." He brushed a kiss on her forehead and walked out of the room. Maggie was growing up so fast, and he was missing out on so many things that would only happen once. Maybe after the holidays, he'd look into hiring another part-time deputy, or move one of the part-timers to full-time work. He needed more time just to be a dad.

Restless, he turned off the living room light and walked out onto the covered porch. Snow was drifting down in powdery flakes. The storm didn't look like a big one, but the roads would be slick in the morning. He'd be smart to get some rest now, while he could.

Back inside, passing the phone, he thought of calling Grace, just to make sure she'd arrived home safely. Where had that notion come from? Grace would probably be asleep by now, and even if she weren't, calling to check wouldn't set well with her or her roommates.

Knowing that he needed to sleep, Sam took a moment to look in on Maggie, then wandered on down the hall to get ready for bed.

Snow was still falling the next morning, not deep on the ground, but sharp and stinging, like windblown sand. Sam made sure that Maggie was bundled into her warmest coat, with boots on her feet and mittens on her hands, before driving her to school and letting her off at the curb in front.

"Be safe, Daddy." She kissed his cheek as she turned to go.

"I will. And you stay warm. I'll see you after school."

He watched her until she vanished through the double doors. There was no sign of Grace, but she would have parked in the lot out back and entered through the rear of the building.

As he drove away, headed for work, Sam found himself wishing he'd said more to her last night. Alone with her in the parking lot, he'd had the perfect opportunity. But he'd chosen to be cautious. Maybe he'd been too cautious.

At work, it was all hands on deck. He called in his two deputies to help him handle the rash of accidents on the snow-slicked roads. A pair of teenage boys had cut school and stolen a battery from a parked car. They were behind bars now, waiting for their parents to arrive. Ruth McCoy had shown up at the clinic with a broken arm, and Sam had taken a deputy with him to bring in her husband. Maybe this time Ruth would let the bastard rot in jail for a while, though he wouldn't bet on it.

It was late afternoon before Sam got enough of a break to run the errand he'd been planning. Hank Miller was going to AA meetings and making a genuine effort to sober up. It was time for Sam to keep his end of the bargain.

He'd checked with Doris Cullimore last night to make sure the feed and hardware still needed help. But he had yet to talk with her husband, Walt, about giving Hank a job. He wasn't due to pick up Maggie for another forty minutes. That should give him plenty of time to drive to the store, talk with Walt, and get to the school.

Braced for a hard sell, Sam climbed into the Jeep and headed for the store at the south end of Main Street, on the way out of town. As he drove, he rehearsed what he was going to say.

You know Hank's a good man, Walt. He gets along with people, and he knows the farming business. He was doing fine before he lost his leg and his family. Now he's trying to turn his life around, but he needs a job. You could hire him on probation. If he doesn't work out, just show him the door. All I'm asking is that you give him a chance.

Sam pulled onto the gravel strip in front of the store and climbed out of the Jeep. Two other vehicles were parked next to his. One of them, a battered red Ford pickup, belonged to a young farm family. The other vehicle, a souped-up black Camaro with Texas plates, was unfamiliar, most likely an out-of-towner. Walt's truck was usually here, too. But there was no sign of it. His wife had probably taken it to run an errand.

As he walked toward the front door, Sam was struck by how quiet the place appeared. And something about the presence of that black Camaro, a stranger's car, made him nervous. Sam had learned to trust his instincts. Right now those instincts were telling him that something was off.

The ads that covered the windows, along with reflected light, kept him from looking inside the store. But if there was trouble, barging in through the front door wouldn't be smart. There was a loading dock in the rear of the building. The overhead metal door would be closed because of the weather. But the regular door next to it was kept unlocked during business hours. Sam could go in that way and scope out the place to make sure everything was all right.

It occurred to him that his Jeep might've been seen by someone inside the store, looking out between the ads posted on the windows. That might explain why the place was so quiet. Someone could be waiting to see what he would do.

Pretending to leave, he got back into his vehicle and drove it a dozen yards down the road, where it couldn't be seen from the store. Parking it again, he took a moment to radio Dispatch, letting them know where he was and what he was doing. Then he climbed out of the Jeep, closed the door quietly, and circled around to the back of the store.

Maybe he was jumping at shadows. After all, he'd been wrong before. Hopefully everything was fine. But he couldn't be too careful. If the situation was dangerous, it was his job to take care of it.

Wearing no protective gear except for his leather uniform jacket, and armed with nothing but his service revolver, he stepped through the door into the cavernous space that served as a warehouse. It was filled with boxed tools and equipment, stacked lumber, fencing, lengths of PVC pipe, salt blocks, and piled bags of animal feed.

Sam made his way through the maze to the wall that separated the storage from the sales area. The door stood ajar. He slipped through and crouched behind a rack of power tools. From there he could see all the way to the counter in front. As he took in the situation, his heart slammed. His muscles tensed. His hand tightened on the grip of his gun.

A pale and shaking Walt Cullimore stood behind the

old-fashioned cash register, stuffing bills into an orange plastic grocery bag.

A single gunman stood at the counter. Young, with bleached, punk-style hair and a slightly crazed look, he was pointing his heavy semiautomatic pistol toward something on the floor. The displays blocked Sam's line of vision, but he remembered the red farm truck outside and the young family struggling to make a living off their land.

"Hurry up, old man," the gunman's voice was high-pitched, his speech slightly slurred. "No tricks, or you'll be scrapin' bodies off your nice, clean floor. Which one do you think I should shoot first? The little snot-faced brat, maybe? Or the mom?"

"You can have the money and anything else you want." Walt's voice quivered as he lifted the tray out of the register and scooped out the bills underneath. "But please, for the love of God, don't hurt them. Just take the cash and go. We'll say we never saw you."

Sam shifted his position. Raising his head a few inches, he could see where the robber was pointing his pistol.

A terrified-looking young woman crouched against a display rack, her body shielding two small boys.

Chapter Eleven

Sam made a quick assessment of the situation. The gunman appeared to be high on drugs, which meant his behavior could be erratic. He might take the money and leave, or he might get nervous and start shooting. Anything could happen.

There was something else to consider. The young man had walked into the store unmasked. There were two adult witnesses who would have no trouble describing him to the police or picking out his mug shot. Either he hadn't given a thought to what might happen, or he was a cold-blooded murderer, planning to kill everybody in the place before he left, as he'd already threatened to do.

Training and experience had taught Sam to assume the worst. If he were to speak and identify himself, even a word could trigger a shooting frenzy. He would be risking the lives of four innocent people, including two children.

As he was debating his options, all hell broke loose.

The older of the two boys tore away from his mother and bolted for the front door. With the robber distracted for an instant, Walt whipped a pistol from under the counter and fired.

Wounded in the shoulder, the young man staggered, reeled, and dropped his weapon. Sam charged in and kicked the semiautomatic pistol out of reach. Jamming his gun against the young man's neck, he forced him to the floor.

"Run!" Sam shouted to the mother. "Grab your boys and get out!"

The woman scrambled to her feet, scooped up her youngest, caught her other boy at the door, and raced outside.

Sam reached back for the handcuffs on his belt. "Get that pistol, Walt. Then get to the phone and call—"

The words died in his throat as he caught a flicker of movement behind him. The gunshot rang out before he had time to react. He felt the sickening burn of the bullet piercing his body as he pitched sideways, onto the floor.

Through the enfolding darkness, he heard voices.

"Jeez, Trixie, you just shot a cop! We got to get out of here! Grab the money!"

"Forget the damned money! The old guy's disappeared and he's got a gun! Come on!"

Sam heard the sound of running footsteps and the slamming of car doors. As the Camaro roared into the distance, the images in his mind faded to black.

With ten minutes to go before the bell, Grace was leading her class through the verses of "It's Beginning to Look a Lot Like Christmas" when one of the office volunteers opened the door a few inches.

"Excuse me, Miss Chapman," she said. "You're needed in the office right now. I can stay and supervise your class."

"Thanks. They're just singing. If I'm not back by the time the bell rings, please make sure they have everything they need, then line them up and let them go."

Worry gnawed at Grace as she hurried down the hall. What could be urgent enough for the office to call her out of class? Had Ed Judkins found some crime to pin on her? She felt in the pocket of her blazer for Jess's mini recorder.

It was there, and she knew how to use it. Whatever the problem, she needed to be prepared.

But it wasn't the principal who met her at the entrance to the office. It was the school secretary, Emmaline Spicer.

"We have an emergency with one of your students, Grace," she said. "It's Maggie Delaney, the sheriff's daughter. Her father's been shot."

The shock slammed Grace like a head-on collision with a glass wall.

Oh, no! Not Sam. Please, not Sam!

She fought to hide her reaction from the secretary. "What can you tell me? How did it happen? Where is he?"

"It was the clerk at the sheriff's office who called. There was a robbery at the feed and hardware store. The sheriff happened to be there and got shot trying to stop it. He's been taken to the hospital in Cottonwood Springs for surgery. That's all I know. But that poor little girl has no other family at home. She lost her mother just last year. Her only grandparents are out of state. If you could take her in hand—"

"Of course. I'll give her the news and take care of her. Right now I need to find her before she goes outside to wait for him."

Oh, Maggie, Maggie . . . Grace knew that as terrible as the news had been for her, it would be devastating for Sam's little girl.

She heard the bell as she raced back down the hall. Her students were already leaving. She caught Maggie in the doorway. "Come back into the room with me, Maggie." She laid a hand on the girl's small shoulder. "I need to talk to you."

She resisted. "But my dad—he'll be waiting to pick me up."

"No, he can't be here. There's been a problem. Come on

in." Grace ushered her gently back into the room and closed the door as the last student left.

"Has something happened to my dad?" Maggie's green eyes were wide with fear. She was a perceptive child. It came as no surprise that she'd already guessed the truth.

"He's been taken to the hospital, in Cottonwood Springs," Grace said. "He was shot. The doctors will be operating on him to take the bullet out."

"Will he be all right? He's not going to die, is he?"

Oh, Maggie . . .

"I certainly don't think so." It was the best answer Grace could manage.

"I want to go to the hospital. Can you take me, Miss Chapman?"

"Yes." Grace took the small, cold hand in hers. "I'll take you and I'll stay with you until your dad is better. Come on. Let me get my coat and purse, and we'll go."

They walked out to the parking lot. Maggie, pale and silent, had not shed a tear. Grace could imagine the little girl struggling to be brave for her father. She could only pray, silently, as she drove, that this was not the day when they would lose him.

Even before he opened his eyes, Sam felt the raw sensations in every part of his violated body—the sting of needles, the pull of tubes and bandages, the beeping monitors, the oxygen clip on his nose, the lights that penetrated his closed eyelids, and the deep, hard pain at the core of it all.

Like a scene from a bad crime show, the memory swam into focus—the crazed-looking gunman, the mother and her boys, Walt with a gun, the wounded, struggling young man, and then . . .

Stupid . . . Why hadn't he checked for an accomplice? That was how cops got shot.

With a groan, he forced his eyes open. The doctor studying him as if he were a lab specimen looked young enough to be in high school. "Welcome back, Sheriff," he said.

Sam was in no mood for chitchat. "Tell me everything," he said.

The doctor nodded, glancing at the chart in his hands. "You were incredibly lucky. Clean shot. The bullet went in from behind the shoulder and out below the collarbone without hitting anything vital. We got you cleaned up, but you lost a lot of blood—that was our big worry. It took two pints to get your vitals up. We've got you on antibiotics and some morphine for the pain. You can expect to hurt a lot when it wears off. There's a drain in the wound. If it looks good, we'll take that out in the morning."

Sam stirred, but moving hurt. He was propped up at a slight angle with pillows behind him. A thick dressing with a drain lay over his right shoulder. His arm was in a sling to keep the wound stable.

"What's next?" he asked. "I need to get out of here."

"We'll be keeping you over the weekend, at least. When you do get home, you'll need to take it easy for a few weeks while you heal."

Fat chance of that. He had work to do and a daughter to take care of.

His heart lurched. Where was Maggie? He'd been planning to pick her up before he was shot. Had she walked home and gone to the McDermotts'? Had anybody thought to tell her what had happened to him? She had to be worried sick. He had to get a phone and make some calls. He needed to make sure Maggie was all right and that things were covered at work.

Sam could see the time on the wall clock. The hands said 10:15 but there were no windows in the room. He didn't know whether that meant A.M. or P.M. He'd lost all track of time.

"Get me a phone," he demanded. "I've got people depending on me. I need to make some calls."

"Take it easy, Sheriff. It's nighttime. The world can get along without you for a few more hours. Right now, you're in recovery. First thing in the morning, we'll be moving you to a regular room. But first, there's a visitor in the waiting room who's very anxious to see you."

As the doctor stepped out into the hall, Sam lay back on the pillows and closed his eyes. Now that the shock of waking up had worn off, he felt exhausted. He began to drift.

"Daddy?" Maggie's voice brought him back. She stood by the bed, gazing at him with her wise, worried eyes.

"Hello, honey." He reached out with his left hand and touched her cheek.

"Oh, Daddy!" The tears began to flow, welling in her eyes and trickling down her cheeks. "I was so scared that you might die."

"Don't cry, Maggie." He brushed a tear away with a fingertip. "I'm going to be fine. I'll just be here for a few days. Then I can rest at home." He took her hand and held it in his. "How did you get here? Who's taking care of you?"

"Miss Chapman brought me here from school. She's going to take care of me until you're home. Then I'll take care of you. I'll cook and everything."

Sam looked past Maggie, toward the door. Grace was standing in the open doorway. She looked tired, but she was smiling like an angel.

"Thank you, Grace," he said. "Coming here, bringing Maggie—it can't have been an easy decision for you."

"You're wrong, Sam," she said. "I knew Maggie would

want to be here. I wanted to be here, too. It was an easy decision. The nurse said we could only stay a few minutes. Then I'll be taking her home and bringing her to school with me tomorrow. If she's not too tired, we'll come back here later in the day."

"I owe you big-time, Grace," he said, beginning to drift again.

"It's nothing," she said. "It's what a friend would do. We have to go now. Get some rest and don't worry."

"Thanks again . . ." His voice trailed off as his eyelids closed.

It's what a friend would do. Her words lingered. Even groggy as he was, Sam knew that what he wanted from her was much more than friendship.

When Sam woke, the sun was shining through slatted blinds. An orderly walked in with his breakfast on a tray. The scrambled eggs, toast, and oatmeal didn't have much flavor, but he was surprisingly hungry. His shoulder wound hurt like the blazes, but the pain was preferable to being on morphine. He'd moved the tray aside and was finishing the coffee he'd asked for when the middle-aged nurse came in to check his vitals.

"You're doing great," she said. "If the doctor gives his okay, we should be good to take that drain out. You'll be more comfortable then."

"What I really want is to get out of here, go home, and get back to work."

"All in good time, Sheriff. Your body's had a terrible shock. You need to give it time to recover. You're not Superman."

Sam sank back onto the pillows. The nurse was right; he'd be a fool not to rest for a few days after taking a bullet and needing two pints of donated blood. But the thought of all the things he'd left undone made him want to jump out of the blasted bed, find his clothes, check himself out, and hitch a ride back to Branding Iron.

The drain had been taken out of his wound and fresh dressing applied when the door to his room opened and a welcome visitor walked in.

"Good heavens, Sam." Helen was all smiles. "You look like a hard case if I ever saw one. How are you feeling?"

"About the way I look. I hope you're here to catch me up on things at work."

"Actually, I'm here to see for myself that you're really alive. As for work, you can rest your mind. Everything's under control. I brought in Buck Winston full-time to cover for you."

"Good choice." Buck, a local boy and Sam's senior deputy, worked as a ranch hand when he wasn't needed by the sheriff's department. He had the makings of a good lawman and would do fine at his temporary post. If Sam could get approval from the county budget folks, it wouldn't hurt to make Buck's job permanent.

"What about the folks at the hardware and feed store? Is Walt all right?"

"Walt's fine." Helen chuckled. "But his wife's a basket case. She was off doing some shopping when that robbery went down. By the time she got back, it was all over. Junie Cardona and her little boys are all right, too. That girl's got one cool head on her. She wrote down the license number of that Camaro before those two birds took off. The state police picked them up around midnight. They're wanted for armed robbery in three states."

Sam shook his head. "I can't believe I didn't see that second shooter."

"They were pros. They knew what they were doing. But they should've known better than to mess with Branding Iron. Oh—there's even a TV crew in town. They'll be talking to Walt and Junie. You can expect a visit, too."

"Oh, hell."

Helen laughed. "I knew you'd be thrilled. That's why I brought something to sweeten your disposition." Reaching into her big flowered purse, she pulled out a one-pound gold foil box of Sam's favorite gourmet chocolates. "Enjoy."

"Wow, thanks." Sam took the box, opened it, and offered Helen her choice, which she waved away. "I'll bet you didn't get these in Branding Iron."

"No, I didn't. Actually, I was saving them for your birthday next month. So happy birthday early. And now I need to get back to relieve Buck at my desk."

"You're the best, Helen. Tell Buck to call me if he has any questions."

"We'll be fine. Get some rest." She was out the door.

Sam polished off two chocolates and willed himself not to take a third. He was getting drowsy again. He hadn't meant to sleep so much, but his body was in charge.

When the TV crew arrived half an hour later, he was fast asleep. They woke him long enough to get a few mumbled words about his not deserving credit for stopping the robbery. "All I did was get shot," he said. "I'm just glad they caught the bastards. Now go and let me sleep." He drifted off, wondering whether the word *bastards* would be bleeped from the news broadcast.

"Sam?" The voice that woke him was familiar. He opened his eyes. Walt was standing by his bed. "They said it was okay to wake you because they'll be bringing lunch around. How are you doing?"

"I've been better, but I'll mend." Sam pushed himself up on the pillows. "Have a chocolate."

"Don't mind if I do." Walt helped himself to a raspberry cream. "Just wanted to come by and thank you. I don't know what might've happened if you hadn't been there."

"You did pretty well yourself."

"I tried. But that crazy bugger would probably have shot me after I hit him. Or his girlfriend would've. And you're the one who got the woman and her boys out."

"Let's just call it a team effort and be glad nothing worse happened."

"One thing I was wondering. What were you doing at the store in the first place? Did you just happen along and see a strange car?"

"Now that's a good question." Sam launched into his pitch about why Hank should be hired to work at the store. "You'd be doing me a favor, Walt," he concluded. "But if it all works out, you'll be doing Hank the biggest favor and yourself, too."

Walt scratched his ear. "I'll think on it. I knew Hank before the bad times. He was a good man, and smart. I reckon he still is. But Lordy, Sam, what if I hire him and he won't stop drinking?"

"Then you fire him on the spot. Hank would have to understand that he's on probation. One slip-up, and he's gone. So, what do you say?"

"I'll have to ask my wife. But we're not getting any younger, and we do need help. She's been after me to cut back on work. Hank would be a godsend if he could do the job and stay sober."

"Okay, talk to Doris and let me know. I should be out of here early next week. If it's a yes, I'll give Hank the word."

"No need," Walt said. "I know where to find Hank. If I'm thinking about hiring him, I'll want to talk to him first. Right now, I hear the lunch cart coming down the hall." He turned to go, then paused. "Thanks for being where you were needed, Sam. I mean it. I think maybe the Man Upstairs was looking out for all of us."

"Maybe so, Walt." Sam had pretty much lost his belief when Bethany died. But he could appreciate the faith of men like Walt. He could still count his blessings—good friends, the chance to be of service, and a daughter who was the sunshine of his life. With Grace, that life could be complete once more—but only if she felt as strongly as he did.

Today they'd both be in school. Sam couldn't help hoping they'd come back to see him afterward. But it was a long drive for a tired teacher and a little girl still worn out from last night.

After some exercise walking the hall and a lunch of tuna casserole, canned peas, and pudding, Sam finally had a chance to rest. Not only was he exhausted, but it was still dawning on him how close he'd come to death. Lying in his bed, he replayed the robbery, imagining what might have happened if any one thing had gone differently.

He remembered seeing Maggie in the hospital last night, her eyes shedding tears of relief. He pictured her as a lonely orphan going to live with Bethany's parents or falling through the cracks into the foster system.

Being sheriff in a small, rural community like Branding Iron couldn't be called a dangerous job. There were accidents, domestics, a few disputes, maybe some shoplifting or vandalism from misbehaving kids—nothing to threaten a lawman's life.

Not until yesterday when, in a heartbeat, everything had changed.

What if that bullet had killed him, leaving his daughter motherless, fatherless, and scarred by loss?

Then again, what might have happened if he hadn't been there to do his job?

Struggling with unanswered questions, his reason dulled by painkillers, Sam sank into sleep.

"Daddy! Wake up!" Maggie's hand, patting his cheek, roused Sam from a jumbled dream. His sleep had been so deep that it took a moment for him to remember where he was. Outside the window, the sky was dark. Someone had turned on the light above his bed.

"Hi, honey." He reached out and rumpled her curls. His body felt stiff from lying in one position, but he could tell he'd had a good rest. "I didn't think you'd be coming tonight. You must be tired after being up last night and then going to school all day."

"We're both tired." Grace was standing a few feet behind her. "But Maggie insisted on coming. She didn't have any trouble talking me into it. I wanted to see you, too."

Grace's words warmed Sam as he took her in with his eyes. She stood in the shadows, dressed in gray slacks and a simple black sweater. When their eyes met, a little smile played around her lips.

"Have some chocolates. Helen brought them this morning." Sam opened the box and held it out. Maggie chose a chocolate truffle.

Grace declined with a slight shake of her head. "I'm sorry we didn't think to bring you anything," she said.

"You brought yourselves. That's all I need." Sam was looking at Grace as he said it. She lowered her gaze. Was it a signal for him to back off?

"It looks like I'll be going home on Monday," he said. "I'm getting around fine, just sore and a little tired."

"Will you be needing a ride?" Grace asked.

"You'll be in school. Helen can pick me up and drop me off at the house. And there's no need for you to come here over the weekend. It's a long drive. I'll be fine."

"I can take care of you at home, Daddy," Maggie said. "I'll do laundry and even cook your food. Grace is going to help me learn."

"We'll learn together," Grace said. "I've never been much of a cook. But I hope you don't mind my staying at your house over the weekend. Maggie slept at my place last night, but I know she'll be more comfortable sleeping in her own room."

So she would be sleeping in his bed. Too bad he wouldn't be there with her. "Maggie can show you where the clean sheets are. And thanks. That's a lot of bother for you."

"No bother at all. We're going to have girl fun, aren't we, Maggie?"

"Lots and lots of girl fun." Maggie danced a little jig step.

"I'm hoping you'll at least let me pay you back with a nice steak dinner, Grace," he said.

"As you're fond of saying, Sam, we'll cross that bridge when we come to it."

A nurse, rushing into the room, broke the awkward pause. "Turn on the TV. The evening news just started. They're going to broadcast the interviews about the robbery. You don't want to miss it."

"Daddy—are you going to be on TV?" Maggie grabbed the remote off the side table and handed it to Sam.

"Not for long, I hope." Sam clicked on the TV. "I can't say I was at my best."

The news of the crime had broken the night before. But the interviews were new. The TV reporter talked to Walt and to Junie Cardona. Both of them praised Sam for his role in stopping the robbery.

"I wounded the punk with the gun," Walt said. "But it was the sheriff who took him down and got shot for it."

"The sheriff made sure we got out all right," Junie Cardona said. "If it wasn't for him, my boys and I might not be here."

The next shot showed Sam in the hospital, gazing sleepily into the camera and muttering something about teamwork. Sam shook his head. "Great. My fifteen seconds of fame, and I was on drugs."

"You were a hero, Daddy," Maggie said.

"A smart hero would've thought to look for the gunman's partner. And he wouldn't have let himself get shot."

"It's all right." Maggie gave him a careful hug. "We're just glad you're okay."

Behind her, Grace was smiling. "We'd best go and let your dad rest now, Maggie. Remember, I promised you we'd get ice cream on the way home."

"And you don't need to come all the way back here tomorrow," Sam said. "I'll give Grace the phone number. You can use it to call me anytime, okay?" Sam scrawled the phone number and his room number on a notepad by his bed and handed the paper to Grace. "I can't thank you enough," he said.

"Anything for a friend." She tucked the paper into her purse.

Anything for a friend. Grace's words lingered in Sam's memory long after she and Maggie had left. The message was clear. Grace might have stepped in to care for his daughter, but he couldn't expect any more from her. She was still not ready for any kind of commitment. Maybe she never would be.

But after having held her in his arms and having kissed her sweet, willing lips, Sam knew he wasn't ready to settle for less.

After a stop at Maggie's favorite ice cream parlor for strawberry sundaes with sprinkles, Grace buckled the little girl into the backseat of the Cadillac, turned on the heated seats, and headed for home. A few miles later, when she pulled over to check, Maggie had toppled to one side and was sound asleep with her head on Grace's folded coat.

The last time she was home, Grace had packed a suitcase with enough clothes and other essentials to last through Monday. She'd included some items like pink nail polish, scented lotion, and bubble bath to make the weekend fun for Maggie. They'd be cooking, and although Sam's house wasn't messy, the place could use some cleaning before he got home from the hospital. That, along with a little Saturday shopping, a meal at Buckaroo's, and Sunday church, if Maggie wanted to go, should be plenty to keep the little girl occupied.

Grace had seven years' experience teaching first grade. She'd loved all her students in a detached, teacherly way. But she'd never engaged closely with a child outside of class. This weekend with Maggie would be a first.

Maggie was bright, well-behaved, and eager to please. Getting along with her would be no problem. But Grace had another, more pressing worry.

Sam was a wonderful father to his little girl. But Maggie's heart hungered for the motherly love she'd lost. In the time they'd spent together, Grace could already feel the bond forming between them—and it wasn't just one-sided. Her attachment to Sam's daughter was tender and real.

But what if she couldn't overcome her fear of commitment? What if things weren't right with Sam and she had to walk away?

How would she live with herself if she were to break Maggie's vulnerable young heart?

Chapter Twelve

It was after 10:00 when Grace pulled the car into the driveway behind Sam's off-duty pickup truck. Maggie was still asleep in the backseat, but she roused when Grace tried to unfasten the seat belt and lift her.

"Are we home?" she asked.

"We're home." It crossed Grace's mind to wonder if this place would ever be home to her. The thought was both exciting and frightening. What if she were to attempt to make things work with Sam, only to fail? The hurt, especially to Maggie, would be far worse than if she hadn't tried at all.

Maybe she shouldn't try.

"I can get in by myself." Maggie scampered up the porch steps and lifted the rubber doormat to get the key. Grace took her suitcase out of the trunk. By the time she'd followed Maggie into the house, the little girl had the living room light on. The house was chilly, but Maggie had already turned up the thermostat.

"I'll show you where my dad's room is, Miss Chapman," she said. "The clean sheets are in the hall closet, top shelf. Don't worry about me. I can get myself ready for bed."

While Maggie busied herself in the bathroom, Grace left her suitcase on a chair in Sam's room, then took a moment to explore the layout of the house. There were three bedrooms off the hallway, but one had been converted to Sam's office with a desktop computer, a couple of file cabinets, and a leather chair worn to the shape of his body. A bulky cardboard box had been shoved into a corner. Grace recognized it as the box that held the Santa costume. It was unopened.

Maggie's framed school picture and another photo of her as a toddler in her mother's arms hung on the wall above the military surplus desk. Maybe it was that photo that made Grace feel like an intruder. She closed the door and made her way back down the hall, where she found a set of queen-sized sheets in the linen closet.

"I'm going to bed now," Maggie called from her room. Was she asking to be tucked in?

Grace turned toward the bedroom door, then hesitated. No, she mustn't do it. Tucking Maggie in, as a parent might do, would send the wrong message to the trusting little girl. Instead, Grace stood in the open doorway. "Good night, Maggie," she said. "Tomorrow's Saturday, so you can sleep late. Then we'll have ourselves a fun day."

"Good night, Miss Chapman. Thanks for taking care of me. Leave the night-light on in the hall and the door open just a little bit." Maggie snuggled into the covers and closed her eyes.

And that was that. As Grace walked back to the living room to lock the front door, she felt her body give way to exhaustion. It had been a long, hectic week. Only now did she realize how tired she was. All she wanted to do was sleep. In Sam's bed.

She opened the suitcase and took the travel kit with her toothbrush, makeup, and other needs into the bathroom. After brushing her teeth and splashing her face, she returned to the bedroom and put on her pajamas. The room was spare and neat. There were no photos on display, not even one of his wife, although Grace had noticed the picture on Maggie's nightstand.

Sam had made the bed before leaving Thursday morning, unaware that he wouldn't be back that night. Grace shuddered, thinking how close he'd come to dying, and that the few words she'd exchanged with him after the Wednesday night meeting could have been their last. Life was so short and uncertain. She wanted more time with him, time for them to know each other, time for love to grow, if only she could get past her fears and let it happen.

The jeans and flannel shirt he'd worn Wednesday night were piled with other clothes in a laundry basket on the floor. She would wash everything in the morning to leave it clean for him when he came home.

The fresh sheets lay in a folded stack on a corner of the bed. Grace had meant to change the linens before going to sleep; but she was dead on her feet. The temptation to just fall into bed, between the sheets where Sam had slept, was more than she could resist.

She lifted the covers, slipped into bed, and closed her eyes. Sam's clean, manly aroma crept around her, seeping into her senses. She breathed him in, feeling strangely safe and cherished, the way she'd felt when he'd held her that night in the fog—the way she'd felt when he kissed her.

She drifted into sleep, Sam's sheets wrapping her in a cocoon of warm contentment and sensual dreams.

By the next day, Sam was feeling stronger, but the pain was still there, shooting arrows into his chest and back whenever he changed position in the bed. "Damn it," he groused to the nurse who came in to change the IV drip that supplied antibiotics and glucose through a needle in his hand. "I'm sick of lying here. I need to get out of this place and get back to work."

"Give it time, Sheriff." Today's nurse was young, pretty,

and visibly pregnant. "You're dealing with a serious injury. It's not going to heal overnight, especially if you don't rest it."

"So, how long do I need to be hooked up to these blasted tubes?"

"Until tomorrow, at least. Maybe longer if you don't behave. I saw the story and the interviews on the news. You should count your lucky stars that you didn't die. People are calling you a hero. At least you can feel good about that."

"Don't remind me. A real hero would've been smart enough to keep from getting shot."

The nurse chuckled. "At least you're well enough to complain. And your vitals are looking good. So just take it easy. That's the best thing you can do."

Sam lay back and used the remote to turn on the TV and flip through the channels. At this hour there was nothing on but game shows, kiddie cartoons, and infomercials. He turned the TV off. The phone sat on the table next to the bed. He could use it to call Helen and see how work was going—but no, that would be meddling. He wanted Buck to know that his boss believed he could do the job. He could call Maggie at home. But she would be busy having fun with Grace. Maggie would call him when she wanted to talk.

Last night he'd gone to sleep imagining Grace in his bed. His dreams would've gotten him slapped, or maybe even arrested. Damn it, he'd had enough of the games he and Grace were playing. When he got back into shape, he would do whatever it took to convince the woman that they needed to make their relationship real.

His brush with near death had reminded him that life was too short to put happiness on hold.

Despite his restlessness, Sam managed to doze through

much of the morning. Toward noon, the sound of stiletto heels clicking on the tile startled him awake. He opened his eyes as the mayor and his wife walked into the room.

"Hello, Sam." The mayor's voice was loud enough to carry three doors down the hall. "How's our hometown hero doing?"

Sam stifled a groan. "No hero, Rulon. Just a cop who made a bad call and got in the way of a bullet."

"I saw the interviews on TV. That story has put Branding Iron on the map as a town where folks stand up to crime. It might even drum us up some new business, maybe even a big-box store on that empty lot south of town."

"The story could've been about five shooting victims, including a couple of kids," Sam said. "We were damned lucky."

"Maybe. But I believe in giving credit where it's due. We're planning an award ceremony with a medal when you're healed. The press will be there, of course."

"Forget that," Sam said. "I don't even—"

"Oh, my, look at those!" Alice had spotted the open box of chocolates. Dressed to the nines in high heels and a fox fur stole, she came clicking over to the bedside table, helped herself to two walnut truffles, and popped one into her mouth. "Yum! These are decadent! Try a couple, Rulon." She held the box out to her husband, who took the last vanilla nougat.

Alice put the box back on the stand. "Actually, Sam, we came to ask you a question," she said. "The Cowboy Christmas Ball, as it's now being called, is a week from tonight. We're wondering if you'll be well enough to play Santa Claus."

"I honestly don't know," Sam said. "I'll do my best to be ready, but I've just been shot. If the wound hasn't healed enough for me to wear that costume and put up with kids climbing all over me for a couple of hours, it's not going to happen."

Alice gasped. "But Sam, what about the little ones? What will they do if there's no Santa to hear their wishes?"

Maybe you'd like to wear the damned outfit, Alice.

"I told you I'd do my best to be ready, and I will," Sam said. "But I won't be good for many ho ho ho's if I'm bleeding or in pain under that red suit. Sorry, but that's the best I can do. The costume's at my house. You're welcome to pick it up and give it to somebody else."

"There's nobody else who can wear it. You know that."

"Then you'll just have to hope for the best. I'll keep you posted."

As the couple left, Sam released the smile he'd been holding back. The truth was, for Maggie's sake, and for the sake of Branding Iron's kids, he would put on that blasted Santa suit and go to the ball no matter what condition he might be in. But Rulon and Alice didn't have to know that. He'd enjoyed making them squirm a little. He could only wish he'd had a chance to hide the chocolates before they walked in.

He'd settled back to wait for lunch when the phone rang.

"Daddy!" Maggie's happy voice warmed him like sunshine bursting through dark clouds. "Guess what? Miss Chapman and I are going to make Christmas cookies. We went to the store and bought cookie cutters and colored icing and sprinkles and everything. And we're going to make a whole bunch. We'll take some to Mr. and Mrs. McDermott and save some for you." She paused to catch her breath. "How are you? Are you getting better? When are you coming home?"

"The doctor still says Monday. I'm getting better. It's

just going to take a little time. Is Miss Chapman close by? I'd like to thank her."

"She's right here." Maggie paused. Her voice came through the hand she'd put over the mouthpiece. "My dad wants to talk to you, Miss Chapman."

"Hello, Sam." Grace's voice stirred his senses like the slow stroke of a fingertip. He wanted to tell her how sexy she sounded over the phone, but this wasn't the time. "How are you feeling?" she asked.

"Like hell, but a lot better than yesterday. I'm still due home Monday. I just wanted to thank you and ask if there's anything you or Maggie need."

"We're fine. We went grocery shopping, then to Buckaroo's for lunch, and now we're going to cook up a storm all weekend."

"I wanted to talk to you about that," Sam said. "I know you're spending your own money keeping Maggie entertained. Please keep track of how much and I'll write you a check as soon as I get home."

"I wouldn't dream of asking you to repay me. We're having a great time. It's my pleasure."

"Then, when I'm back on my feet, I want to take you someplace really nice for dinner, and I won't accept no for an answer."

"We'll see," she said. "It sounds like Maggie needs me in the kitchen. I'll check in later. Get well, Sam."

We'll see. Sam pondered her words as he hung up the phone. Why couldn't Grace have simply said yes to his invitation?

She'd been honest with him about her fear of commitment. But he was just beginning to realize how deep that fear went. He'd fallen hard for her—so hard that he'd blinded himself to what could become a real problem between them.

And right in the middle of that problem was his sweet, trusting, love-hungry Maggie.

Grace had told him about her issues, but he'd never told her how strongly he felt about her. They needed to lay everything on the line in a heart-to-heart talk. It couldn't happen while he was in the hospital and she was taking care of his little girl. But it needed to happen soon, before damage was done and hearts were broken.

"I found the cookie recipe." Maggie knelt on a chair at the kitchen table, the red and white five-ring binder cookbook spread open in front of her. "They're called sugar cookies. Have you ever made them, Miss Chapman?"

"Never." Grace's mother had owned the same cookbook, but she'd never been much of a cook, especially after the breakup of her marriage.

"I've never made them either," Maggie said. "But we can learn together. It's too bad this recipe doesn't have pictures."

Grace looked over the little girl's shoulder. The pages of the popular cookbook were stained, spattered, and worn where the binder rings passed through the holes. "Somebody must've used this book a lot," she said.

"My grandma gave the book to my mom," Maggie said. "I remember when Mom made these cookies. I was too little to help. But I'm big now, and the book is mine. I'm going to make them every year for Christmas."

The words triggered a tightening in Grace's throat. "Let's get started," she said. "You read me the ingredients. I'll find them and set them out."

"Shortening . . ." Maggie read. "Sugar . . . grated orange peel . . ." She paused.

"Here's the orange we bought," Grace said. "Do we have a grater?"

"Uh-huh. I know where it is. Let's see . . . eggs, milk, flour, baking powder, and salt. Got it all?"

"Got it. Grace glanced at the recipe and decided to do some teaching. "This recipe makes two dozen cookies. Do you know how many that is?"

"Twenty-four. My dad taught me how much a dozen is. But that doesn't sound like enough cookies."

"We could make more. Do you want to make two batches, or one big one?"

"One big one. Come on, let's turn on some Christmas music and get to work."

Rolling up their sleeves, they let the fun begin. They sang and giggled as they worked, getting flour on their clothes, on their hands and faces, and all over the kitchen. Maggie was in heaven. Grace had never seen the little girl so happy.

The two balls of dough they'd made from the doubled recipe needed to be chilled in the fridge for at least an hour before rolling and cutting. After Grace and Maggie cleaned up the mess they'd made, they were both tired. They took the microwaved popcorn Maggie made into the living room, where they put their feet up and nibbled their way through a Christmas video they'd rented from the store. By the end of the movie, Maggie had dropped off to sleep with her head resting on the arm of the sofa.

Let her sleep, Grace decided. The cookies could wait. It was a pleasure just to sit here with the Christmas tree glowing in the corner, Christmas music drifting from the radio in the kitchen, and the blaze she'd lit crackling in the fireplace. She felt safe and warm in Sam's cozy home, and she'd had a great time shopping and mixing cookies with Maggie.

But could she imagine a lifetime here, in this house, with the man and child who'd stolen her heart? Unless she could make it real, the kindest thing she could do would be to walk away.

She loved Sam—there, she'd finally put the words together. She loved being with him, hearing his voice, feeling his touch. But given Sam's situation with a daughter to raise, she knew he wouldn't settle for having her as a steady girlfriend—not for long, at least. What Sam needed was a wife.

Sam Delaney was an all-or-nothing man. If she wanted him, it would have to be all the way, with open eyes, an open heart, and no barriers to hold her back.

If she couldn't let go of her fears, it was time for their story to end.

By Sunday, Sam was feeling stronger. He still had some pain, but the IV drip was gone. He was up, walking the halls, sitting in a chair to take his meals, and champing at the bit to go home.

Buck Winston, Sam's deputy, dropped by to visit him that morning and catch him up on what was happening at work. Sam appreciated the visit. Young and cowboy tough, Buck was doing well as acting sheriff. Since Sam would be at home for at least a week, the job would be Buck's for a while longer.

"I do have some good news," Buck said. "I talked to Walt. He wanted me to tell you that he gave Hank a job at the hardware store. Yesterday was Hank's first day, and he did fine."

"That's great. What a relief. Let's just hope Hank can stay sober and keep going to those AA meetings."

"My older brother went to AA," Buck said. "It saved his life. He's got a good job and a family now."

"I never thought I'd miss being at work," Sam said. "But I do, especially the people. Is there any good gossip going around?"

Buck's tanned cheeks took on a little pink. "Well, since you're bound to hear it from Helen, I'll tell you myself. I've met this girl. And things are lookin' good."

"A girl, huh? Where does a homely cowpoke like you find one of those?" Sam was teasing. Buck was blond, blue-eyed, and good-looking enough to suit any woman.

"She works in the bakery," Buck said. "I went in to buy some doughnuts, and we just clicked. I knew her a little in school, but she was three grades behind me, so I didn't pay her any attention. Now she's all grown up, and boy howdy, did I notice. We've only had a couple of dates, but I think I'm in love. Her name's Wynette, by the way. Wynette Gustavson."

Sam grinned. "I know the lady. You've got good taste. Don't know if I can say the same for Wynette, but I wish you luck."

"Thanks. There's just something about her and those doughnuts . . ."

Five minutes after Buck left, Sam was still smiling. Wynette was a great girl, and they'd make a handsome couple. But the road to true love always had a few bumps.

As did Sam's own road—if it even led in the right direction.

He hadn't heard from Maggie since yesterday's phone call. He was wondering whether to call her when the door opened and Maggie herself scampered into the room.

"Daddy, I brought you some Christmas cookies! Miss Chapman and I made them, and I decorated them all by myself!"

Grace walked in behind her. She was smiling. "Maggie couldn't wait to show you her cookies. Try one. They taste as yummy as they look."

Maggie was carrying a plastic container. She thrust it at Sam. "Open it, Daddy," she said.

The cookies inside, layered between sheets of waxed

paper, were decorated with colored icing and candy sprinkles. The icing might be smeared in spots, the sprinkles uneven, but to Sam, the stars, bells, Christmas trees, and snowmen were beautiful. He sampled a star with pink icing. "Yum," he said. "These are really good. You sure brought me plenty of cookies. How can I eat them all?"

"We thought you could share with the doctors and nurses," Maggie said. "We made four dozen cookies. I took some to Mr. and Mrs. McDermott, but there are still a lot left over."

"We're going to the mall for some window shopping," Grace added. "When we get home, we're going to make lasagna, so you'll have something to warm up when you get home."

"You ladies are too good to me." Sam took another cookie, mostly to please Maggie. "I'm getting spoiled. Grace said you were going to the mall. Are you going to talk to Santa?"

"Ugh!" Maggie crinkled her nose. "The mall Santa is gross. Everybody says so. And the lines are awful. I know who'll be the best Santa, Daddy. It'll be you."

"But you'll know it's me."

"Uh-huh. But that's all right. Some kids in my class still believe, but I know Santa is just for fun."

"Will you be all right playing Santa this Saturday, Sam?" Grace gave him a concerned glance. She looked delicious today, in a bright red sweater, jeans, and a navy blue peacoat.

"I'll manage fine," he said. "But you can make my excuses to the committee on Wednesday. I won't be feeling up to the meeting."

"Oh, dear, that's too bad. I can tell you're just crushed." Grace's eyes sparkled with mischief. She knew how Sam disliked those meetings.

"Yes, I'll miss Alice's masterful reading of the minutes.

But it can't be helped." Sam suppressed the urge to reach out and make an indecent grab at her. *Damn,* he must be getting better.

He almost mentioned the romance between Buck and Wynette, but decided against it. Buck had told him in confidence. And if Grace didn't already know, she would soon get the news from her roommates.

"Can we go to the mall now, Miss Chapman?" Maggie asked.

"You're the boss today," Grace said. "We'll go when you want."

"You ladies run along," Sam said. "I'm going to share my cookies with those nice nurses and then take a nap. I'll see you at home tomorrow after school."

Maggie leaned into his chair and kissed his cheek. "I'll take care of you, Daddy," she said. "You won't need to worry about a thing."

"I know, honey." Sam hugged his daughter, then looked up at Grace. "I'm going to make this up to you," he said.

Her smile flickered. "No need," she said. "It's my pleasure. Come on, Maggie, time for us to be a couple of chicks hanging out at the mall!"

To Maggie, the Cottonwood Springs Mall was a Christmas wonderland. Giant painted candy canes decorated the storefronts. Miniature colored lights, strung above the walkways, twinkled like ten thousand stars. Christmas songs were playing, and the heavenly aromas of bayberry, pine, cinnamon, and fresh pastries drifted through the air.

Those familiar fragrances stirred a memory. Maggie remembered walking through the mall as a small child, clasping her mother's hand as holiday shoppers scurried past. Her mother had taken her to see Santa, who was big and gruff and had smelled of cigarettes. He had frightened her a little.

When she thought of her mother, Maggie still felt an ache in her chest where she thought her heart must be. But she was a big girl now, and she was here with Miss Chapman, who was more like a girlfriend than like her mother. Maybe someday Miss Chapman really would be her mother. But the magic between her teacher and her father had yet to happen. Maggie was getting worried, but she wouldn't think about that now. Today she was here to have a good time.

In the very center of the mall was the biggest Christmas tree Maggie had ever seen. It was even taller than the one in the Branding Iron park. The lights and oversized ornaments were all gold in color. The tree was so dazzling that Maggie had to stop and stare at it for a moment.

"Do you like it?" Miss Chapman asked.

Maggie thought for a moment. "It's pretty," she said. "But our tree at home has things on it that mean something. This tree doesn't mean anything. It's just big and fancy."

Miss Chapman gave her a smile. "Well said, Maggie. I think you're going to get along fine in life. Now, I know you're hungry. What would you like to eat?"

"How about those big, giant pretzels? I've always wanted to try one."

"Come on. I know right where to find them."

The pretzels were delicious, soft, warm, and chewy, flavored with butter and salt. Maggie and Miss Chapman ate them sitting on a bench outside the food court, while they watched the Christmas shoppers go by. When they'd finished eating, they washed their hands and went up to the mezzanine of the mall. Miss Chapman had mentioned that she had a special surprise. Only now did Maggie discover what it was.

They walked along the mezzanine until they came to a store called Lemonade and Lollipops. "Here we are,"

Miss Chapman said, and took Maggie inside. It was a clothing store for young girls.

"When I asked you what you were going to wear to the Christmas ball, you told me you didn't have a nice dress that would fit you," she said. "If we can find one here, I'd like to buy it for you. They're having a big half-price sale, but if you find the perfect dress, and it isn't on sale, that's fine, too."

"Thank you!" Maggie almost hugged her teacher but wasn't sure that would be proper. "My dad can do a lot of things, but I don't think he knows much about buying girl clothes."

"Look around. Pick out some dresses to try on. This is going to be fun."

Maggie walked over to a long rack marked SALE and began looking through the dresses. She knew that some people at the ball would be wearing cowboy clothes. But she'd be better off with a nice dress she could wear other places, too. And she certainly didn't want Miss Chapman to spend much money.

Many of the sale dresses in Maggie's size were too summery for Christmas. And most of the Christmas dresses, which weren't on sale, were too fancy. Satins and velvets with glittery trim were definitely not her style.

It took some looking, but she finally did find the perfect dress. It was a dark green cotton knit, printed with tiny blue and yellow flowers. It had a long skirt and a white collar trimmed with a bit of lace. When Maggie tried it on, it fit perfectly. It was even on sale.

"And you know," Miss Chapman said, smiling, "that dress even looks a little bit western. It'll be perfect for the Cowboy Christmas Ball. Now, shall we go home and make some lasagna?"

They trooped across the parking lot to the red Cadillac. Maggie clutched the shopping bag with her new dress against the icy wind that had sprung up. The sky was overcast—no storm clouds yet. But something was blowing in.

"If it snows, do you think they'll close school?" Maggie asked as they buckled themselves into their seats.

"That's not up to me." Miss Chapman started the car. Maggie could feel the leather seat beginning to get warm. "You know, Maggie, when we get back to school, I'll just be your teacher. You'll be treated the way you always have, as one of my students. Do you understand?"

"Uh-huh. Besides, I don't want the other kids to know that you took care of me and bought me a dress. They'd start calling me the teacher's pet. Nobody would be my friend, maybe not even Brenda. That would be awful."

"Then we're good." Miss Chapman glanced back with a smile before turning the car onto the highway. "How about some nice Christmas music?"

She punched the radio button. The sounds of a choir singing "Silent Night" wafted into the backseat where Maggie sat. She was already tired, and the song was like a lullaby. By the time it ended, she had drifted off to sleep.

Chapter Thirteen

On Monday, Grace was up before first light. Dressed in her gray slacks and red sweater, she changed the sheets on Sam's bed, threw some last-minute laundry into the washer, and packed the suitcase she'd brought to tide her over the weekend. Sam would be coming home today. He was more likely to rest if the place was in good order. Leaving it that way was the least she could do.

Before waking Maggie and starting breakfast, Grace paused to open the blinds and gaze out the front window at the gray, windy dawn. She'd spent a sleepless night, tossing, turning, and staring up into the dark. But she had yet to come to a decision—one that would affect her life and the lives of two precious people.

Should she commit to building a lasting relationship with Sam, or should she end things now, before any more damage could be done?

She loved Sam. And she loved Maggie. But was love enough to keep her here, with them, for the rest of her life? Or would fear drive her away—as it had sent her fleeing from every relationship in her past.

It wasn't Sam she doubted. He had the truest heart of any man she'd ever known. She'd seen it in his devotion to his late wife and his love for his little girl. He would never hurt his family the way her own father had.

What frightened her was her own insecurity—her tendency to bolt like a spooked horse at the first sign of trouble. She'd made so many mistakes. The wrong decision now could turn out to be her biggest mistake ever.

"Good morning, Miss Chapman." Maggie, still in her nightgown, stood at the entrance to the hallway. Her curls were tousled, her eyelids still droopy from sleep.

"Good morning, Maggie." Grace gave her a smile. "I was about to make some breakfast. Is there anything special you'd like?"

"Could we have waffles? There's some mix in the cupboard. The waffle iron is in the cabinet by the dishwasher."

"Waffles it is. Anything else?"

"Could we have cocoa, with marshmallows? This will be our last breakfast together before you go home. Cocoa will make it special."

Oh, Maggie! Grace struggled to ignore the tug at her heart.

"Go get washed up and dressed. By the time you're ready for school, your breakfast will be on the table. Do you need any help?"

"No. I always get ready by myself."

Wide-awake now, Maggie skipped back down the hall toward her room. Grace took a moment to put the laundry in the dryer, then busied herself with fixing breakfast. Between the syrupy waffles and the cocoa, Maggie would probably be on a sugar high for the rest of the day, but what did it matter? As the little girl had said, this morning was special.

She planned to take Maggie with her to school this morning and drive her home at the end of the day. By then, Sam would be there. Grace would be expected to come in, of course, but she didn't plan to stay long. With the pressure of her unresolved decision weighing on her mind, she wouldn't feel much like talking. She could only hope Sam wouldn't press her for any future plans.

After breakfast, they loaded the dishwasher and tidied up the kitchen. While Maggie was gathering her books for school, Grace put on her tweed blazer, with Jess's cassette recorder still in the pocket, slipped her warm winter coat over that, and loaded her suitcase into the trunk of the car. After a last-minute check of the house, she gave Maggie the key to hide under the doormat, and they left for school.

"I'm sorry you aren't coming back tonight," Maggie said as they turned onto the street that led to the school. "We had such a good time. I wish you could stay forever."

"Now, Maggie, you know better than that," Grace said.

"Yes, I know." Maggie sighed. "But I can still wish."

True to her word, Maggie behaved naturally at school and did nothing to call attention to herself. But with less than three days of school left before the break, the Christmas crazies were in full swing. With twenty-five chattering, wiggling, teasing children in her charge, Grace had her hands full.

It didn't help that she hadn't slept the night before, or that she'd been too busy over the weekend to go over her lesson plans. But she was experienced enough to be resourceful. She divided the students into teams and set up a math competition that kept them busy until time for morning recess.

After helping her students bundle up and shooing them outside to run off energy in the cold, Grace retreated to the teachers' lounge for a much-needed cup of coffee.

Finding herself alone, she filled her mug from the carafe and drank it black. The coffee was barely warm, but at least the caffeine jolt would help her feel more alert. The day wasn't going to get any easier.

"Grace."

She turned, her heart sinking at the sound of an all-too-familiar voice. Ed Judkins had stepped into the room. He wasn't smiling. "Do you have a few minutes? I'd like a word with you," he said.

"Can it wait? Recess is almost over. My students will be coming back inside."

"Fine. Drop by my office at lunchtime. I'll be expecting you."

He walked out, giving her no chance to reply. Grace's nerves were crawling. This wasn't his usual creepy-friendly approach. Something was up, and she had the feeling she wasn't going to like it.

After recess, she ran the class through the songs they'd be singing in the Christmas program. There was an old piano in the room and Grace could play well enough to manage the simple arrangements in the Christmas songbook. They'd have a better accompanist for the Wednesday morning program, after which the students would go home with their families to begin the two-week holiday vacation.

As she played the piano, Grace couldn't help glancing at the clock. Lunchtime was getting closer. She probably wouldn't have time to eat after her meeting with the principal, but given her nervous stomach, food might not be the best idea.

She remembered Jess's mini cassette recorder in her pocket. She had yet to use it, but that was about to change. Whatever Ed Judkins had in store for her, she needed to do everything possible to protect herself.

She'd begun to read the class the story of the Grinch who stole Christmas, giving voices to the characters, when the lunch bell rang. Promising to finish the story after lunch, she lined the students up and marched them to the cafeteria. From there, she turned around and walked back to the principal's office.

The volunteer manning the reception desk gave her a nod as she passed through the outer office. Outside the principal's door, Grace reached into her pocket and switched on the recorder. It vibrated slightly against her hand. Hopefully, it was working. And hopefully, it wouldn't be needed.

Ed Judkins sat behind his desk. He stood as she entered the room, then took his seat again. "You'll want to shut the door for this," he said. "Then sit down."

Grace closed the door, then settled in the chair that faced his desk. Forcing herself to appear calm, she asked him, "Is something wrong?"

"You might say that." He scowled at her as if she were a misbehaving sixth grader. "I received a disturbing phone call this morning from someone in the office of the district where you used to teach."

"Someone?" A name sprang to mind. "Can you tell me who it was?"

"I'm not at liberty to say."

"Was it Nick Treadwell?" Nicky had threatened to get even with her for jilting him. It appeared that he was serious.

"Was it?" she demanded.

"Well . . . yes," Judkins admitted. "I take it you know him."

"I do." She would save the details for later in case she needed them. "What did Mr. Treadwell have to say?"

"According to him, you have an arrest record for illegal drug use. As you know, that's grounds for dismissal from your job here."

"Wait—what?" And then Grace remembered. She'd been sixteen, going through a rebellious phase. At a rock concert, someone had offered to share a joint—her first.

She'd taken a couple of puffs when an undercover cop had busted her. Since it was a first offense, she'd been sentenced to probation. She hadn't touched weed since that night, and the charge had been expunged when she turned eighteen. But she'd told Nicky about it. Now he was trying to use the story to get her in trouble. *Good luck with that, Nicky, you narcissistic little jerk.*

"Well," Judkins asked, "is it true?"

Grace took her time. "Didn't the district do a background check before they hired me?"

"Of course."

"Did they find anything, like an arrest record, that might be grounds for dismissal?"

"No. But sometimes these things slip through the cracks." He leaned back in his chair, his demeanor shifting. "Is it true, Grace?"

"That I was arrested? Yes, it is." She would save the circumstances for later, after she knew where Judkins was going with this.

"And that you actually used drugs?"

"One time. Yes." Grace paused. "So, what happens now?"

"You're aware that, for what you just admitted to, I could have you fired on the spot."

She nodded. "So, is that what you plan to do?"

"Maybe. Maybe not." He leaned toward her, a slight flush creeping over his face. "If you play your cards right, our little conversation doesn't have to leave this room."

"I don't understand." Grace could feel her pulse racing.

"I think you do, Grace. Be nice to me, and we can pretend this never happened. Your job will be secure for as long as you want it."

"Tell me more."

"I shouldn't have to draw you a picture. I drop a note in your mailbox. You show up at my apartment that night, and we take things from there. You're a beautiful woman, Grace. I'm looking forward to knowing you better." He gave her a sly wink. "So, do we have a deal?"

Grace rose from the chair. "Let me offer you a better deal," she said, taking the cassette recorder out of her pocket and switching it off. "Don't you ever say an inappropriate word to me, or any other teacher, or I take this recording to the district superintendent. Oh—and that drug arrest happened when I was sixteen, so it's not on my record. And Nick Treadwell is my creepy ex-fiancé. That's the only reason he knew about it. So, Mr. Judkins, do we have an understanding?"

His face had taken on the gray-white hue of old-fashioned library paste. He cleared his throat. "Yes, Miss Chapman, I believe we do."

"Good." She opened the door. "One more thing. It might not be a bad idea for you to find another job. Meanwhile, this"—she held up the cassette recorder—"this is going into a safe place."

She walked out, closing the door behind her. Somehow she made it all the way to the women's faculty restroom before her legs began to shake. She shut herself into one of the stalls and leaned against the metal wall. She could feel the cold sweat on her body. She had faced Ed Judkins and won. She should be congratulating herself. But she felt as if she'd just waded through a slime pit and barely survived. Chalk up one more treacherous, conniving man in her life.

She felt drained of emotion and energy. But she wasn't finished. She still had to deal with Nicky. She would do that when she got home.

By the time the bell rang to call her back to class, Grace had regained her composure. She finished the story of the Grinch and even managed the voices. After that, she marched her students to the auditorium for a rehearsal of the Christmas program. With the music teacher in charge, Grace's only job was to keep her students quiet and get them on and off the stage in an orderly fashion. There'd been no sign of Ed Judkins at the rehearsal or in the halls. Maybe he was avoiding her. Good.

Tomorrow would be a dress rehearsal, with her class wearing the star hats they'd made out of picnic plates and yellow construction paper. For now, the school day was over.

Maggie stayed after the other students had left, waiting for Grace to drive her home. Grace took a few minutes to lay out some lesson materials for tomorrow. Then she and Maggie put on their coats and went out to the car.

The house was only a few blocks from the school. Maggie chattered all the way. "Do you think my dad will be home?"

"He said he would," Grace drove out of the parking lot and into the street.

"How do I heat the lasagna we made? Do I put it back in the oven?"

"It's easier if you just cut a piece, put it on a plate, and put it in the microwave for a couple of minutes. Just make sure it's warmed all the way through."

"Oh. I should have figured that out."

"You'll figure out a lot of things, Maggie." Grace pulled up to the curb in front of the house. She helped Maggie out of the backseat. The icy wind whipped at their coats as they trudged up the walk and climbed the steps to the porch.

"I can hear the TV!" Maggie exclaimed as they reached the door. "Daddy's home!"

Flinging the door open, she dashed inside. Sam was on the couch watching the news. He put up an arm to protect his shoulder as Maggie hurled herself into his lap.

"Whoa, there." He laughed, wincing as she hugged him. "Careful, honey. I'm still pretty sore."

She backed off, staying close. "I'm sorry. I'm just so glad you're home."

"I'm glad, too." He tousled her curls and kissed her cheek.

Grace had followed Maggie into the house and closed the door behind her. The room was pleasantly warm. She hadn't planned on taking off her coat, but she slipped out of it and laid it over the back of the couch.

"Are you all right, Sam?" she asked. "Is there anything you need?"

His gaze took her in, welcoming, questioning. Grace sensed that he was anxious to resolve things between them. But after today's encounter with her boss, she was emotionally drained. How could she tell Sam that this wasn't a good time?

"I don't need anything at the moment," he said. "But I've got some news for you, Maggie. The McDermotts came over to bring me some homemade bread this afternoon. You remember their granddaughter, Ann Marie, don't you?"

"Sure. We had a lot of fun when she was here last summer."

"She's staying here for a few days while her parents take a trip. When you get time, she wants you to come over."

"That's great! Can I go over now, just for a little while to say hi? I'll be back in time to fix you some lasagna."

"Stay as long as you want," Sam said. "I'll be fine."

Still wearing her coat, Maggie dashed out the door, leaving Grace and Sam alone.

Now what? Should she tell him about her encounter with Judkins? Should she make a hasty excuse and leave? Or should she stay and face what had to be faced?

Looking at Sam, she felt her heart overflow with love. But her nerves were still raw from the facedown with her boss. And the fear was still there—the fear that she didn't have what it took to stay in a relationship. Not even with this wonderful man.

"Come here, Grace." Sam motioned to the spot beside him on the sofa. His expression told her that he wouldn't take no for an answer.

Grace sat down next to him, close, but not too close. Maybe he'd gotten tired of her games. Maybe he would be the one to end things between them here and now. "Is something wrong?" she asked.

"Not really. But I've got something to say, and I want you to hear me out. No interruptions, all right?"

"All right. I'm listening." Grace prepared herself for his good-bye. It wasn't what she wanted, but maybe it was what she deserved.

"When you come as close to dying as I did last week, it brings some truths home," he said. "You realize that time and life are uncertain gifts, and you can't expect anything to last forever. Before I lost my wife, I thought that we'd grow old together. I thought we'd have years to have more children, to watch them grow up and have families of their own. Then she went shopping and never came home. She was gone, just like that. I never even had the chance to tell her good-bye."

"Sam—" She laid a hand on his arm.

"No, let me finish," he said. "I don't know how much time I have left on this earth—or how much time any one of us has. I only know that I don't want to waste any more of it waiting around for happiness. Life is too short and too precious."

He turned toward her, his gentle eyes gazing deep into hers. "Grace, I know we can't make any big decisions until we know each other better. But I don't want to wait around playing these silly games. I want to end this damned stand-off and start spending serious time together." He paused, searching her face for answers. "Blast it, woman, I'm in love with you."

Stunned, she let him cup her face between his palms and bring his lips to hers. His tender, seeking kiss went through her like a warm spring flood, stirring pulses of buried desire in the depths of her body. She wanted him. She needed what he was giving her. But the fears were there, too, the raw nerves sending out alarm signals. Grace could feel them holding her back like invisible chains, blocking her response.

Sam could feel them, too. Abruptly, he released her.

"So that's the way it is," he said.

"Sam, it's not you—"

"Don't bother to explain. At least I know where I stand. I laid my cards on the table and came up short. But we can deal with this like civilized adults, can't we?"

"I need to go." She took her coat off the back of the couch.

"Don't worry about getting Maggie to school tomorrow," he said. "If I can't drive, I'll walk with her."

Grace could feel tears welling. Before they could betray her, she fled out the door and down the walk to her car. This time she knew that Sam wouldn't be coming after her.

Ten minutes later she arrived home. Jess's car was parked in the driveway. Grace found her roommate in the kitchen, brewing a cup of the Earl Grey tea she enjoyed. She glanced up as Grace walked in.

"Would you like a cup? I can brew you a different kind. I know you don't care for Earl Grey." She stared at Grace. "My word, girl, you look like you've been through the wringer. Did something happen to you?"

Grace put her purse on the table and sank onto a chair. "Oh, Jess, it's been a long day. And it isn't over."

"I'm always willing to listen if you want to tell me about it." Jess poured steaming water into another mug and added a bag of the herbal tea Grace preferred. "Did your weekend with Maggie go all right?"

"Oh, yes. Maggie was delightful. It's just . . ." Grace sighed. "Sam and I just broke up—if you can call it that. Not that there was much between us to break. We just agreed not to see each other."

"That's too bad. You and Sam would make a great couple. What was the problem? Was it that he's still mourning his wife?"

"No, the problem was me. He wanted to move ahead with our relationship. But I got cold feet. I couldn't handle the thought of another breakup, especially knowing that Maggie would be hurt if it happened."

"So, you're afraid of commitment?" This was Jess, the counselor, talking.

"Afraid? I'm terrified. That's how I came to leave a trail of wrecked relationships behind me. I love Sam and Maggie too much to risk ruining their lives."

"You've tried therapy?"

"I have. I understand that I'm afraid to trust because my father cheated on my mother and left us. But that doesn't fix my problem."

Jess passed Grace the mug of brewed tea. "I want you to think about something, Grace. Who made the decision that you were going to have this issue with trust? Was it your father? Was it maybe your mother? Or was it you? And who has power over that decision?"

"You make it sound so simple." Grace sipped her tea.

"In a way, it is. Just take your time and think about it."

"Thanks, I will. But it won't change things with Sam. That bridge has been crossed and burned."

"I'm sorry. I really am. Especially since Wynette has been walking on air the past few days. She's out-of-her-mind in love with Sam's deputy, Buck Winston. And evidently, he feels the same about her. You won't see her till later tonight. She mentioned they were going out after work."

"That's great news. I'm happy for them." Grace's smile was real. "Buck seems like a good guy, and any man would be lucky to have Wynette. Oh—one more thing." She fumbled in her blazer pocket for the cassette recorder. After the devastation of her breakup with Sam, she'd almost forgotten today's victory over Ed Judkins.

"It worked." She laid the recorder on the table. "I got him dead to rights, and he knows it. He'll never bother me again. I just hope he's learned his lesson. I hate to think he'd try this with another woman, but if he does, I'll have this recording to back her up." Grace popped the cassette out of the small machine. "Here's your recorder. I'll be glad to replace this cassette with a new one."

"Don't bother. I have plenty of spares."

"I can't thank you enough, Jess."

"You already have." Jess finished her tea and stood. "Now, what sounds good for dinner?"

When Maggie came back from the neighbors' house, Sam was alone. He gave her a smile, but his eyes were sad. Maggie knew that look. She'd seen it in the weeks and months after her mother died. Maybe she was seeing it now because Miss Chapman wasn't here.

Maggie wanted to ask him why Miss Chapman had left so soon. But something told her this might not be a good time.

"Are you all right, Daddy?" she asked him, taking off her coat.

"Fine. Just a little tired. But I'm happy to be home with my best girl."

"Are you hungry? I could warm up some lasagna or bring you some cookies and milk."

"Later maybe. Right now, why don't you sit down here and tell me about your weekend?"

"Can I plug in the Christmas tree lights first?"

"Sure. That would be nice."

Maggie squeezed into the corner behind the tree, found the plug, and pushed it into the wall outlet. The colored tree lights came on, casting a rainbow glow that made the room feel more like Christmas. Maggie could only hope it would make her father feel more like Christmas, too. But something was clearly wrong.

"When will your shoulder be better?" she asked, sitting next to him. "Do you think you can drive your truck?"

"I don't know. The Jeep might be easier to shift. But we'll figure it out. I do plan to go to your Christmas program on Wednesday, even if I have to walk."

"Our class is supposed to be stars. We made star hats. They're kind of lame."

"That's all right." He slipped an arm around her shoulders. "So, what did you learn to cook this weekend?"

"You know about the cookies and lasagna. But Miss Chapman showed me how to make scrambled eggs and cook bacon in the microwave. I already know how to make toast, so I can fix breakfast now. I can even make instant coffee for you."

"And what did you do besides cook? What did you do at the mall?"

"We looked at decorations and ate giant pretzels. And Miss Chapman bought me a pretty dress to wear to the Christmas ball. Let me show it to you." Maggie jumped up and hurried into her room. She had intended to take the dress to show Sam, but then decided to put it on. She waltzed into the living room and made a slow circle, like a model, in front of her father.

He gave a low whistle. "My, don't you look beautiful," he said. "You'll be the prettiest girl at the ball. Come here. There's something I want to see."

Maggie walked to the couch where he sat. A paper tag showing the brand and price dangled from the sleeve of her dress. Sam frowned as he studied it.

"Maggie, this dress was expensive."

"But Miss Chapman said it was on sale. See that red sticker?"

"Yes, but even on sale the dress was expensive. I can't allow Miss Chapman to spend that kind of money on you."

Maggie clutched at the dress, thinking how pretty it made her feel. "Miss Chapman said it was a present. You aren't going to make me give it back, are you, Daddy?"

"Nothing like that, Maggie. You can keep the dress. But I'm going to see that your teacher lets me pay for it."

Your teacher. That's what he'd called her—not Grace or even Miss Chapman. Yes, something had gone wrong. And this time, Maggie didn't know how to fix it. She had run out of ideas.

Chapter Fourteen

Grace waited until after 10:00 to call Nicky. By then she had built up a cold, quiet rage. Nicky had bent the truth to get her in trouble. He had wanted to damage her reputation, or worse, get her fired. But the trap she'd set to shut down Ed Judkins had caught Nicky, too. What he'd done—calling her boss from his work with a damaging lie—had been highly unethical. She had the evidence to prove he'd done it. But she didn't care enough to punish him. She just wanted him to leave her alone.

She punched in his number and waited for his answering machine to come on. "Nicky," she said, "I have my principal, Ed Judkins, on tape, saying that you called and told him I'd been arrested for drug use. If you ever contact me again, even once, I will send a copy of the tape to your supervisor. Good-bye."

She ended the call and waited, half expecting to hear the phone ring. When it didn't happen, she sank onto a kitchen chair and rested her head between her hands.

What if she'd married Nicky Treadwell? What if she hadn't listened to the inner voice that told her to cut and run before she made the worst mistake of her life?

She hadn't cancelled her wedding because she was a flighty, damaged woman who couldn't commit. She'd cancelled it because, at some gut level, she'd finally realized that behind the charming façade he'd shown her, Nicky was a jerk.

But what had happened today with Sam was a different story. The most wonderful man she'd ever known had offered her his heart—and she had panicked.

What was wrong with her? Why couldn't she heal and put the past behind her?

She heard voices from the porch. A moment later, the front door opened and closed. Wynette came dancing into the kitchen after her date with Buck. Her face was flushed, her makeup smeared. She was the picture of glowing, giddy happiness.

"Hi, Grace. We missed you. How was your weekend of babysitting?"

"Fine. Jess told me your exciting news. She said you were walking on air."

Wynette giggled. "That's how it feels. Back in school, I had a crush on Buck for years. But I was too young for him. I guess I finally caught up." She dropped a pink box on the table. "These doughnuts were left over from work. Help yourself."

"Thanks, but I'll pass. I don't have much appetite tonight."

"Oh, no." Wynette studied Grace's face. "Did something happen with Sam?"

"What happened with Sam was . . . a great big nothing. We barely got out of the starting gate before it was over. All I can do is wish him well."

"And here I am, gushing all over the place while you're hurting. I'm so sorry, Grace."

"Gush away, girl. You're entitled. I couldn't be happier for you." Grace stood. "And now, I think I'll turn in. It'll feel good to sleep in my own bed again."

Too bad it isn't Sam's bed.

Fifteen minutes later she was turning off the light and nestling under the covers. After four days and nights of worrying about Sam and taking care of Maggie, along with the Christmas crazies at school, she was bone weary. Only one full day and one half day of school remained before the start of Christmas break. Two empty weeks stretched before her, without Sam and without Maggie. What would she do with her time?

Staying here would be a waste. Maybe she should take a trip somewhere. She would miss the Christmas ball, but seeing Sam as Santa and Maggie in her pretty new dress would only be awkward and painful. Why not get away? Clara and the other volunteers could manage the children's activity room.

Where could she go? Tonight she was too tired to think. But she would get on her computer tomorrow after work and do some checking. There had to be some last-minute deals on winter getaways—someplace like Galveston, maybe, with a beach, where she could just sit on the sand, watch the waves, and try not to think about Sam.

On Tuesday morning, as the students were coming into the classroom, Maggie walked up to Grace and handed her a sealed envelope.

"My dad asked me to give you this." Her expression betrayed nothing. But Grace sensed the emotions that lay behind it. The little girl was hurt.

"Thank you, Maggie. I'll open it later." Grace reached into the bottom drawer of her desk and slipped the envelope into her purse. Maggie was already headed for her seat. By the time she reached it, the students were standing for the national anthem and the Pledge of Allegiance. As they took their seats, Ed Judkins's voice boomed over the speaker with the day's announcements. He was trying to sound jolly, like Santa. The kids seemed to like it. But what a phony, Grace thought. Maybe he'd find another job over the break.

For math, she had the students make up and solve Christmas math problems: Santa has eight reindeer; if he hitches Rudolph in front, how many reindeer will there be then? The class had fun. But Grace's mind was on the sealed envelope that Maggie had given her. What was in it? A letter? Did Sam want to give her another chance?

But that didn't seem likely. Sam was a proud man, and nothing about their situation had changed.

When the class went out for recess, she withdrew the envelope from her purse. Sam had written her name on the front—not *Grace,* but *Miss Chapman.* It sounded cold. But what else could she have expected?

She ran a finger under the flap. Inside was a check from Sam, made out to her, for the price of Maggie's new dress. Attached to the face of the check was a yellow Post-it note with a hastily jotted message.

For the dress. Thanks.

That was all. And that was when Grace knew Sam had given up on her. There would be no reunion, no second chances. He was finished.

Stifling a sob of frustration, she tore the check in two, stuffed the pieces back into the envelope, and put it back in her purse. She would mail the check back to him later. But recess was almost over. Any minute now, the bell would ring to call her students inside. For now, all she could do was get on with her day, as if nothing had happened.

Gritting his teeth against the pain in his shoulder, Sam had driven Maggie to school and let her off in front. She'd given him a smile and a hug, but he could tell she was dejected, and he knew why.

He'd promised to give his daughter a happy Christmas. So far, the season had been a disaster, from the terrifying gunshot wound to the fizzle of his relationship with Grace. It amazed him that Maggie was even able to smile.

At least the tree was up. But there was not one present under it. He hadn't even asked Maggie what she wanted—besides a happy ending for her father and her teacher. Shopping would have to wait a few more days, until he was stronger. But then he planned to pull out all the stops for his little girl. Whatever Maggie wanted—a bike, maybe, or even a puppy—was going under that tree.

He watched TV for a while, then switched it off and tried to lose himself in a new mystery novel from the library. But he wasn't used to being stuck at home alone. He was already suffering from cabin fever. At least Maggie would be on break in a couple of days. Life was never dull with his daughter around. Maybe Wednesday night they could order pizza, rent some videos, and invite her friend, Ann Marie, over to watch them.

Anything to keep him from thinking about Grace.

Last night he'd lain awake for hours, remembering the feel of her in his arms, her warm body molding to his. He remembered the taste of her lips, the fragrance of her hair, and the flash of her smile when he said something that struck her. He'd fallen hard for the pretty schoolteacher. But he had too much pride to pursue a woman who couldn't return his feelings. Grace would have to deal with her issues in her own time, and in her own way.

But who was he kidding? If she were to come back and want to try again, he'd take her on in a minute. That was why he'd left a message scrawled inside the envelope he'd sent with his check. If she ignored it, he would know that things were really over between them.

Sam's musings were interrupted by the chime of the doorbell. He answered it to find the mayor standing on the doorstep.

"Hello, Sam." He was all smiles. "How are you feeling?"

"Better every day, Rulon. Come on in and have a seat." The mayor had never been Sam's favorite person, but today any company was welcome.

"I'll stand, thanks. Just dropped by to check on you."

"As you see, I'm fine." Sam remained standing. "Still feeling some pain, but I'm putting up with it. No more heavy drugs for me."

"And when will you be back doing your job?" His voice held a note of impatience.

Sam curbed the impulse to remind the mayor that the question was out of line. As sheriff, he worked for the county. Rulon Wilkins wasn't his boss. "The doctors want me to take it easy for another ten days, at least. I'm planning on sometime after Christmas. Meanwhile, Helen tells me that Buck is doing a fine job, so everything should be covered."

"And the Christmas ball? Will you be fit to play Santa?"

"I'll do my best—for the kids."

"Have you tried on the suit?"

"I haven't even opened the box." Sam shifted his position. His injured shoulder was beginning to ache. "As long as you're here, Rulon, there's something I've been meaning to mention. That street on the north edge of town—I was up that way a couple of weeks ago. The road has so many potholes that I could barely drive on it. The gutters are clogged, and the empty lots are so full of weeds that fire is a real danger. In a dry winter like this one, some fool tossing a cigarette could burn the whole neighborhood to the ground. And somebody mentioned to me last month that when we do get a storm, the street is never plowed. I'm hoping you'll send a crew up there to make some improvements."

The mayor shook his head. "I'm aware of the problems, Sam. But Branding Iron isn't a wealthy town. We don't have money to fix up a neighborhood whose residents won't lift a finger to fix it up themselves. Maybe if they generated more tax revenue, things would be different. But for now, we don't have funding to help folks who are nothing but a drag on society."

"I see." And Sam did. Rulon Wilkins could spend city money to refurbish his office and take his wife to New York, but he wouldn't pay to help the poor people in his town. Something needed to be done. But what?

One more thing to think about.

"Well, it's time I got back to running my town," Rulon said. "You let me know if you need anything, hear? Oh, and I guess I'll see you at the Wednesday meeting. Maybe you can model the Santa suit for us."

"I won't be there. Doctor's orders. But Buck will be taking care of security at the ball, so my only job will be to play Santa."

"But Alice specifically told me she wanted to see that suit on you."

"Don't worry, Rulon, I've got this covered. I'll see you Saturday night." Sam edged the mayor out the door and closed it behind him. Then he wandered into the kitchen, swallowed a couple tablets of ibuprofen for the pain in his shoulder, and cut a square of lasagna to put in the microwave.

What would Grace be doing for the holidays? Sam wondered. She didn't have any family here, and she'd mentioned to him that she was estranged from her father and rarely communicated with her brother. Would she be spending Christmas alone?

He imagined how much fun it would have been, sharing

Christmastime with Maggie and Grace—shopping, cooking, wrapping gifts, snuggling in front of the fire. But now that wasn't going to happen. All he could do was try to make this the happy Christmas his little girl deserved.

For the last hour of the school day, Grace had passed out colored paper and had her students make Christmas cards for their families. She was looking forward to going home and booking vacation plans when the secretary's voice came over the intercom.

"Miss Chapman, you have an urgent phone call in the office. Someone will be coming to supervise your class while you take it."

Urgent? What was that supposed to mean? Grace hurried down the hall to the office. The volunteer who'd be watching her class passed her on the way. Grace could feel her heart racing. Urgent calls were never good news. But she couldn't imagine who'd be calling her at school. Had something happened to Sam? Was she needed to take care of Maggie again?

Mrs. Spicer, the secretary, was waiting for her. "You can take the call in the conference room," she said. "It's quiet and private in there."

"Did the caller give you a name?"

The secretary shook her head. "He only said he was your brother. I'll transfer the call."

What could Cooper want? They hadn't spoken since August, when she'd called to tell him about her new job and her planned move to Branding Iron. She'd given him the number of the school because, at the time, it was all she'd had.

Grace walked into the conference room, sat down at the table, and punched the blinking button on the phone. "Cooper? What is it? Is everything all right?"

"No. That's why I'm calling you. It's Dad. He's in the

hospital in Salt Lake City. I flew here from Seattle to be with him."

"What happened? An accident?" Grace pictured her handsome, vigorous father on the day he'd walked out of the house, leaving her and her mother weeping in the front hallway. "Is he all right?"

"His heart is failing, and he's too weak to survive a transplant. He's dying, Grace. The doctors told me he has just days left, if that." Cooper cleared his throat, his voice hoarse with emotion. "He wants to see you."

"No." The response sprang from years of bitterness. "I lost my father when he walked out of the house and drove off to be with that woman. The man in that hospital bed is a stranger. I don't even know him."

"And you never will if you don't get on a plane and come. He knows how much he hurt you and Mom. He never got a chance to tell her he was sorry, and he's never forgiven himself. Give him some peace before he dies. You won't get another chance in this life."

"And what about his wife? Is she there with you?"

"She's long gone. I'll tell you the whole story when I see you."

"I didn't say I was coming, Cooper. Dad ruined my childhood, and he ruined my relationships with men." Grace had never told her brother about the day she came home and heard her father in the bedroom with his girl-friend. Maybe she should tell him. But what good would it serve now? It would only open old wounds.

"Grace, if you don't come, you'll spend the rest of your life wondering whether you could've made a difference. I've got a cell phone now. I'll give you the number. Call me when you've booked your flight, and I'll meet you at the airport. Got a pen and paper?"

Grace grabbed a pen and notepad off the nearby cre-denza and copied the number as he gave it to her. In turn, she gave him the number of the landline at the house. "I'll see you, hopefully sometime tomorrow," he said, and ended the call.

Grace sat still for a long moment, staring down at the phone and the paper with her brother's number on it. How could she go and be there to comfort a man she hadn't seen since she was Maggie's age, a man whose betrayal she'd blamed for all her doubts and insecurities?

Then again, he was her father. How could she *not* go?

After a word with the secretary, Grace hurried back to her classroom. The bell hadn't rung. With luck, she'd have a moment to tell her students why she wouldn't be here for the school program tomorrow.

She stepped into the room, excused the volunteer, and gave the students a quick explanation. "I just got word that my father is in the hospital. I need to go to him, so I won't be around to hear you sing tomorrow. Do your best, have a wonderful Christmas, and I'll see you when school starts again in the new year."

There wasn't time for more. The bell rang, and Grace excused the class. As her students filed out of the room, Maggie met her eyes and gave her a sad little smile. At least Sam's daughter would know what had happened, and she would tell her father.

Not that it mattered. Sam was finished with her. He had no reason to care.

When Maggie came out of the building, Sam was waiting in the truck. He climbed out to help her into the backseat. "Careful," she said as he lifted her. "You don't want to hurt your shoulder."

"I'll be fine. I'm using my good arm. But I think you must be getting heavier."

"I'm growing, Daddy. Soon I'll be big enough to climb up by myself."

"And someday, when you grow up, you won't need me at all. I'm not looking forward to that."

"But that won't be for a long time."

"I hope not." He closed the door and went around the truck to get in. She needed to tell him about Miss Chapman's father, Maggie reminded herself. But that could wait. He seemed to be in a happy mood. Why risk spoiling it?

"How would you like to go to the hardware store with me?" he asked. "After that we can stop by Buckaroo's for an early dinner. Okay?"

"You bet." Maggie liked going to the hardware and feed. It was fun, wandering the aisles, looking at the different tools and trying to guess what they were used for. And the smell of the place was a wonderful mix of machine oil, leather, tobacco, burlap, fertilizer, sawdust, and other aromas she had yet to name. Once she had licked a salt block to see if it tasted like table salt. It did.

"What do you need from the store?" she asked.

"I don't need to buy anything, but I want to see how Hank is doing. I talked Walt into giving him a job."

"If he stops drinking?"

"That's right. Hank deserves a break, but he has to keep up his end of the bargain."

They parked in front of the hardware store, and Maggie followed her dad inside. Only then did she remember that this was where Sam had been shot. She tried to imagine the spot where his blood had stained the floor, but she knew better than to ask him where it was. The kids at school were saying he was a hero. But Maggie had learned that Sam didn't like talking about the robbery.

The store wasn't busy this time of day. Walt Cullimore, the owner, was rearranging a shelf when Sam and Maggie walked in. Hank was nowhere in sight. Maggie's heart sank. What if Hank had already been fired?

Walt gave them an easygoing smile. "Howdy, Sam, Maggie. If you're looking for Hank, he's out back, helping some folks with a lumber order."

"Don't bother him," Sam said. "I just wanted to ask you how he's working out."

Walt nodded. "He's doing fine. Gets along great with the customers and knows the products almost as well as I do. And he's already come up with some ideas for getting more business. Next year we're going to clear out that weed patch on the south side of the store and put up a Christmas tree lot, so people can get their trees right here in town. That was Hank's idea."

"That would be great," Sam said. "What about the drinking?"

"No sign of it so far. I'm crossing my fingers that he'll stay off the bottle and keep going to those meetings. Otherwise, he'll get fired, and I'd hate to lose him."

"If you see any sign that he's getting discouraged or slipping up, give me a call," Sam said. "We both want to help the man, but he has to help himself, too."

"I'll do that." Walt excused himself to welcome a new customer who'd just come in. While they were talking, Sam and Maggie went outside to the truck.

"It's nice that you help people like Hank," Maggie said as they drove back uptown to Buckaroo's. "Is that part of your sheriff's job?"

"Not really. I just like to help folks who need it. It makes me happy."

"Does catching bad guys make you happy?"

Sam sighed. "Most of the arrests I make are just good people doing bad things. Like kids who shoplift and get into mischief, or cowboys who get in fights out at Rowdy's Roost. Real bad guys, like the ones who tried to rob the hardware store, don't come around here very often—

thank goodness for that. You know the state police caught them, don't you? They're going to prison for years. They'll never hurt anybody again."

"I know, Daddy. But still, sometimes I wish you had a different job. When you have to go out at night, I get scared that something will happen to you."

"Nothing's going to happen to me, sweetheart."

"Something did happen. You got shot. You almost died."

"But I didn't die, did I? Look, here we are at Buckaroo's. How does a burger and a big chocolate shake sound to you?"

Maggie enjoyed the meal at Buckaroo's, although the place was too noisy for much talking. After that, they drove home and watched TV together, with the Christmas lights on, until bedtime. It was so nice, she thought, having her dad here and knowing that he wasn't going to be called away in the night, leaving her to sleep at the McDermotts'.

She was in her bed and almost asleep before she remembered that she hadn't told Sam about Miss Chapman leaving to be with her father. But that could wait until morning. Tonight it might just make him sad.

The nearest major airport, Lubbock International, was a two-hour drive from Branding Iron. Last night, Grace had booked the only available flight to Salt Lake City, leaving at 10:15 A.M. today, with a layover and plane change in Las Vegas. Between driving, flying, and waiting, her trip would take almost nine hours.

She'd done her best to cover the responsibilities she was leaving behind. A volunteer would take charge of her students, getting them on and offstage for the Christmas program. Clara Marsden had graciously agreed to fill in for her at tonight's committee meeting and take charge of the children's activities at the ball if Grace didn't get back in time.

She'd spent a long moment staring at the phone, wondering whether she should call Sam. But given their broken relationship, that could be a bad idea. Maggie would let him know where she'd gone and why.

At the airport, she parked the Cadillac in the long-term lot, checked in with her carry-on bag, and walked down the concourse to her gate. The flight would be on time—one less worry. But there were plenty of other reasons to be anxious.

She'd never been in Salt Lake City and had no idea how to get around. She could only hope that Cooper would be at the airport to meet her and that she would arrive in time to see her father—although she still had mixed feelings about that.

As she waited to board, she tried to remember the good times with him—and there *had* been good times, when they'd been as close as Sam and Maggie appeared to be. He had called her his little princess, bought her treats and toys, and read her stories at bedtime. He had taken her out to eat and to Cooper's high school football games, where he'd taught her the rules and plays and how to watch the sport. Sometimes he would take her hiking on easy trails, pointing out the different plants, birds, and animals they saw. Her mother, who'd disliked the outdoors, had hardly ever gone along. Mostly it had just been the two of them, pals in the best sense of the word.

Grace had idolized her dad—all the more reason she had been crushed when he'd cheated and left. In her childish grief, she had vowed to stop loving him. After a time she almost had.

* * *

The sun was low in the sky when the plane flew over the snow-capped Oquirrh Mountains and descended into the Salt Lake Valley. Beyond the vast flat expanse of the Great Salt Lake, the city spread eastward, all the way to the towering Wasatch Range with its jagged peaks and deep canyons. As the plane taxied to the gate, Grace could see blowing snow. Cooper had warned her about the winter weather, and she was ready with her boots and her warm down parka. But just looking outside was enough to make her shiver.

Pulling her wheeled carry-on, she came out of the jetway and headed for the baggage claim area, where Cooper had said he'd be waiting. She was on her way down the escalator when she spotted him in the crowd below—tall and rugged, looking like James Bond in the Burberry overcoat he'd bought years ago in a London secondhand shop. Seeing her, he waved. Seconds later, Grace was off the escalator, rushing through the crowd toward him.

He gave her an easy hug. The two had never been close, but they got along—although he had yet to forgive her for the botched wedding fiasco last June. "Thanks for coming," he said, taking her bag. "I knew you would."

"How is he?" She couldn't manage to say the word *Dad*.

"I called the hospital a few minutes ago. He's stable and sleeping for now, so there's no rush. The car's in the short-term garage. If you're hungry, we can grab a bite on the way to the hospital. Or there's a twenty-four-hour snack bar at our hotel if you need it. I took the liberty of reserving you a room."

"I'm fine. I had time for a meal in Vegas."

"Then let's have coffee somewhere quiet. We need to talk before you see him. You need to know what to expect."

"All right. Lead the way." Grace lengthened her steps to keep pace with his long strides as they left the main terminal and headed for the parking garage. She hadn't seen her father, or even known what his life was like, for more than twenty years. Cooper was wise to prepare her. There were things she needed to understand before she saw him.

Chapter Fifteen

Falling snow battered the windshield of the rental SUV, faster than the wipers could clear it away. In the gathering darkness, Grace could barely make out the traffic lanes ahead. But Cooper seemed to know where they were going. Tired and emotional, she settled back into the seat and let him take her.

After fighting rush-hour traffic from the airport and winding through a maze of streets, Cooper pulled into the nearly empty parking lot of what appeared to be a small coffee shop. The lights were on, the OPEN sign glowing through the front window.

Cooper, always the gentleman, came around to help her out of the vehicle. "Careful, it's slippery," he said, taking her arm as they crossed the snowy parking lot. "The hospital, St. Mark's, is just a few blocks from here. I discovered this place by accident. The coffee's good, and they sell great oatmeal-raisin cookies."

Inside, the place was rustic and cozy. A potbellied stove, with a cleverly disguised gas burner, provided heat and a cheery glow through the mica panes in its door. Old-fashioned Christmas lights were strung above the counter. A pine candle scented the room with holiday fragrance.

Cooper ordered two coffees and two cookies at the counter, then led the way to a corner booth. They hadn't said much on the way here, mostly just small talk about her flight and her new life in Branding Iron. But Grace sensed that the serious conversation was about to begin.

Their order arrived on a tray, the coffee steaming. Grace added some cream from a hand-thrown pottery pitcher and took a careful sip. "So, are you going to fill me in on our father?"

Cooper broke off a chunk of cookie and dunked it in his coffee, something she remembered him doing years ago, at home. He looked good, the wrinkles deepening around his hazel eyes and a touch of silver showing in his dark hair. He'd been single since his divorce nine years ago and had a teenage son who lived with his ex-wife. He made a good living as a freelance magazine writer.

"When was the last time you had any contact with Dad?" he asked.

"The day he walked out. I believe my last words to him were 'Please don't go, Daddy.' "

"But he did try to stay in touch with you, didn't he?"

"He sent me a few letters, birthday cards, little gifts. Mom always sent them back. I let her. After a while he stopped trying."

"Did he phone you?"

"I don't know. Mom always answered the phone. If he called, she never told me. But when she got sick and he never came to see her, never even showed up for the funeral, even when I knew you'd phoned him about it, I vowed I would never forgive him."

"He sent flowers. Remember that bouquet of two dozen pink roses, with no card? Those were from him. He didn't come because he knew his being there would upset the family, especially you."

"It doesn't matter. He destroyed our family. Things

were never happy after he left." Grace resisted the urge to tell him about the day she'd come home from school. No need, she told herself. The situation was already painful enough.

"Things weren't happy *before* he left," Cooper said. "He and Mom hid it from you, but I knew about the fights they had. And whatever you might think, Dad paid for what he did. His new wife left him after going through his money. He and Mom had agreed to split a property cash-out in place of alimony and child support, so his loss didn't affect you, but that second divorce left him penniless."

"Couldn't he make enough selling real estate? He was always good at that."

"He tried. But the housing market was down. Nobody was buying. And he didn't have the drive anymore. It was as if he'd lost his magic touch. He'd call me every few months to catch up. That was how I found out all this.

"We kept in touch over the years, although we didn't get together. He'd tell me he was back on his feet, selling property again, living in a nice condo, and he'd met a terrific woman.

"Last year, I was passing through Salt Lake City on business and decided to surprise him. I found out it was all a lie. When I tracked down the address he'd given me, I found him living in a run-down motel room on the west side, cleaning a bar after hours to make rent. I took him out for a good meal and gave him some cash. It was all I could do. I didn't know he was sick until the hospital called me this week." Cooper finished his coffee and set the mug on the tray. "Our father paid for what he did, Grace. He lost everything."

"He didn't lose it. He threw it away. Why didn't you tell me all this before now?"

"Because I knew you wouldn't want to hear it. Every

time he called me, he asked about you. He was so proud that you were a teacher."

"You didn't tell him I was a wreck in the relationship department?"

Instead of answering, Cooper glanced at his watch, pulled a couple of bills out of his wallet, and laid them on the table. "We need to go," he said. "I can't tell you what to do, Grace. I just wanted you to understand the man you're about to meet."

"I know. Thanks for the heads-up."

The snow was up to her boot tops and still coming down as he forged a path to the SUV and helped her climb inside. After he'd cleared the windows, they headed for the nearby hospital. Minutes later they arrived at a complex of buildings set amid tall trees in what appeared to be a mostly residential neighborhood.

Cooper let her off at the covered main entrance, where she waited while he parked in the visitors' lot and slogged back through the storm to join her. As they crossed the lobby to the elevators, they passed a brightly lit Christmas tree in one corner. On a night like this, in a place like this, it was all too easy to forget that Christmas was almost here.

Waiting for the elevator to take them to the second floor, Grace sensed the tightening of a cold, hard knot in the pit of her stomach. How would she feel when she saw the man who'd broken her heart, destroyed her childhood, and shattered her trust? What would she say to him? Maybe this whole trip was a mistake. Maybe she should just turn around, walk back to the lobby, and wait for Cooper to end his visit.

Cooper had said he couldn't tell her what to do. But Grace knew what he wanted and why he'd asked her to be here. He wanted to give their father peace in his final hours. How could she do that? How could she give peace to the man who'd taken so much from her?

"Come on." Cooper nudged her through the sliding door and pushed the button for the second floor. As the elevator hummed upward, Grace gazed down at her wet boots, too conflicted to speak.

On the second floor, they left the elevator and walked down the hall to the nurses' station. "Your timing's fortunate," the nurse on duty told Cooper. "He's awake and lucid, but it may not be for long. His vital signs are getting weaker."

Grace felt the urgency as Cooper strode down the hall. Heart pounding, she raced after him. They walked into the room together.

The man in the bed was in his late sixties, but he looked much older. His eyes, now closed, were sunk into hollows. His scalp showed pink through the thin gray hair that had once been thick and dark. His cheeks were frosted with stubble. A mask that covered his nose and mouth fed hissing oxygen into his lungs. An IV drip sent fluids through a needle in his arm. Tubes and sensors connected his failing body to a softly beeping monitor above the bed.

Was this man really her father? If she hadn't known who he was, she would never have recognized him.

Then he opened his eyes—the beautiful, blue eyes that were exactly as she remembered. Grace felt her heart contract.

"Hi, Dad." Cooper touched his shoulder. "There's somebody here to see you."

"Hello, Dad." She leaned over him so he could see her without having to turn his head. "I'm your daughter. I'm Grace."

He moved the mask to one side. "Grace? But you've grown up. You're a beautiful woman now." His voice was a feeble rasp, laboring over every word. "Thank you for coming to see this old wreck."

What should she say now? There seemed to be no point in telling him how he'd hurt her. He knew what he'd done.

His hand, the one that was free of needles and monitors, reached up to her. Grace forced herself to take it. His fingers were cold against her skin, the bones like fragile, knotted twigs.

"I'm sorry for what I did, Princess," he said, using the old name. "I've been sorry every day since. Leaving you the way I did was the worst mistake of my life. If you hate me for it, I can't blame you."

"I never hated you, Dad." As she spoke the words, Grace realized they were true. "I was hurt. I was angry. But I didn't hate you. I loved you."

"I wrote. I tried to call." He coughed slightly; the monitor beeps accelerated, then slowed again. "But I didn't expect to hear back. I knew how much I'd hurt you."

"You did hurt me. You left me to grow up without the father I loved. My school activities, my prom, my graduation, all the times I needed hugging or scolding—you weren't there for any of them. I missed you so much."

"I know. I missed you, too, Princess. More than you can imagine. When I left, I ruined lives—yours, your mother's, and my own. But I can't go back and do it over. All I can do is hope that one day you'll forgive me."

Grace felt the arthritic fingers clutching her hand. She tried to imagine what it would take to walk away from a child who was begging you not to go. She tried to imagine Sam walking away from Maggie. She couldn't fathom it. Sam would never do that.

But what if, in a moment of terrible judgment, he were to do that very thing? Would Maggie ever forgive him?

Grace searched the depths of her wounded heart for the

answer to that question. Then like the glow of a half-hidden light, buried beneath the bitterness of years, she found it—in the innocent, unconditional love of a little girl for her father. She sensed what Maggie would do. It was what she needed to do.

She pressed his hand to her cheek as the words welled out of her—words that had been there all along. "I forgive you now, Dad," she whispered, her tears spilling over. "I forgive you and I love you."

Sam had gone to Maggie's school Christmas program on Wednesday morning. Sitting for more than an hour on a hard metal chair, watching while the different classes, and then the entire school, performed songs and choral readings, had been torture on his injured body. But the fatherly thrill of seeing Maggie in the back row of her class, wearing a silly paper star hat, and singing her heart out, had been worth the pain.

His eyes had searched for Grace, but he hadn't seen her. Could she have been avoiding him? It wasn't like her to hide. She'd probably just been busy backstage.

Now it was Wednesday night. Maggie had gone to bed after a busy time playing with her friend Ann Marie. Too tired to move but too restless to sleep, Sam sat alone on the couch, using the remote to flip through the TV channels.

Surely, by now, Grace would have seen what he'd written inside the envelope when he'd sent the check to school with Maggie. His best hope was that she would read it, call him, and give him a chance to apologize for wanting too much too soon. But it was getting late, and no call had come. Maybe it was time he faced reality—he wasn't going to hear from her.

He almost wished he'd forced himself to go to the final

meeting of the Christmas ball committee. At least he might have been able to talk to her there. But if she didn't want to see him, his presence would only make things awkward. Anyway, he hated sitting through those damned meetings.

He yawned. Maybe it was time to drag himself to bed. He had switched off the TV and was about to get up when he heard the patter of small bare feet. Maggie stood before him in her blue snowman pajamas.

"Aren't you supposed to be asleep, young lady?" he asked.

"Uh-huh. But I can't sleep 'cause I remembered something I was supposed to tell you, Daddy. Promise me you won't get mad."

"How could I ever get mad at my best girl? Sit down here and tell me." He made room for her next to him on the couch and waited for her to sit down. "Now, what's this you were supposed to tell me?"

"It's about Miss Chapman. She had to go away."

"Go away? Go where?"

"I don't think she said where. Yesterday she got a phone call in the office. When she came back, she told us that her dad was in the hospital. She had to go and see him. That's what I forgot to tell you."

"So, she wasn't at school this morning?"

Maggie shook her head. "We had a substitute."

"And you say this was yesterday. Did you give her the envelope with the check in it?"

"Uh-huh. She said she'd open it later. I think she put it in her purse."

"Okay." That would explain why he hadn't heard from Grace. "Did she say what was wrong with her father?"

"No." Maggie took a deep breath. "Daddy, did you and Miss Chapman have a fight?"

"No, honey. We're still friends."

"But something's wrong. I can tell. Why did you have me give her that envelope? Why didn't you give it to her yourself?"

She wasn't making things easy. "Nothing's wrong. We've just decided not to see each other, that's all."

"But why?" Maggie looked stricken. "I know you really like her. And I'm pretty sure she likes you. What's the matter?"

Sam sighed, knowing that only the truth would satisfy Maggie. "I do like Grace," he said. "I like her a lot. But there's a problem. When she was about your age, her father left the family to marry another woman."

"That's awful," Maggie said. "I bet she was really sad."

"She wasn't just sad. She was scared. Ever since then, she's been afraid to trust men. She's afraid she'll fall in love with a man and he'll turn out to be like her father."

"But you wouldn't do that, Daddy. If you loved her, you would stay forever."

"I know that. And Grace knows that. But she can't stop being scared. And when she's scared, she runs away, even when she doesn't want to. Does that make any sense, Maggie?"

She frowned. "Kind of. But it's . . . complicated."

"Complicated. That's a good word for it." Sam pushed himself to his feet. "Come on, let's both get some sleep. If I'm feeling strong enough tomorrow, I'll take you and Ann Marie to a movie at the mall. Popcorn and sodas and everything."

"Yay! I know just the one we want to see!" Maggie scampered off to her room.

Sam followed more slowly, lost in thought. If Grace's father was in the hospital, and if she had left to be with him . . . He was too tired to finish the thought. But the implications hung in his mind.

Grace was a strong woman. But facing her father, especially if he were dying, would be a wrenching experience. How would she deal with it?

Would it change her? Sam wondered.

When it was over, would she come back to him?

Michael Aldrich Chapman died peacefully at 4:46 A.M. on Thursday morning. Grace and Cooper, who'd been there through the night, sat on either side of him, holding his hands as he slipped away. Grace was weeping freely, but her tears were good tears, a release of the anger, grief, and fear that had festered since that long-ago day when he'd walked out of the house for the last time.

Arrangements had already been made with the mortuary. They would collect the body and prepare it for cremation on Friday. There would be no service, but his children would be there for a final farewell. Cooper would keep the ashes until next summer when they would be scattered.

Drained and exhausted, brother and sister walked out of the hospital to a clear dawn. The storm had passed, leaving a foot of glistening snow that lay like an ermine robe over the ground, the roofs, and the trees. Grace had seen snow in Oklahoma and Texas, but it had never looked like this.

"Thanks again for coming." Cooper used his arm to sweep the snow off the SUV. "I know it was tough in there. But I hope you're glad you made the trip."

"You were right—I needed to come." Grace scooped a handful of snow. It was so fluffy it almost floated away. "Thank you for talking me into it. It's good to know Dad's at peace. And now, if you don't mind, all I want to do is go back to the hotel and sleep."

"Same here." Cooper opened her door and gave her a hand up. "Let's touch base around four o'clock. We can make plans over dinner. When's your flight home?"

"It leaves on Saturday at eight-fifteen with a stop in Denver."

"I'll be staying a couple of extra days but I can drive you to the airport. Good luck with Denver. The weather can be dicey. Lots of delays when it's bad."

"I'll cross my fingers." When she'd booked the flight, Grace had known that she might miss the Cowboy Christmas Ball. But the children's activities were covered. And given her strained relationship with Sam, she welcomed any excuse to stay away.

Friday evening, after the cremation, Grace and Cooper shared a last dinner in the hotel dining room. The past three days had been emotionally draining, but the two of them had developed a closeness that Grace had missed all her life. That alone would have made her trip worthwhile.

Tonight he appeared troubled. When she mentioned it, he sighed. "When I got back to my room this afternoon, I had a message that Carol had called."

"That doesn't sound like good news." Carol and Cooper had been divorced for nine years. They both lived in the Seattle area and shared custody of their teenage son, Trevor.

"It wasn't good news. Trevor got arrested for vandalizing his school with spray paint. He'll be getting probation and a fine, but Carol says he's out of control. She wants me to take him full-time for a while."

"I'm sorry," Grace said. "I hope you can turn things around."

"So do I. It doesn't help that his mother's getting remarried to a man he doesn't like. I think Carol wants Trevor out of the way so she can get her marriage off to a good start. He's a good kid, but he can be a handful, and he's got a lot of anger in him."

"But you're taking him, of course."

"Of course. He's my son. And I want to do a better job with him than my dad did with me." Cooper tasted his broiled salmon and added a squeeze of lemon juice. "I'm thinking it might help to get him out of Seattle. I can do my work anywhere. Maybe a move to some small town where he can be outdoors, make some new friends, and learn some new skills, like horseback riding."

"A small town? Like Branding Iron, Texas?" Grace asked.

He shrugged. "I'll give it some thought. I'd have to sell the condo. And Trevor might hate the whole idea." He paused, then changed the subject.

"But we haven't talked much about you. For what it's worth, I was sore about your cancelled wedding. But looking back, you did the right thing. The guy was a jerk. You should've dumped him sooner."

"Thanks. I know. If I'd gone through with that wedding, I'd probably be seeing a lawyer by now. Commitment phobia to the rescue." Grace sipped the iced tea she'd ordered with her meal.

"Maybe you've just never met the right man," Cooper said. "Not that I'm an expert, but if you fall in love, and he's the one, maybe you won't get cold feet."

"You're wrong about that, Cooper. I did meet the right man in Branding Iron. I did fall in love. And when he wanted more from me, I froze. I drove him away."

Tears welled in Grace's eyes. She wiped them away with the back of her hand. "Being here, seeing Dad again, I realized how much blame I'd put on him, when I should have taken responsibility for my own feelings. When I forgave him, it was as if I was forgiving myself, too."

"Then maybe you can try again with this man. Maybe the second time will be the charm. I want to see you happy, little sis." He hadn't called her that in years.

Grace shook her head. "It's too late. When I walked

away from him, I burned all my bridges. He'd have to be crazy to give me another chance."

Cooper raised a dark eyebrow. "Don't be so sure. You never know about love."

Later, in her room, Grace packed her carry-on bag for tomorrow's flight back to Texas. The forecast on TV had assured her that the weather would be clear over Salt Lake City, but the storms had moved east, causing flight delays in Denver. That was a worry, but all she could do was get on the plane and hope for the best.

There wasn't much to pack. Just a pair of jeans, a pair of nice slacks, a couple of extra sweaters, some pumps she hadn't worn because of the snow, some underclothes, a nightgown which she'd add in the morning, and the dress she'd worn to honor her father at the cremation.

Though she'd been estranged from her father most of her life, she felt his absence even more keenly now that he was gone—the talks they could've had, the visits they could've shared. But maybe he would only have lied to her, as he'd lied to Cooper. Maybe it was right that they'd only been together on his last night in the hospital.

She paused to stand at the window. Her room, on the ninth floor, gave her a panoramic view of the city lit up in a glory of Christmas lights. To the east, the moon rose over towering peaks blanketed in snow. It was a beautiful scene. But she was finished here. She was ready to fly back to the little Texas town that was becoming home.

Ready to fly back to Sam—if he would have her. But after the way they'd parted, she couldn't expect him to want to try again.

Turning back to the bed where she'd laid out her things, she emptied her purse to organize it for the flight. The plane ticket and her ID would go in an outside zipper pocket. The used boarding pass, a couple of candy wrappers, and a crumpled tissue could go in the trash.

The envelope Maggie had given her lay on the bed with Sam's torn check inside. She'd meant to mail it back to him. Maybe she could do that from here—one less thing to worry about.

A table in the room held some sheets of hotel stationery with matching envelopes. Sam's address was on the check, and she had a few stamps in her purse. It would be simple enough to address an envelope and drop it in the mail slot at the desk on her way out in the morning.

She slipped the torn pieces of the check out of the envelope and was about to drop it in the wastebasket when she noticed something written inside the envelope, half hidden by the flap. It was just three simple words, but her throat tightened with emotion as she read them.

Grace, I'm here.

Chapter Sixteen

On Saturday morning, Sam took Maggie with him to run a few errands. He dropped some bills off at the post office, picked up bread, milk, and eggs at the grocery store, and filled the gas tank in his truck. His shoulder wound was improving with each day. By now he felt pain only when he made a wrong move or tried to lift something heavy.

"Daddy, don't forget to stop at the bakery," Maggie reminded him as they drove down Main Street.

"No way would I forget that." Sam pulled into a parking place, helped her to the sidewalk, and held the door for her as they entered the bakery. He wanted to accustom his daughter to the way a gentleman should treat a lady. Hopefully, she would never settle for less.

They found Wynette working behind the glass counter in her pink smock. She was glowing like a woman in love. "Hello, you two." She gave them a smile. "You're just in time to try our fresh gingerbread men. We're giving away free samples."

She handed each of them a cookie. The warm gingerbread melted in Sam's mouth. "So, what's your pleasure today?" Wynette asked.

"That's up to Maggie. She's the boss." Sam finished the cookie. "But we'll want more of these gingerbread men. Say, a half dozen."

"And doughnuts," Maggie said. "A box of them, with lots of sprinkles. Oh—and some brownies."

"You've got it." Wynette bent to scoop fresh doughnuts out of the case and arrange them in a box. "So, are you two ready for the big shindig tonight? I hear you have a beautiful new dress to wear, Maggie."

"Yes, I do. You'll see it. I bet you'll look pretty, too."

"And Sam, I hear rumors that you're going to be our Santa Claus."

"I thought it was a secret," Sam said. "Who told you?"

"Buck. He tells me everything."

And Wynette had probably spread the word, Sam thought. If she knew, so would everybody else at the Christmas ball. "Have you heard from Grace?" he asked, trying to sound casual.

"Not a word since she left for her flight to Salt Lake City. She told us her father was dying. She was pretty emotional, as you can imagine."

"Did she say when she'd be back?"

"She booked a return ticket for today. But who knows when she'll make it home? Anything could be happening with her father. And her flight has a stopover in Denver. According to the news, there's a big snowstorm expected there. Lots of flights are being cancelled."

"Well, all we can do is hope for the best." Sam tried to ignore a prickle of worry. Airlines didn't take chances with their passengers' lives. Grace was bound to be all right. But he wouldn't breathe easy until he knew she was home safe.

Had she read the note in the envelope? Would it make any difference if she had?

But the answer to that question would have to wait. Even if she were to make it to the Christmas ball, there'd be no way for them to talk. For the sake of the children, he would need to play his Santa role the whole time.

Wynette bagged the baked goods and rang up the sale. Sam paid with his credit card, thanked her, and escorted Maggie back to the truck. He gave her the bag to hold, closed the door, and went around to the driver's side. Before opening the door, he paused a moment to gaze up at the sky. Clouds were rolling in from the northwest, blown by a cold wind. Maybe the Denver storm would move south to drop Christmas snow on Branding Iron. But only one thing really mattered now—more than snow, more even than Christmas.

As he watched the changing sky, his thoughts sent out a silent message.

Come home to me, Grace.

Grace stood in the Denver terminal, gazing out the window at the flying snow. The short flight from Salt Lake City had landed ahead of the storm. But her connecting flight to Lubbock could be delayed for at least two hours. The plane had yet to come from Cheyenne, where the storm had already struck in full fury. For now, the plane was stuck on the ground, waiting for the runway to clear. By the time it arrived, the storm would be worsening here in Denver, causing more delays.

Would she make it home in time for the Cowboy Christmas Ball? Until she'd read Sam's message inside the envelope, that question hadn't mattered. Now it had suddenly become all-important.

On the flight from Salt Lake City, she'd come up with a plan—a perfect way to let Sam know exactly how she felt about him. It was an audacious plan—an all-or-nothing plan. But it depended on her being at the ball.

The flight to Lubbock wasn't a long one, but after it arrived, and she got back to her car, she'd be faced with a two-hour drive back to Branding Iron. Grace did the math in her head. The dinner would start at 7:00. The family activities, including Santa Claus, would start about 7:20 and continue until 9:00, or whenever all the little ones had taken turns with Santa. The dancing would begin at 8:00 and end at 10:00. Sam would probably be worn-out after two hours of playing Santa. He would most likely take Maggie and go home as soon as he was finished.

Grace sighed. At best, it would require a near-miracle to get her to the ball, especially if she took the time to go home and change from her jeans into the dress she'd planned to wear.

The snowfall was getting heavier. She could be stuck in this airport for hours, even overnight. Feeling dejected, she sank into a nearby seat and closed her tired eyes to rest them. The public address system was blaring Christmas music, interrupted every few minutes by announcements. The song playing now was "Here Comes Santa Claus." She tried to imagine Sam in the red suit with a pillow, a hat, and a fake beard. Even as Santa, he'd be a gorgeous hunk.

A hunk who would wear an embarrassing costume and pretend to be jolly just to make a bunch of kids happy— that was her kind of man, and she wanted him to know it.

But the way her trip home was going, she wouldn't get to see him at the ball. Maybe it was time to abandon her plan and think of something more practical.

Sam sat on the couch with the open cardboard box on the floor in front of him. He'd stalled for as long as he could manage. It was time to take out the blasted Santa costume and put it on.

"How do I look, Daddy?" Maggie twirled in her pretty new dress.

"Lovely," Sam said. "I'll be the proudest dad at the ball."

Maggie stopped twirling. "Here's the thing," she said. "Promise you won't get your feelings hurt."

"Okay. What is it?" Sam asked.

"I can't be with you at the ball. You'll be Santa Claus. If I'm hanging around with you, everybody, even the kids, will know who you really are."

Sam frowned. "I hadn't thought of that. But you're right. So, what are we going to do about that? Any ideas?"

"Uh-huh. The McDermotts are taking Ann Marie. They invited me to go with them. Okay?"

Sam suspected she just wanted to be with her friend, but he'd have to get used to such things. Maggie was growing up. "Okay, fine," he said. "But I'll miss being with my best girl."

"You'll be Santa Claus. All the little kids will want to sit on your knee and talk to you. You'll be too busy to miss me."

She was right. This was all about the kids. He'd have to remember to keep from grumping at the little ones or scaring them with too much *ho, ho, ho.*

"So, when are the McDermotts picking you up?" he asked.

"I thought I'd go over there now and help Ann Marie braid her hair. We'll go after that."

"Okay. Have fun. Don't forget your warm coat. It's cold out there."

"You don't need to remind me, Daddy. I'm not a baby." Maggie took her coat off the hook, put it on, and skipped out the door.

With a sigh, Sam stared down into the open box. He'd attended enough Christmas parties to know the drill.

Santa would make his appearance after most families had been through the serving line. He would sit in the big chair in front of the Christmas tree, and the kids would queue up to climb on his knee, tell him their wishes, and get a candy cane from his bag. Somebody was supposed to stand next to him and pass out the candy canes. Maybe Alice Wilkins would do it. Whatever.

But it was getting late. Rulon was probably pacing the floor, wondering where he was.

Taking a pillow from his bed, he used the sash from his robe to hold it firmly in front. The red velveteen pants had elastic in the waist and fit without a problem. The legs were a little long but they could be tucked into the boot tops. The jacket, trimmed with white fake fur, fit nicely over the pillow. A black leather belt held everything together.

Putting on the black boots was awkward with the pillow strapped in front, but Sam managed with effort. Even with thick socks, the fit was loose. But there was no time to add more padding.

Next came the tricky part. A bottle of spirit gum with a brush was included in the plastic Ziploc bag that held the fake whiskers and eyebrows. Standing before the bathroom mirror, Sam glued the beard, moustache, and shaggy brows to his face. Getting them off would probably hurt like hell, but he would worry about that later.

The hat had a layer of white hair, long enough to cover his neck and ears, sewn to hang below the inside of the wide band. Sam tugged on the hat, adjusted it, then walked back down the hall to view himself in the full-length door mirror.

He stood still, jaw dropping as he stared at the image in the glass.

He was looking at Santa Claus.

* * *

The last colors of sunset were fading to twilight as the plane from Denver touched down on the runway at Lubbock International Airport. Grace glanced at her watch. The flight delay had been shorter than expected. There was still a chance she could make it to the ball—not for the beginning, but at least before the end. Otherwise she'd be faced with finding another way to break the ice with Sam.

As the plane came to a stop at the gate, she looped her purse over her shoulder and lifted her carry-on down from the overhead bin. Minutes later she was literally racing toward the exit to the long-term parking lot.

Keys. She fumbled in her purse, fingers groping for the weight and feel of them before she remembered zipping them into her coat pocket, where they'd be in easy reach. By the time she found the red Cadillac, the wind was blowing hard. Clutching her coat around her, she put her bag in the trunk and climbed into the car.

When Grace turned the key, the starter ground but didn't catch. Grace's heart sank. She tried again. This time the engine roared to life. Limp with relief, she put the car in reverse, backed out of the parking stall, and headed out of the airport. The dash clock read 7:05. She had a chance, but barely. And now it was starting to snow.

Fully dressed as Santa, Sam entered the high school through a side entrance. The mayor was waiting for him. "Where have you been?" he sputtered. "The kids have been asking where Santa Claus is. Alice has been out of her mind with worry."

"You said seven-twenty, Rulon," Sam replied calmly. "I said I'd be here, and I am—right on time."

The mayor looked him up and down. "Not bad. I see the suit fits."

"I told you it would."

"Are you ready to do this?"

"I'm here." Sam's heart was pounding but he willed himself not to show it. "Let's get the show on the road."

"Oh, thank heaven!" Alice, dressed in ruffled red and green plaid taffeta, came clicking down the hallway in her stiletto-heeled pumps. "I was afraid you'd gotten cold feet. Come on, Sam. I'll introduce you and then you'll make your entrance. Do you know what to do?" She handed him a green bag filled with cellophane-wrapped candy canes.

"Don't worry, I've seen Archie McNab play Santa half a dozen times. I'll just do what he did." Sam could only hope he didn't sound as nervous as he felt.

He followed her to the gym entrance and waited outside the door while she walked to the front of the Christmas tree and rang a handbell for attention.

"Boys and girls, a special visitor just arrived from the North Pole to hear your Christmas wishes. When you're ready to sit on his knee and talk to him, get in line over here. If your mom and dad want to take your photo with him, that's just fine. Now here he is—everybody cheer for Santa Claus!"

As the applause rose, Sam strode into the gym. "Ho, ho, ho! Merry Christmas, boys and girls!" The voice came from somewhere so deep inside him that Sam barely recognized it himself. "I've been checking up on you. I know that you've been good. So tell me what you want to find under your Christmas tree."

Most of the families were still at the tables eating, so the line was slow at first. The lull gave Sam a chance to scan the crowd. He spotted Maggie sharing a table with the McDermotts. She grinned and gave him a thumbs-up. At another table, Wynette and Buck seemed lost in each other's eyes. He didn't see Jess, Grace's other roommate, but she'd never struck him as a social person.

Sam knew that Grace wouldn't be here, although he looked for her anyway. Right now she could be anywhere—stuck in an airport, flying through clouds and snow, or driving on a dark road. With a storm in the forecast, travel could be a beast tonight.

Damn it, he wanted her safe. And he wanted her back in his arms. Whatever relationship issues she had, he loved her. There had to be a way to make things work for them.

He felt a tug at his sleeve. A wide-eyed little boy stood at the head of the growing line, waiting to be noticed. It was time for Santa to get back to work.

Being careful not to frighten him, he boosted the child onto his knee. "Well, young man," he said in his deep Santa voice. "What can I bring you for Christmas?"

By the time Grace drove into the high school parking lot, snow was falling in thick, downy flakes. According to the dashboard clock, it was fifteen minutes after 9:00. Sam would likely be gone. But no—there was his truck. He was still here, though probably not for long.

She'd been racing ahead of the storm all the way from Lubbock. A few miles outside of Branding Iron, it had caught up with her. For safety's sake, she'd been forced to slow to a crawl. Now she was finally here. But she'd arrived late.

There'd been no time to change her clothes. She'd be walking into the gym in her jeans. But if her crazy plan worked, Sam wouldn't care, and nobody else mattered.

Sam had expected to finish by 9:00. But he should've known better. The kids had just kept coming, and he couldn't deny any one of them a chance to talk to Santa. By now the tables had been put away and the floor cleared for dancing. The ball idea had been a great success. People of all ages were enjoying the country music and dancing as couples or in lines. Everyone seemed to be having a great time.

Playing Santa had gone better than he'd expected. But he was getting tired. His shoulder was aching, the suit was hot, and the whiskers had begun to itch. He was ready for a break.

Even Alice had given up and quit handing out candy canes. What was left of the Christmas treats rested in a bowl on a nearby table.

There was just one little freckle-faced boy left in the line, with no more coming forward. Last one. He could do this, Sam told himself. Then he could call it a night and go home.

"And what's your name, young man?" he asked in a voice that was getting hoarse.

"Jed. And I want a horse."

"A real horse?"

"Yup. With a saddle and everything."

"I don't know if I could get one of those in my sleigh."

"You could hitch him up with the reindeer. Then you could turn him loose at my house. You can do anything, Santa."

"I don't know about that, Jed, but I'll do my best."

"You'd better, 'cause I really want that horse." Jed slipped off Sam's knee and made for the candy bowl.

Too tired to laugh, Sam slumped in the chair. At last he was finished—or so he thought. Glancing at the floor in front of him, he saw a pair of slim leather boots, surrounded by a puddle of melting snow. His gaze traveled upward—long legs in faded jeans, a red sweater, then warm brown eyes, velvety soft behind those funky John Lennon glasses.

Was he hallucinating? Sam thought he might be, but then Grace spoke in a low voice.

"Hello, Santa. Would you like to hear my Christmas wish?"

Still dazed, he decided to play along. He patted his knee. "Why don't you sit down here and tell me?"

She slipped into place. Snowflakes were still melting in her hair.

"So, what can I bring you for Christmas, young lady?" he asked. "What do you want to find under your Christmas tree?"

"Can I whisper it in your ear?"

When he nodded, she leaned forward and moved aside the fake hair that covered his ear.

"I want you under my tree, Sam—and under all my trees to come. All I want for Christmas is you and me together. So, what do you say, Santa?"

Sam didn't care that people were watching or that his fake whiskers would tickle her face.

He kissed her.

Epilogue

Christmas morning, the same year

For as long as she lived, Maggie would never forget the joy of this Christmas. And it wasn't just because of the presents—although her dad had gone overboard with a shiny blue bike and the puppy she'd been secretly wanting for ages. The little mutt pup was soft and brown with big feet, floppy ears, and sad eyes. Maggie had named him Banjo after a dog in a book she'd read. She already loved him.

But the best thing about this Christmas was seeing Sam's happy face as he sat on the sofa with his arm around Miss Chapman. Now that she was his girlfriend, Maggie had debated what to call her. *Grace* seemed a little too familiar for the woman who was still her teacher. She would stick with Miss Chapman until school was out. After that, maybe it would be time to start calling her *Mom.*

A little while ago, Maggie passed by the kitchen door, where they'd gone to check on dinner. She'd caught a glimpse of them kissing, just like in the movies. Maggie had snuck away with a grin on her face. The plan she'd made a month ago had hit some rough patches along the way, but it had finally worked out—for always, she hoped.

The dining room table, which hadn't been used in more than a year, had been opened up all the way and set with Maggie's mother's good china and linens. It had been Sam's idea to host a Christmas dinner for their friends. Grace's roommates would be coming, and Wynette would be bringing Buck. Hank Miller, who had no place else to go, would be coming, too.

The mouthwatering smells of baked ham, cheesy potatoes, hot rolls, and spiced apple cider filled the air. Maggie breathed them all in as she snuggled with Banjo next to the Christmas tree. Could any time be more wonderful than this?

"Maggie." Sam called her name from the couch, where he and Miss Chapman were taking a break before the final dinner preparations. "Listen up. I have one last present to give you, and it doesn't come in a box."

"What is it?" Maggie asked.

"It's something I know you've wanted for a long time. I've talked this over with Grace, and she agrees that I'm making the right decision."

"Tell me."

"It's this. You've told me you wished I had a different job, so I wouldn't have to get up in the night or be in danger. Getting shot made me do a lot of thinking. I want to be here to watch you grow up, Maggie. I don't want to risk your losing me."

"Daddy, just tell me."

"All right, here goes. Next month I'm going to turn my sheriff's job over to Buck. After that I'll be doing other work for the county—work that won't call me out at night. But here's the exciting part. Next fall I'm going to run against Rulon for mayor."

Maggie clapped her hands. "Daddy, you'll make a great

mayor. You're always helping people and getting things done."

"Then it's settled," Sam said. "I just wanted to make sure you liked the idea."

Maggie hugged her puppy. Her eyes felt wet. But that was all right. Sometimes, when there was more happiness inside you than you could hold, it spilled out as tears.